FORGOTTEN MEMORIES

A LUCKY TOWN NOVEL
BOOK 5

AMANDA SIEGRIST

McCord Family Novel

Protecting You

Trust in Love

Deserving You

Always Kind of Love

Finding You

Dare You to Love

Mona & Mason

The Paranormal Chronicles, Volume 1

Perfect For You Novel

The Wrong Brother

The Right Time

The Easy Part

The Hard Choice

Psychic Love Novel

Exploding Love

Captured Love

Slaying Love Novel

Won't Let You Go

Doomed Love

Deadly Crazy

Evidence of Sin

Finding Redemption

Obsessed Hope

Short Stories

Paint By Murder

Follow Me, Sweet Darling

Sleighville Novel

Dashing Through the Fear

Here Comes Chaos

The Last Noel

Standalone Novel

The Danger with Love

———

Conquering Fear Novel

CO-WRITTEN WITH JANE BLYTHE

Drowning in You

Out of the Darkness

Closing In

SHE ISN'T LOOKING FOR TROUBLE...

.

1

He counted down slowly, from ten all the way to one, before opening his eyes. No sunshine peeked through his windows. No bright wake-up call to announce a new day. He liked it that way. Dark. Because if he didn't have blackout curtains to keep the sun away, he'd never get the chance at attempting to get decent sleep on his day off.

Except he didn't like it when he finally woke up and the darkness surrounded him. Enveloped him in an eerie way. Slithering and sliding around until his heart started pounding and images popped into his head, unable to be erased.

Easily solvable. Take the damn curtains down. Or keep them open on his days off. He only closed them when he knew he'd be able to sleep in. Or attempt to, anyway.

He wanted that sleep. That elusive will-it-happen-this-time sleep.

Bolt reached over to his phone on the nightstand and groaned when the screen lit up.

7:27 AM

So much for sleeping in. Of course, he wasn't surprised.

One, he usually got up around six to get ready for work and out the door so he made it to the station by seven. Two, no matter how many times he used the blackout curtains on his days off, they never worked. He could never manage to get past seven thirty, and he was lucky if he even got that close.

Sleep never came effortlessly. He could go to bed at ten and not manage to fall asleep until two—if luck was on his side—and wake up at six on the dot. Most nights he tossed and turned, hoping for a good solid hour of sleep, knowing he wouldn't get it.

He'd tried it all. Meditation, staying away from caffeine, no alcohol, putting his phone away an hour before bed. Not watching TV. Then he switched gears and tried numbing his mind with alcohol, getting so drunk he'd pass out. Nothing worked. His mind wouldn't shut off and let him rest.

Not since he got shot ten months ago.

No matter how many times he told himself to move on and forget what happened, he replayed it over and over. What could he have done differently? Why didn't he call for backup? How could he have been so stupid? Each time, he didn't see a better answer. He was an idiot for letting Wayne Barten get the jump on him, and it didn't make a difference what anyone said.

Not that anyone tried to convince him otherwise. Because he didn't talk about it. He didn't tell anyone about his struggles. They didn't inquire, assuming he was okay. Not the sheriff, not his friends. Definitely not his family. His mom and dad would only worry if he said he was having trouble moving on. And Carson, his brother, Bolt hadn't talked to him in four months, since the last brief call asking if Deke and Charlotte could use his cabin.

But he was good. He was fine. He'd get through this all on his own.

Bolt sat up and flicked his lamp on, welcoming the light and hating it all at the same time. Because it meant he was getting up to start a new day instead of sleeping in like people loved to do on their day off.

No sense in sulking over it. He swept the curtains open, wanting to smile at the sun shining, and settled for a short grin that lasted a few seconds. A shower came next and then breakfast.

Eggs and toast with a large cup of black coffee. Quitting caffeine for three weeks had been tough. To make up for it now, he drank as much as wanted as strong as he wanted.

He had no plans for his day off. A beautiful sunny Saturday in late July. It'd be hot and humid again. Maybe he'd run down by the lake and then take a swim. He grabbed his coffee mug from the table, put his dirty plate in the sink, and refilled his mug. It felt like a two-cup kind of day.

He'd gone to bed around midnight after bingeing a few episodes of the latest crime show he was watching, barely catching any sleep. Typical night for him. With his insomnia, he didn't mind working late into the evening or being on call more than Pepper. She had Seth to go home to. He had no one. It didn't bother him to keep his energy and time focused on work. Living in such a small town—and a small county—they didn't get a lot of late-night calls to respond to a crime in progress, a disturbance, or someone needing help.

Of course, in the past four months, since the last showdown with the Cheetah gang, things had settled down. They'd found all the bunkers on Mr. Barten's residence and shut them down. No more drugs running in and out of Lucky. Brett Nelson, one of the Cheetahs who tried to kill Charlotte and Deke, died a month ago. He'd lain in a coma for three solid months before his neurological signs deteriorated. His sister made the difficult decision to pull the plug. Nobody was sad about it in his circle. As far as Bolt knew, Brett's sister wasn't that heartbroken about it either. She'd seemed irritated she had to fly out to Minnesota to even acknowledge her brother. Odd family dynamics, although Bolt wasn't going to judge. He didn't have the best relationship with his brother either.

Mr. Barten was still sitting on drug charges and looking at serious time. Bolt didn't think he'd be getting off. It was only a matter of time before his trial finally came and he was found guilty and sentenced. And his only remaining son, Evan, pled guilty to aiding and abetting when he tried to lead everyone to their deaths on Brett's orders. Being his first arrest—and his reason behind it to help save his girlfriend—the judge went easy on him. Gave him one-year probation and thirty hours of community service. Evan was still around, running the only garage in town, yet not many people were friendly with him anymore. Especially not Seth, his former best friend.

Life was back to normal—for everyone else.

Bolt felt stuck in limbo. Locked in his own personal hell that he had created. If he hadn't been careless and gotten shot, he wouldn't be where he was now—trapped in his own personal hell.

He took his mug outside to the porch and sat in the old rocker his grandfather had built. Solid and sturdy. Just like the man himself. He had passed away three years ago, and it hit everyone in the family hard. He'd like to think him most of all, but he knew Carson had also been close to their grandfather. Back then, they talked. Acted like brothers.

The light breeze brushed over him, soothing in a way, until it disappeared and the already high temps saying hello rushed in and attacked him. Yep. It was going to be a scorcher today. Since he woke up so damn early, it'd be better if he got his run over with before the day was too hot to handle.

He finished his coffee, changed into his running outfit, locked up, and jaunted down the steps, heading down his driveway. He lived on the outskirts of town, nestled in the woods. Long driveway, no close neighbors. Plenty of privacy. He had to drive about a quarter mile of dirt road from the main road before he hit his driveway. From there, the main road leading into town could be found. About another half-mile down that road was a nice lake. That's usually where he ran. No need to drive, and it was a great workout. From his house to the lake and then circling it, then back to his house, it was about two miles overall. He loved the sweat that rolled down his neck and back. The ache in his muscles. The feeling that he was strong enough, powerful enough to make the run. In the beginning, after recovering from the gunshot wound, it had been pure hell. Intense torture he'd never dealt with before. But he persevered. He worked hard to get stronger, to get even better than his former self had been.

Getting shot had taken more out of him than just his ability to sleep. It had knocked him down completely. Mentally and physically. He'd never let anyone get the jump on him again. And he hadn't. He took charge when Joshua Barten—Wayne's half-brother—tried to kill Danny and Kat in the cabin. Bolt didn't hesitate to fire his weapon. He took a life with one squeeze of a trigger. He figured he should be struggling with that too. But nope. He wasn't that sorry Joshua Barten was dead. He'd been a bad guy with no morals. He had tried to hurt Bolt's friends. He'd never feel sorry for saving his friends.

He hit the road and turned right toward the lake. Left would've taken him to town. He didn't get very far before he saw an old beat-up yellow car sitting on the side of the road with the hood up and the finest legs he'd seen in a long time.

The woman peeking under the hood wore shorts so short, it showcased her asscheeks in a very arousing way. She had on a bright-pink tank top and white flip-flops with silver rhinestones covering the threads. And long blonde hair that trailed down her back and on her shoulders in gentle waves. When she turned at the sound of his feet hitting the ground, oh, boy. He nearly tripped in his stride. High cheekbones. Lovely red lips. And green eyes that sucked him right in. Those eyes pulled him in so hard, he knew he'd do anything for her. All she had to do was say the word.

The woman was drop-dead gorgeous and not from around these parts. He would've remembered seeing her somewhere for sure. Not necessarily would've talked to her, but he would've taken a second look. Or three. Or four or five or as many as he could without her noticing. Bolt wasn't one to chat up women. Talk about fumbling every single time.

He slowed down, breathing heavily, and stopped in front of her.

"Car trouble?"

Well, no, shit. He was a deputy, for goodness' sake. Figuring crimes out was part of his forte. It didn't take a genius to figure out she was having problems. He couldn't believe he said that, although wasn't surprised. Women had never been his strong suit. He either got tongue-tied or said the stupidest shit. People didn't think he was the best deputy, and they knew he wasn't smooth with the ladies either. He was a joke. To everyone.

"Yeah, it started smoking and making this weird..." She made a funny face and then laughed. "I don't know. It sounded like it was dying. And I think it did. Because it won't start now. I stopped when it started smoking, but maybe I should've kept going until I hit town. If I'm close to it, that is?"

She looked hopeful, yet defeated.

He nodded, smiling. "About five more miles and you would've been driving down Main Street in Lucky. But it's better you didn't keep driving with it smoking like that. Want me to take a look? Not that I'm a super huge car expert, but..." He shrugged. He didn't want to make it seem like he knew better than her. Some women didn't like that— men acting all superior and macho and like they had to save the world.

She waved a hand toward the hood, a smile in her eyes. Good sign he hadn't offended her.

Yeah, he really wasn't a car expert at all. But the engine looked old with cracks here and there. It was still smoking, and the fact it wouldn't start didn't bode well. He plopped to the ground and took a look under the car. Yep. Not good at all. Oil was leaking from below.

He stood back up. "There's already oil pooling on the ground. I think your engine went kaput."

"Kaput?" She frowned. "Like, you don't mean died? Like never going to work ever again kind of kaput?"

He winced. "I'm not a mechanic, so I can't say for sure, but everything you told me, with the oil on the ground says it's an engine problem. That's never good. I can give you the number to the garage in town and they can tow it for you."

She bit her bottom lip. "Can you call them for me? You'll be able to explain things better anyway."

"Yeah, sure." Bolt tilted his lips into an easy grin, hoping to ease her discomfort. He knew it didn't work by the severe frown still puncturing her beautiful face as she stared at the engine.

He pulled out his phone from where it was strapped around his forearm and dialed Barry's Garage. Now Evan's after Barry was murdered and left it to him, but he hadn't changed the name yet. Bolt had no idea if he intended to. Not that he ever planned to ask.

He said a short hello to Evan when he answered, offered a rundown of the problems, and then threw another optimistic smile toward the woman.

"He'll be here shortly."

She shoved her hands in her back pockets, which thrust her boobs toward him, making him take notice. Hell, he was a man and couldn't help but look, especially when she made such a movement as if daring him to.

He could feel his cheeks burning as he looked around, trying to get his mind off how beautiful she was and how much he wanted to kiss her. He'd never had such a strong reaction to a woman before. It was odd. Sure, he'd look and envision things, but not this hardcore. Not to the point where he could feel himself getting hard by one simple look at her boobs pointing directly at him as if she *wanted* him to touch them.

"So, Bolt, is it? Like the movie with that dog and little girl."

He met her gaze once again. Wow. He was fantasizing about kissing her breathless and his cock getting so hard it was so damn painful, and she had to compare his name to a kid's movie.

This was why he didn't date much. Women never saw him as more than a pathetic loser.

SHE REGRETTED SAYING anything when his expression shattered with pain. Although he had gone from frowning to smiling within seconds, she would've missed it if she hadn't been paying close attention to him. But she had hurt his feelings somehow. No surprise there. She was always screwing up everywhere she went.

"It's a nickname. Nothing to do with the movie. My name is Thomas Bolten. People have always called me Bolt since I can remember."

She swayed on her feet, thrusting her chest out a bit more, smiling even brighter, hoping she could erase the last traces of heartache out of his baby-blue eyes. "I like it. It's cute."

His brows puckered, and she wanted to kick herself for saying cute. Men didn't want to be labeled as cute.

"Thomas is a great name too." She drew her hands out of her back pockets and shoved one of them toward him. "I'm Cherry. Thanks for coming to my rescue."

He hesitated, then shook her hand, a slow smile reappearing. He had the most gorgeous smile too. Two dimples lit up his face. Perfect white teeth. Those baby-blue eyes that shined with such kindness. His light-brown hair wasn't quite a buzzcut, but short enough where she itched to rub her hand over it to feel the softness. Toned legs. Ripped arms. She could only imagine how chiseled and firm his chest was. And she should seriously stop ogling him before he left without finishing helping her.

"It's nice to meet you. You're welcome. It's my job."

She laughed. "To rescue women on the side of the road?"

His deep, rich laughter filled her heart with joy. "Well, in a way, yes. I work for the sheriff's department. I'm off duty right now, but I'm a deputy."

Her smile died. "Oh, okay." When he started to frown, she knew she had to keep her cool. Her lips arced into a wide half-circle once again. "That's cool. I got lucky then."

In more ways than she could count. He knew Pepper.

Before she could segue into a topic she was nervous to breach, a tow truck stopped next to them.

The man who jumped out of the truck nodded at Bolt, who did the same in return, then he smiled at her. "Hi, I'm Evan. Can I take a look?"

"Oh, by all means." She swept her hands at the car and took a step back.

Her feet tangled around a long stick she didn't see and she tripped. Bolt threw out a hand, cupping her arm, stopping her from tumbling down the ditch. He pulled her closer.

"You okay?"

"Call me clumsy. It's my middle name. Cherry Clumsy Chapman." She giggled.

His laughter filled her soul again at her silliness, letting go of her arm. Then he frowned as it dawned on him what she had said. "Chapman?"

Oh, shit. She hadn't meant to reveal that so soon.

"Yeah, Chapman. I was kidding about the clumsy part." Her laughter sounded fake, even to her.

Evan stood up from the hood and looked at her, while Bolt continued to frown. "Looks like your engine might be blown."

"What?" She took a step away from Bolt, grateful she

couldn't see his frown anymore. It only reinforced how much this was a bad idea that she came here. "That sounds...not good."

Evan half-grinned. "It's not. You're going to need a whole new engine."

"That sounds expensive."

Evan nodded. "This looks like an old car. Nineties?"

"Something like that. It's a good thirty years old." Because that's all she could afford. She was grateful the old beast got her this far.

"You might be better off buying a new car."

Ha! The man had jokes.

"Well, why don't you take it to the garage and give me a quote on a new engine first."

She wouldn't be able to pay for a new engine *or* a new car, but he didn't need to know that.

"I'll hook it up."

He jumped back in his tow truck while she and Bolt moved so he could hook up her car to the back of it.

"So are you related to Pepper?"

The way he asked it told her he already knew the answer. This wasn't going as she had planned. What a disaster in the making.

Cherry nodded, yet still couldn't look him in the eyes. "We're half-sisters." She cleared her throat. "Not that she knows that. I didn't know it either until recently."

"Hmm."

She jerked her head at him. That's all he had to say.

"What?"

He peeled his gaze off the tow truck and toward her. There was a mixture of distrust and...maybe her being too hopeful, but desire mingled in his gaze. "I'm sorry?"

"What was the hmm for?"

His brows drew low. "How did you find out you're sisters?"

"Why?" She crossed her arms, hating how it sounded like he was interrogating her. She didn't do anything wrong. She wasn't here to hurt Pepper in any way.

"Because she's my friend and I want to know."

Her eyes narrowed. "I don't think it's your business."

She wanted to rewind everything between them and go back to when he was checking her out, his eyes dilating with pleasure. She might've put her hands in her pockets on purpose to get him to look. She liked how his eyes glided across her body in a subtle, slow way. Not full-on gawking like guys enjoyed doing.

"It's my business when it deals with my friends. Ones that had a rough few months recently. I won't let anyone hurt my friends."

She inhaled deeply, knowing he was talking about Pepper's twin, Lillian. The evil bitch.

"Car's all hooked up. I can give you a ride to the garage," Evan suddenly said, breaking the hard stare they were leveling at each other.

She smiled at Evan. "Thank you. I—"

"I'll bring her into town."

Her head snapped at Bolt. The determination in his gaze said he wouldn't be swayed by anything.

Okay, she'd listen to him. For now.

"I'll pop in later and chat with you about my car. Can I grab my purse and bag?"

Evan nodded, and she opened the door awkwardly, figuring she should've done this before he hooked it up.

They stood quietly on the side of the road as Evan drove off. As soon as they couldn't see him anymore, Bolt turned to her.

"Come on. My house isn't far from here. You can tell me everything as we walk."

She threw the thin strap of her purse over her shoulder and head, along with her small duffle bag, then crossed her arms. Her lips formed a fierce frown too. He could be all dominating and controlling, telling her what to do, but she didn't have to be happy about it.

This was the worst idea ever. She could be following a serial killer home. How did she really know if he was a deputy? She was taking his word for it. Even though Evan didn't argue with her about going off alone with him, he hadn't been friendly with Bolt. There was animosity between them.

Because Bolt was bad news?

She was about to find out.

2

So much for his run and dip in the lake. And relaxing on his day off. Here, he walked next to a rigid woman, the tension radiating off her in heavy waves. Another maniac sister? He hoped not. Pepper didn't deserve to deal with more turmoil like that.

"So, tell me."

She huffed, yet didn't speak.

That wasn't going to deter him. He made mistakes in the past, but he'd make up for them now. By being smarter. More focused. He wasn't about to let another psycho woman get the jump on anyone in town. Lillian Chapman, evil twin to Pepper, had duped them all. Almost killed Pepper and had taken over her identity. Bolt was grateful Cherry looked nothing like Pepper. Sure, they both had blonde hair, but that was about it. Of course, she said they were half-sisters, so it made sense.

"You know Pepper is a twin right?"

She snorted. "Yeah, and I'm not an evil bitch like her." She stopped walking. "I'm not here to hurt her."

"Then why are you here?"

She threw her arms out wide. "Because she's my sister. I've never had one before. Wouldn't you want to know your siblings if you found out one day you had one?"

Yeah, probably. Not that he did so well with the relationship he had with his brother.

"She almost killed Pepper." He'd never forget the downright demonic look Lillian had carried. It was as if pure evil lived inside her.

"I saw it in the papers. The whole thing with the Cheetahs and stuff. I swear I'm not here to hurt her."

Bolt nodded and started walking again. Cherry followed suit. "Then just tell me how you found out she's your sister."

"The news article. It gave a breakdown of Pepper and Lillian's history. Mentioned their dad's name. I never met him, but my mom told me about him. Real winner, that one."

Interesting. So they shared the same dad. Not that he knew anything about Pepper's background. She was tight-lipped about her life. Bolt imagined Seth was the only one who knew most things about her.

"What do you want from Pepper?"

She stopped again. He was forced to stop as well. They were on the dirt road leading to his driveway. It wasn't much farther, but if they kept stopping and walking, they'd be at this all day.

"Maybe to feel like I have a family for once. Grew up with no dad, though for some strange reason, my mom gave me his last name. That's the only thing I ever got from the guy. Hell, as far as I'm concerned, he was nothing more than a sperm donor. My mom's a stripper, still to this day. I'm impressed she keeps her body so toned in her late fifties. But more power to her. I wouldn't exactly call our relationship close. She's a woman that birthed me and then made sure I got to adulthood without dying. She expected me to follow in her footsteps. She named me Cherry!"

Bolt flinched when she hollered. A bit from the sound and from the pain he heard echoed through each word.

"I like your name."

She scoffed, crossing her arms again, and stared off into the woods.

"It's different and unique."

Her gaze slowly came back to his. "You sound sincere."

He felt his cheeks burning red again. "I don't form the habit of lying. I don't usually be rude to people I just met either. But Pepper's my friend and I'm only looking out for her."

Cherry dropped her arms. "It's nice that you are. I promise I'm not here to do anything bad. I wanted to meet my sister. That's it."

He jerked his head toward the direction of his house. "Then let's meet her." They started walking again. "I can't guarantee she'll be receptive to meeting you. Like I said before, a few months ago, she had it rough."

"Well, it can't hurt to try."

They walked quietly until they hit his driveway.

"You run a lot?"

"When I find time. I thought I'd run to the lake nearby, then take a swim. It's a nice day for it."

She lifted her head and basked in the sun's glory. "It really is. It's so hot. I thought Minnesota was always cold."

Bolt laughed. "Oh, no, it can get hot and humid here. Summers can be brutal. Though, I know we're known for the cold." He stopped at his porch. "Do you want something to drink? There's bottled water and pop in the fridge. I'm going to change quick."

"I'm good. I'll wait outside."

He didn't say it, but he was glad about that. He changed quickly into jeans and a blue T-shirt, then dialed Pepper's number. Despite telling himself not to, he was warming to Cherry. It had nothing to do with his attraction to her. He couldn't be attracted to her. It'd be wrong. Because as soon as he found out she was Pepper's sister, that had turned off as if an ice-cold bucket of water had been tossed over his head. Well, sort of. She was a beautiful woman, and it was hard to ignore. But her story. The pain he heard. He had an inkling she wasn't lying about why she was here or how she found out about Pepper. Though he couldn't take her word for it. For all he knew, she was working with the Cheetahs— or Lillian—and was here to finish the job that Lillian and Brett couldn't do—kill Pepper.

He had to warn Pepper before he showed up at the station with her half-sister in tow.

She answered with her usual semi-cheerful, serious self.

"I have something to tell you and you're not going to like it."

―――――

CHERRY WASN'T AN IDIOT. She figured Bolt was inside calling Pepper. That was fine by her. She wasn't here to hide anything—much. There were a few things she'd keep to herself for now. She didn't know these people. Until she found out more, and her gut settled down, then she could spill the beans. Maybe. Most of it was embarrassing.

Bolt returned outside a few minutes later. He wore jeans and a blue T-shirt that sculpted his muscles a little too nicely to her liking. If this all went to shit, at least she was able to ogle such a fine-looking man for a while. There was always a bright side to things. Something she tried to find when things weren't going her way, which happened most of her life.

"Come on. We'll take my truck. Pepper's at the station."

Wow. He called her, which she knew he would. But he admitted it. That was a first. People rarely were honest. At least in her experience.

"Okay."

Although this was finally happening, she wasn't brave enough to ask what he told Pepper and how she responded.

The drive into town didn't take long. He hadn't lied when he said she was close to town. She didn't know why she doubted him. He'd been nothing but honest since they met.

When he parked the truck in the parking lot near the sheriff's department, her heart finally started to make some noise. The pounding was so loud, it roared in her ears. He got out and rounded the truck, waiting patiently for her. No bouncing on the balls of his feet. No swaying back and forth. No motion for her to hurry up.

She exited the vehicle and forced out a smile. She might not be ready to do this, but it was time. No more wondering and conjuring different scenarios about how this would go. She was about to find out. She thought she'd have more time to prepare. Practice her speech in the mirror. Puke. Go back and forth viciously through her mind whether this was a good idea.

He opened the door to the station and let her go in first. There was a woman behind the counter with long black hair and deadly eyes. She didn't look friendly. In front of the counter stood Pepper. No smile. No kindness in her eyes. Rigid posture.

It was happening.

This wasn't going to be a pleasant, happy introduction like she had pictured—hoped for.

Bolt tensed beside her. "Pepper."

She nodded. "Bolt."

He put his hand on her back. Not to push her forward, but almost as if offering her a small sign of support.

"This is Cherry."

"Hi." Ugh. That came out meek. Like she didn't know what to say or do, which was the truth. This was new territory for her.

"Bolt says you claim to be my half-sister," Pepper said with tight lips.

She wanted to roll her eyes and glare at him. Claimed? She thought they had come to some sort of understanding. She thought he had believed her.

"Same dad."

"My parents weren't divorced."

Cherry shrugged, hating to paint their father in a bad light, but it was what it was. "I guess...he wasn't faithful. My mom isn't picky when it comes to men."

Pepper's eyes narrowed.

"She's slept with a lot of guys. I don't know what to say. I never met him. She had a picture of him though. She gave me his last name." Cherry shrugged again. Talk about awkward. She had no idea he'd been married. She knew nothing about the guy other than he had knocked up her mom.

"You didn't miss anything. He was a terrible father. Gambled too much, drank too much, and got killed for the former, owing the wrong people."

That was news to her. How he died, anyway. She knew he had passed—the article had been thorough—but she hadn't known how.

"You met Lillian then?"

She felt like she was in an interrogation room, sweating, waiting for the ax to drop and slice her to pieces. Cherry shook her head.

"The article didn't paint a pretty picture about her. I wanted to meet you instead."

The way Pepper stared her down, her eyes thin, her lips tight, her shoulders rigid, it was as if she knew without a doubt she was lying. As if they all believed her to be a part of the Cheetah gang and she was here to do something terrible. Sure, she had secrets, but it had nothing to do with any of that.

"Why?"

Cherry looked at the woman behind the counter.

"Why do you want to meet Pepper?" the woman demanded.

"Because I always thought I was an only child. Now I'm not." Cherry looked at Pepper. "I don't want anything from you. I wanted to meet you. Say hi, we're sisters."

Pepper's posture relaxed a fraction. "I was never close to Lillian. I'm not good at being a sister."

"Plus, we don't know if it's even true."

Cherry didn't look at the woman again. Her hostility was easy to read. She might be a lot of things, but she wasn't a liar.

"I'll take a DNA test or whatever. I have nothing to hide." She threw a smile out to ease the tension in the room.

Nobody budged in their fierce stance or severe frowns. Though Bolt stood tall by her side, not moving an inch as if he didn't want to ditch her side. Not that she believed he was on her side, but still. His presence helped in this tumultuous situation.

"Good. Because we're going to do a deep dive about everything in your life."

"Geez, Charlotte, cool it," Bolt said.

Pepper chuckled. That low sound seemed to decrease the tension in the room by a smidge. "A DNA test couldn't hurt to confirm."

Cherry nodded. Whatever she had to do to make Pepper believe her. Who knew? Maybe her mom lied to her about who her father was. She slept with so many men in her life, she might not know who her actual father was and just picked one as the winner.

"How long are you staying in town?"

Well, considering she had no car now... Until she could find transportation out of town.

"A few days or so. A week." That wasn't quite a lie, but it also wasn't truthful. In all honesty, she had no idea how long she'd be in town.

"I don't know what to say to you, Cherry. This is all a bit much."

Cherry respected that. Considering everything Pepper had been through with her other sister, it made sense she'd be leery with this information.

"I get it. It's okay. Maybe we can have lunch or something on your day off. Get to know each other." She wasn't asking for the moon. She just wanted to get to know her sister.

"Yeah, I'll think about it. I have to get back on the road."

"DNA test," Charlotte snapped.

Pepper tilted her head she heard. "Where are you staying?"

"Umm..." She had no clue. "I barely made it to town. My car died on me, and I haven't had a chance to look for a place to stay yet."

By the look in Pepper's eyes, she wouldn't be staying with her. As if she were family visiting and welcome to stay.

Hopefully, the places around here weren't too expensive. She didn't see any hotels or motels on the way to Lucky or when they drove through town. Which meant she'd have to stay in some sort of B&B or cabin. That sounded expensive. She had no idea how she was going to get around town either without a vehicle. Talk about going up a creek without a paddle or whatever that dumb saying was.

"You can stay with me. I have a spare room."

She jerked her attention to Bolt, as did the other two women.

He couldn't be serious. Yet his gaze looked sincere. He hadn't stumbled on his words. Why would he offer his place to her? What game was he playing? Because in her experience, men were always playing one game or another. Her mother taught her that.

But beggars couldn't be choosers and it would save her a lot of money. Though he didn't live close to town. She couldn't walk five miles every day to find a bite to eat or have a look around. It didn't mean she wouldn't do what she had to do though. *Suck it up and deal with it.* Ugh. She even heard the words in her mother's annoying voice.

"Thank you, Bolt. I'll take you up on that offer."

3

"WHAT ARE YOU DOING?" Pepper hissed as soon as Cherry walked out of the area with Charlotte to swab the inside of her mouth for the DNA test.

"Do you trust her?" Bolt wanted to listen to his gut—which had failed him before—that they could trust Cherry. He knew it wasn't smart to until they confirmed with hard evidence they could.

"No."

"Then doesn't it make sense to keep her close? Keep an eye on her just in case."

Pepper propped a hand to her hip, her eyes narrowing. "It does. You have a point."

"I didn't think you would offer, and it isn't wise, in case she is out to hurt you. So I thought I would. I can handle it."

Pepper's expression softened. She stepped closer and touched his shoulder. "Of course, you can. I never doubted that."

She wouldn't. Pepper wasn't here when he got shot. She didn't know him then. She didn't know how everyone thought of him as a screwup. The backup deputy to the real hero, Derek, and, of course, Sheriff Caldwell who could do no wrong. He had something to prove. Ever since the day in the woods, he'd had something to prove. That he wasn't an idiot and that he could be a hero just as much as the other two. Wayne Barten might've gotten the jump on him, but he saved the day when Wayne's half-brother Joshua tried to kill Danny. Shot and killed him. He didn't hesitate. Didn't falter. Didn't come out the loser that time.

"Your turn," Charlotte said in her usual bossy tone, coming from out of nowhere.

Pepper let her hand drop and turned to Charlotte as she did her thing. Bolt made eye contact with Cherry. She looked annoyed. Not surprising. Charlotte got on his nerves all the time too. Telling him he was doing this wrong and that wrong. Hollering at him for messing up the files in the cabinets, which she claimed were organized alphabetically. Could've fooled him. He found them out of order all the time, so he wasn't the only one messing things up around here. She demanded damn near perfection, and he always fell short. He saved Kat and Danny's life and he still always fell short.

"I'll get this sent out right now." Charlotte left the room.

"I need to get back on the road. I'll...uh..." Pepper shrugged as she looked at Cherry. "Call you, I guess, about lunch."

"I don't have a phone."

Which now made a lot more sense why she asked him to call for the tow truck. Why didn't she have a phone? Everyone had a phone these days. Even his grandma did, though she didn't know how to work it very well.

Pepper narrowed her eyes again. If he could see the suspicion in her eyes, he knew Cherry could too. She had to know it wouldn't be easy to gain Pepper's trust, not with whatever she had read in the article. It had to have been an article in Florida. He didn't recall any of the local newspapers writing a huge story about Pepper like that around here. Everyone would've known and made sure Pepper was holding up okay over it.

"Fine. Since you're staying with Bolt, I'll call him." Pepper then left without another word.

Typical Pepper. She wasn't the best people person. Bolt didn't blame her though. Until they knew more about Cherry, they couldn't trust her.

"So..." Cherry's face lit up with a bright smile. "I don't have a car anymore."

He knew she wasn't smiling about that prospect, but her smile did something to him every time it punctured her lips. It made him want to drop everything he was doing and be at her beck and call. And she liked to smile a lot in the very short time he'd known her.

It looked like he was her personal chauffeur and her secretary to field phone calls.

"Let's see what Evan has to say about your car."

Of course, if she didn't have a phone, he imagined she wasn't going to have the money to fix her car—or buy a new one.

It just kept getting better and better the more he learned about her.

He almost put a hand on her back as they walked out but stopped himself. No matter how gorgeous she was, he had to maintain distance. Shouldn't be too difficult. Women were not his forte, and she seemed way out of his league. Too beautiful, for sure. Maybe even too young. She looked like she was in her early twenties. He wasn't old, but he'd recently turned thirty-two, and dating someone in their early twenties didn't seem like his thing. Sounded too young.

Silence filled his truck as he pulled out of the parking lot. He felt an odd tension build in the small space. A bit of apprehension, distrust...desire. Only his wishful thinking.

"Thanks for helping me out here. I appreciate it."

He nodded, keeping his eyes on the road. "No problem. You'd have a hard time finding somewhere to stay right now anyway. No motel or hotel in town, and it's summer, so lots of tourists in the area staying around the cabins and stuff."

"So..."

He saw her lick her lips out of the corner of his eyes. The simple gesture had his cock twitching. *Down, boy.* Until they knew more about her, until they could trust her, he couldn't make one wrong move. Even after that, he had to stay out of her pants. Nothing good would come from dallying with her. She was Pepper's sister. Off-limits.

"Yeah?" he prompted when she didn't continue.

"You and Pepper have, like, a thing going on?"

Laughter filled the truck. When he glanced at her to see if she was serious, his hands tightened on the steering wheel and his stomach did a belly flip at the annoyance in her gaze. The same expression he witnessed when they came back into the area and Pepper had let go of his shoulder.

Interesting.

Jealousy, perhaps?

No way. They didn't know each other. They just met. He didn't notice her checking him out like he had done with her. Hello? She was wearing the shortest shorts on the planet. Any man would stop and stare.

He turned his attention back to the road and cleared his throat. "Sorry about that. Laughing. That's funny. She's dating Seth, the sheriff's brother."

"Why is it funny?"

He risked another glance her way. The annoyance was gone from her gaze. Well, that was good. Odd, but good. "Pepper and I are complete opposites. I don't see her that way either. She's a good friend. She's like a sister to me."

"What's Seth like?"

Why did she want to know? Because Pepper was her sister? Because she was gathering intel for a far more sinister plan? Bolt didn't like the unknown. He also didn't like how his gut continued to churn and twist around that he could trust her. He couldn't quite pinpoint why he thought so, but while he'd made mistakes in the past trusting his instincts, he was going to give her the benefit of the doubt. It didn't mean he'd let his guard slip. It meant he'd give her a small amount of trust until he saw otherwise.

Or maybe it was his dick talking and not his head.

"He's friendly and outgoing. He loves Pepper. He's the baby of the family. There's him, Logan—the sheriff—and his sister, Kat." Bolt gave a short laugh. "He used to be best friends with Evan. Lot of history there."

"The tow truck guy? The one that you didn't seem too friendly with."

"Not many people like him much anymore. He never worked for the Cheetahs, but he made some mistakes concerning them, and it's hard to forgive what he did."

"So, he's on our shit list?"

He chuckled, glancing at her again, noting the sparkle in her emerald-green eyes. That beautiful smile was back on her face.

"I mean, if Pepper doesn't like him, then I won't either."

"Because you want to be on good terms with her?"

She nodded. "When I found out I had two sisters, I was over the moon excited. When I realized one wasn't so great, my spirits dipped a bit, but life's thrown me many disappointments, so I get over things pretty easily. I want Pepper to like me."

"Give her time. Don't take it personally she wasn't welcoming you with open arms. She takes a while to warm up to most people."

Bolt wasn't going to say too much. He liked Pepper. Never had a problem with her or her brusque manner. He knew others had—still did. But deep down, beneath that tough skin of hers, was a person who wanted to be liked. He knew the feeling well.

He'd lived in the small town of Lucky since the day he was born. When high school hit, he swore he'd move and break free from the torment he lived in. Everyone knowing your business. People talking about you like you didn't know. Kids laughing because he was a nerd. And yet, he never left. Too scared to spread his wings.

He parked the truck behind a beat-up red car with the front end scrunched up like an accordion. It was hard to forget how it happened. A couple of college students joyriding, drunk, crashed into a tree. The driver died. The front seat passenger busted up his legs—no more football for him. The two in the backseat barely had a scratch. A tragedy. An unnecessary tragedy. Bolt wondered how long Evan was going to keep the vehicle hanging around the place when the accident happened a month ago.

Not that he planned to ask.

Cherry jumped out of his truck, and he tried his hardest not to stare at her ass as she walked inside the garage. He felt pretty damn proud of himself that he kept his eyes focused on everything but her.

She beamed a beautiful smile at Evan, who rolled out from underneath a car when he heard them approach. Why was she smiling at him? He thought she wasn't going to like him based on the fact Pepper didn't. Bolt forced himself to keep his expression neutral and not act like a jealous boyfriend because she was smiling at another man. He didn't know her well enough to act in such a manner.

"Did you have a chance to look at my car? I know it hasn't been that long, but we were curious."

Evan wiped his hands on a rag and nodded. Judging by his frown, it didn't look promising. "Engine's blown. You also need a new head gasket for sure. A few other things that ain't working right. You're looking at a pretty penny to get it all fixed."

Cherry sighed. "Well, I don't have that kind of money. Nothing close to anything pretty."

"It's an old car. You're better off buying a new one."

Cherry sighed again at Evan's response. Which Bolt took to mean she didn't have money for that either.

"Look, if you want to get rid of it, I'll buy it from you. I can use some of the other parts and whatnot." Evan looked behind her to where he parked her car and shifted on his feet. "A thousand? And I won't charge you for the tow."

She perked up. "Really? You'd do that for me?"

Evan shrugged. "Cars are my thing. Do you have the title?"

Bolt wanted to pull her into his side when she deflated. He also wanted to shove Evan up against the wall and ask what kind of game he was playing with her. That car wasn't worth a thousand and Evan knew it.

"No, but I can try to get it. Then we have a deal. Can I keep it parked here?"

"Of course."

Then Cherry swiveled her head in his direction beaming a bright smile, and Bolt swore his stomach did a joyous somersault. "I have to use the bathroom and then we can go...wherever we're going."

Evan pointed to the right where the office was located. "Go through the doors and you'll see it on your right."

Cherry left the area.

Neither said a word for a beat. But then he couldn't hold it in any longer.

"We both know that car isn't worth a thousand dollars."

Evan narrowed his eyes. "Since when are you the car expert around here, deputy?"

"She's off-limits to you. You stay away from her."

Evan crossed his arms. "She just rolled into town and you're already staking your claim. That's surprising. When's the last time you even took a woman on a date?"

Bolt took a step closer. "She's Pepper's half-sister. Which makes her family. Considering Pepper is with Seth, basically his family too. I'm doing you a favor by telling you to back off."

He'd give Evan credit. He didn't react much to the news.

"I don't take orders from you, deputy. If I want to ask a beautiful woman like her out, I will. I don't foresee you having the balls to do it. Honestly, I was being nice. It's probably worth about five hundred. But now that you're getting in my face about it, I might see if she wants to go out with me."

"Why are doing this?"

Evan's lips tightened. "Well, it doesn't seem to matter what I do around here. Nobody likes me."

"You brought that on yourself and you know it."

Evan's eyes shattered with pain, then he tore his gaze to the floor, shifting on his feet. "Yeah, I know. It doesn't seem to matter what I do to make up for it, nobody is ever going to forgive me." His jaw was clenched, his eyes narrowed when he looked back up. "You don't know how hard that decision was. I wish I could change it, but I can't. I did what I thought I had to do to save Stacy." He shrugged. "And for what? Now I don't even have her. She left me. Decided to stay in California. She didn't want me following her."

Bolt stared at him, unsure of what to say. Evan's actions were unforgivable. He led his friends to be killed. Sure, to save Stacy's life because she had been held hostage and the Cheetahs forced him to do it. But he had options. He could've told Seth or Logan or anyone else what was going on and they would've helped. They would've gotten Stacy back. He made his choice and now he had to live with the consequences.

"Look." Evan glanced behind him toward where Cherry's car was parked. "I found something else interesting with the car. Considering Pepper's last sister tried to kill her, I thought you might want to know. Despite Seth thinking I don't care, I do. He used to be my best friend, and I wish like hell he still was."

Bolt tensed and nodded for him to continue.

"There was a rag shoved in the tailpipe. That could've messed with the engine. Whether it's the cause of it or not" –Evan shrugged— "or it was already going to shit, I can't say. It's an old car, so anything is possible. But the rag in the tailpipe wasn't helping anything. The engine could've exploded from that."

"Why would she put a rag in the tailpipe?"

"There's no good reason to do something like that. Which is why I'm mentioning it, knowing she's Pepper's half-sister."

Bolt didn't realize he said the question out loud until Evan responded. Of course, what Evan said was what he was thinking himself. It wasn't good.

Before Bolt could say anything else, Cherry walked back into the garage.

"I'm ready. Thanks again, Evan. You're a lifesaver."

Evan smirked, the devil dancing in his eyes as he looked at him, then swiveled toward Cherry. "You're welcome. Welcome to Lucky. How about I take you out to dinner later and show you around?"

Cherry looked at Bolt, no doubt seeing the anger in his expression. He couldn't hide it. And Evan couldn't help himself. He wanted people's forgiveness, yet he had to tango with the devil.

She looked at Evan. "I'd love to, but Bolt told me he was grilling steaks tonight. I got my heart set on that now."

"Another time, then," Evan said smoothly as if he hadn't been rejected.

Although Cherry lied through her teeth about her plans tonight, he decided he'd make it real. She was getting steaks because she took a side when she didn't have to.

Not to mention, he needed to question her about the rag. Why would she do something like that? Was her intention all along to break down and be stuck in town? To what end?

He slammed his door harder than he intended when they retreated to his truck.

"Well, I didn't see any of that coming. But I'll take the money if he's willing to buy it."

Bolt turned to her, his expression hard, unable to smooth it out. "You stay away from him. You need to deal with your car, fine. I'll bring you. But I don't want you alone with him."

He hadn't meant to sound so harsh. Or warn her away from Evan. But until he knew what her endgame was, he needed to keep a close eye on her. And Evan, Bolt didn't trust him whatsoever. No matter what he said and how sorry he was, he didn't trust him.

Cherry stared at him for the longest time, not giving away what she was thinking. No smile touched her lips either.

"Okay, Bolt."

While it sounded like she agreed, he had a feeling Cherry didn't always play by the rules.

PEPPER WANTED to put a hand on Kat's knee but didn't. The constant bouncing of her knee was starting to drive her nuts. While Kat's pregnancy hormones had settled down quite significantly, she still didn't feel like Kat always liked her. Now here she was, bringing new trouble to town. Kat would never like her.

Although, it wasn't her fault some woman showed up claiming to be her sister.

"Kat, knock it off. You're making me antsy with the knee tapping," Seth snapped, then ran a hand through his hair, sighing. "It's going to be fine." Then Seth looked at her. "Everything will be fine."

Pepper smiled to reassure him she understood he was only trying to comfort her. But she wasn't positive everything would be fine. How could it be fine after everything that happened today?

"Well, how long will the DNA results take?" Logan asked Charlotte, who stood near the kitchen with a glass of wine in her hand.

"Two to three days. I asked for a rush, but..." Charlotte shrugged. "You know how that goes."

"Like Seth said, everything will be fine," Logan repeated.

"Danny and Deke ran her name. She has no record. She didn't lie about not seeing Lillian. There's no record she ever visited the prison. No ties that they could see that she has to the Cheetah gang. So far, it looks like she's telling the truth. She found out you're her sister and wants to get to know you."

Seth took a seat next to her and wrapped an arm around her. She didn't know what to say. Charlotte had shared with Logan what happened, and before she knew it, the whole town had found out. She couldn't go anywhere on her shift today without someone saying something about her newfound sister.

Logan decided it would be good if they all met at his house for supper and talked about it. Made a game plan. The only people not in attendance were Danny and Deke, who were working a case out of state at the moment, and Bolt, who was babysitting her...sister.

"I don't like it," Charlotte said, breaking the silence.

Kat rolled her eyes. "You're suspicious of everyone. Bolt will tell us more when he can. He's up close and personal with her right now."

Seth cleared his throat. "He did call me earlier. Told me about Evan asking her out."

Which had bothered Pepper that Bolt called Seth instead of her. Not that she said anything to Seth. She didn't want to cause waves. Not yet, anyway.

"To needle him, Seth," Kat replied. "Evan hasn't been friendly with anyone since everything went down."

"Which is ridiculous because he brought it on himself." Charlotte huffed and took a sip of wine.

"I hate to break up this...chat," Aubrey said, coming from behind Logan in the kitchen, "but it's time to eat."

They all took a seat around the table, passing the dishes

around. Aubrey had made pork chops with green beans and mashed potatoes. Pepper always enjoyed coming over to their house because Aubrey made the best food. She wasn't that cook savvy. Seth wasn't either. These home-cooked meals meant so much to her, especially when she didn't get them growing up.

Seth cleared his throat, scraping his fork around his plate. He'd been tense since Bolt called him before they left for Logan's. She'd asked if everything was okay, and he assured her it was, yet she had seen the tightness in his features. The worry. He was holding something back, and she hated it. Of course, fighting with Seth was the last thing she wanted, so she didn't argue or insist he tell her whatever it was.

Because, honestly, did she want to know? It couldn't be anything good.

Seth blew out a breath. "Bolt told me one more thing."

The room grew silent. No one made a move to eat a bite.

Her entire body grew taut as she waited for him to drop the bomb at their feet.

"Evan told him he found a rag shoved in the tailpipe, which could've caused the engine to break. She broke down on purpose."

Seth turned his head toward her and grabbed her hand that trembled near her plate. "I won't let anything happen to you. Not again."

"Bolt ask her about it yet?" Logan asked, his voice tight with anger.

Pepper appreciated the support and love from everyone, but this was her problem. She should be asking Cherry about it.

"I should ask her."

Seth squeezed her hand. "No, you won't. Bolt said he'd

handle it." Seth looked at Logan. "He said he'd chat with her about it tonight."

Logan nodded, his jaw clenched. "I'll check in with him later. Seth's right, Pepper. Let us handle this."

"My sister, my problem."

Why did she have such a dysfunctional family? Why did it feel like she was cursed?

"That's an order, Pepper. I'm treating it as a crime, and I'll investigate it. Don't fight me on this." Logan's face was filled with tension, yet his eyes were soft with concern.

Pepper didn't want to fight with anyone. "I don't want her hurting any of you either. She shouldn't be staying at Bolt's. It's a bad idea."

Kat tossed her head from side to side as if contemplating it first. "Bolt can handle himself. He's not going to change his mind now that it's settled."

"I know he can. It doesn't mean we should risk it."

"I'll talk to Bolt later. If we agree something else should be done, we'll do it. But I'm with Kat," Logan said, glancing at his sister. "Bolt can handle himself. He's smart and intuitive, and if she makes one wrong move, he'll stop her."

Pepper hoped it didn't come to that.

4

————————

CHERRY TOOK a sip of her water as she watched Bolt flip the steaks on the grill. Despite her telling a small fib to Evan, Bolt made it come true by actually making her steaks. Conversation didn't flow as smoothly as she would have liked though. Ever since they left the mechanic's, there had been a weird tension between them. Even weirder than the beginning. That had felt like some sweet sexual tension she could get down with. This... was something else. Something she didn't like.

He was holding something back from her.

She wouldn't say she always did the smartest things in life. Too many stories to back that up. But Cherry had decent intuition most of the time. She could sense when something wasn't right. Half of the time, she managed to get herself out of whatever sticky situation she had landed in. The other half of the time, she failed and paid the consequences. She wasn't looking to fail this time around.

"So, tell me about Lucky. What's there to do around here? What's the one thing I have to see?"

Bolt turned away from the grill, hanging the tongs on

the side of it. He had a simple grill. Charcoal, not gas. It hadn't taken him long to get it going, indicating he grilled often.

"Not much. It's a pretty small town. Fishing or swimming seems to be the thing to do in summer. We have some nice hiking trails. In winter, there's a hill on the other side of town that's great for sledding, skiing, and snowboarding."

She stood up from the deck chair that wasn't as nice as the rocker on the porch and smiled, walking closer to him. "There's gotta be one thing that Lucky's known for. Every town, despite being so small, is known for something."

Bolt shrugged and didn't return a smile. "Nope. It's a pretty boring town."

"Then why do you still live here?"

He frowned. "Because it's my home."

She nodded, although couldn't relate to that sentiment. She'd never had a home. Not that her mother moved her around a lot, but she didn't make anything in the crap tiny apartment they lived in feel homey at all.

This wasn't working. She didn't like the awkward, icky tension between them. She might never get to know Pepper better, but she wanted—needed—at least one friend in this town. And she decided Bolt would be that person. He'd been so nice to her since the moment they met—until now. She knew the way to get under his skin and get him to confess what was bothering him. She could thank her mother for those skills.

"Well, someone else knows that one fun thing about this town. Evan probably does."

Bolt clenched his jaw, his eyes narrowing. "We already had that conversation. Do you want to be on Pepper's bad side by making friends with him?"

No, she didn't. It was the last thing she wanted to do, but

she at least got a rise out of him. And opening a can of worms she wasn't sure she should touch.

"I don't think we fully finished that conversation."

Bolt folded his arms. "Why do you say that?"

"I might be a blonde, but I'm not dumb." She folded her arms to mimic him. "You're holding something back, and I want to know what it is. Ever since we left the garage, you've been weird with me."

"I don't even know you that well to be weird with you yet."

Her skin tingled and her heart jumped at the way the words left his mouth. Not sexual in nature, but that's how her mind warped it. The intense way he watched her probably had something to do with it as well.

They stared at each other, neither blinking nor barely breathing it seemed.

"Why are you here, Cherry?"

Her stance faltered and her arms slid to her sides. "I already told you why. I want to get to know my sister. Not everyone has a family, you know."

She hated herself for adding that last part. For making herself sound so vulnerable. But the way his eyes bored into her, staring so hard and deep, it came out as if he demanded she spill her guts. Her deepest, darkest secrets.

"You drove all the way from Florida?"

She gave a tight nod.

"Was that the first time you had car trouble?"

"Are you kidding me?! That piece of shit was always giving me trouble. It's the first time it completely died on me. I can only be grateful it happened once I got here." She twisted, needing a moment of not seeing his intense gaze. She stared at the big yard, the woods surrounding the property. It looked so serene and beautiful. And blissfully quiet.

She could get used to this peacefulness. She'd always been surrounded by the loud noises and the hustle and bustle. It got old after a while.

"I might have never met Pepper if it broke down somewhere else. As you no doubt figured out, I don't have a lot of money. I could be stuck in some other small town that has no *one fun thing* to it."

She hated the sarcasm in her tone, but she couldn't stop it. He wanted her to trust him, but she deserved the same respect. If he couldn't tell her what he was hiding, then she wasn't going to return the favor. Not that she was hiding anything. Or anything much. Bottom line, her problems had nothing to do with Pepper.

"Evan found a rag in the tailpipe. That suggests the car was purposely tampered with so it would break down."

She shivered, wrapping her arms around herself. Not from the venom and distrust she heard in his voice for the first time. She knew he didn't trust her, but he'd never so blatantly and vehemently let that distrust out.

Oh, no. Shivered for a totally different reason.

From the knowledge that she hadn't escaped. That this new adventure was merging with her old nightmare.

All she wanted to do was move on with her life and forget her past. Make new memories. Make a new life with a new family.

Was that so hard to ask?

This time as her eyes gazed around the yard, she looked at it differently. Straining to see every tree branch, every stick, every leaf, every little thing out there. Although, nothing stood out. Nothing that didn't belong. Of course, she didn't believe for a moment they were alone. Just the two of them. Not with the information Bolt provided her.

"Nothing to say?"

No, she had nothing. The shivers increased. What could she say? He wouldn't believe her anyway. No one did. Not even her mother.

Which was why she ran.

Far, far away.

Only to learn, not even a full day in town, that she hadn't gotten away at all.

She wanted to turn and throw her arms around Bolt and thank him for saving her. If that rag had been put there to intentionally make her car break down, then he saved her life. He'd come upon her shortly after it happened. Any longer alone and she would've been a goner.

A warm hand touched her shoulder.

This time she shivered for an entirely different reason. His touch wasn't rough, but soft and tentative, as if he wasn't sure he should even reach out. She was so glad he had, but despite wanting to fling her arms around him and show her gratitude, she couldn't. Telling him anything would only put him in danger too. She would never allow that to happen. He might not trust her, but she couldn't see him get hurt.

She turned. His eyes thinned, this time with concern.

That look made it harder to hold in her secret.

"I want to trust you, Cherry. I want to think you're here for no reason other than to get to know Pepper. I want to believe that you won't hurt my friends. But I can't until you trust me and tell me the truth."

She wanted to trust him. She really, really did.

"I didn't put a rag in my tailpipe. I needed that car, so I wouldn't sabotage it myself. How am I supposed to get around now? Walk everywhere? I am telling you the truth. You're choosing not to believe me."

But she couldn't trust him. Trust didn't come easily. She didn't foresee it happening anytime soon, not with the way he still looked at her warily and with the distrust lingering in his eyes. So she held some information back; it couldn't be helped. She was no liar though. She had nothing to do with the rag.

"Well, if you didn't, someone did. The question is why."

Oh, yes, that was a very good question. She didn't know the answer to that either. It seemed silly to strand her in this town. But there was a reason for it, she only had to figure it out.

On her own.

"You're not going to tell me."

"How can I tell you something that I don't have an answer to?"

He frowned. "I'm not an idiot either. I can tell when someone is evading the truth."

"Maybe I shouldn't stay here. Not if you don't believe me. Don't trust me."

Trust went both ways. She understood that. But if he didn't trust her, how could he expect her to trust him?

Bolt took a step back. "Feel free to leave. I'm not sure where you're going to go. I already told you there wasn't much open around here."

Right. She forgot about that. She was stuck. With a man who was wary of her...and who she was attracted to despite it.

———

BOLT WAITED for her to say "Fine, I'm gone." He could see it in her eyes she wanted to go. Oddly enough, as if she wanted to run far away from this town, even Pepper.

Which told him that rag in the tailpipe had something to do with her and nothing to do with her playing games with Pepper. He believed her when she said she didn't do it. But that meant someone else did. Cherry knew who but was refusing to tell him. How could he keep her safe if she didn't share everything she knew? Because he would. It was his job to keep people safe.

And she was Pepper's sister. He wanted to believe so badly she was here for a good reason, not a nefarious one. For that alone, he had to keep her safe.

"Well?"

She looked away at his insistence. He felt bad for pushing her, but he wanted answers. He wanted to show her he could solve her problems. Keep her safe. Fix whatever issue she was dealing with. It couldn't be good if someone was messing with her vehicle like that.

"I don't know what to say. You're right. I have nowhere else to go. I don't even have a ride out of town now."

Bolt wanted to step closer, touch her shoulder again, but knew it was a bad idea. Getting attached to her would be wrong. At least, not until they knew they could trust her. That she wasn't here to hurt Pepper.

"I'm not kicking you out. I want to help."

Her gaze tore away from the woods and back to him. The sadness that spilled out broke his heart. What put that there? *Who* was the better question.

"Being the only nice person so far is helping me. I didn't expect open arms from Pepper, but I also didn't expect..." She shrugged. "Her to be so abrupt with me. I get it though. Her other sister is a psycho. I appreciate your kindness, Bolt."

She was trying to change the subject and doing a half-decent job at it. His heart swelled with happiness at her words. Of course, he shouldn't let her avoid the problem. But for now, he'd let it go. They'd only continue to go round and round in circles and her potentially leaving and that was the last thing he wanted.

"Give her time."

Her eyes flashed with fright, yet she said nothing. It's as if she told him without words she was running out of time. But from what?

Good thing he could be tenacious and bullheaded. Not that many people would attribute that trait to him. But he was. He'd prove to Cherry he could help her with whatever she was holding back from him, and he'd help her connect with Pepper. That's how determined he was to get her to trust him.

"Those steaks smell delicious."

"Shit!" He chuckled and turned back to the grill.

They had to be done, and when he checked them, he confirmed he was right. Thank goodness she decided to change the subject once again. Dodging and deflecting. For now, he'd let it slide because otherwise, they would've been eating burnt steak.

The meal was wonderful—in Cherry's words—and the conversation flowed easily. They stayed away from any car talk and Pepper talk, so no tension surrounded them. She told him about growing up in Florida with a mom for a stripper. Life had sounded tough and unhappy at times, yet she made it through to adulthood without failing school. She skipped college and hadn't settled on any specific vocation. After she left Lucky, she wasn't sure where she intended to go, other than knowing she didn't want to go back to Florida.

Bolt told her about growing up in Lucky where everyone knew your business, where gossip ran wild, and where people could jump in without a moment's notice if someone needed help. Small-town life had its perks, and it had its turn-offs. He stayed away from talking about his brother, not wanting to get into it. They also didn't venture into any Cheetah territory or the things that had happened in the past few months. That would only bring Pepper into the conversation, and as good as things were going, he didn't want anything to mess with it.

Once done eating, they cleaned up together, had a drink on the deck without much conversation that time, and then he showed her the spare room.

"Sheets are clean. They were changed last week." Because his mother could be a control freak at times, wanting to run his life, no matter how many times he told her he was fine. She couldn't hover over Carson, so she decided he was the next best thing. Plus, she'd barely given him time to breathe since he was shot. Of course, he didn't mention any of that. Awkward.

"You know where the bathroom is. I only have one. The hallway closet next to it has towels and such. I work tomorrow, so I'll be getting up at six and to work by seven. I can swing by at some point and bring you into town if you want to explore and whatnot."

Her eyes widened. "Oh, my gosh. It's like after ten. You should've told me you had to get up early. You didn't need to stay up on my account."

He waved his hand in the air as if it weren't a big deal. Which it wasn't. He wouldn't sleep much anyway, but there was no point in telling her that.

"I enjoyed the evening."

A shy smile appeared, which looked so odd on her normally vibrant, outgoing face. "I did too." Then she bit her bottom lip. "Do you mind if I come into town with you in the morning?"

"So early?" Not much would be open.

"Yeah, I'd love to explore. Why wait?"

Despite the cheeriness in her tone, he saw the slight panic in her eyes. Did she not want to be alone out here? He lived out of town surrounded by woods. It was quiet. Too quiet?

"Okay. That's fine. I'll wake you after I get out of the shower and you can take one."

"Perfect."

Her smile filled his heart with joy...and his cock jumped to attention that he didn't need her seeing.

"Right. Okay." He turned around. "Uh, good night."

He walked out without another glance, mentally berating himself for being so abrupt with her. But hell, he didn't want her to see his sudden attraction that he'd had a hard time hiding most of the night.

Why did he have to be attracted to her? Why did she have to be so beautiful? Why did he feel this strong, sudden allure toward her when he never had with a woman before?

The hardest question to answer was could he keep his distance?

5

———

SHE GROANED before acknowledging Bolt with mostly intelligible words that she would get up when he knocked on her bedroom door. The hot water helped to wake her up some more. Mornings and she usually didn't agree. But there was no way she wanted to be stranded in his house so far from town—alone. She had seen the question in Bolt's eyes, yet he chose not to interrogate her about it. She was grateful for his self-control.

Breakfast was lovely and surprising when she walked into the kitchen to see he made eggs and toast. She normally had a bowl of cereal and called it good. The strong cup of coffee—straight black—did the trick to wake her up even more. She liked creamer to tame down the taste, but being up so early, she needed a pick-me-up as much as possible.

Bolt looked dashing in his uniform. The gun resting on his hip made her heart skip a beat. Not that she'd seen many guns in her life, but they made her nervous. Just eyeing it now as he put his mug in the sink brought one particular memory to mind that would be best left forgotten.

He turned around, jerking. Then he was by her side,

sweeping a hand across her cheek. The touch came out of nowhere, startling her and sending her insides to goo. He didn't touch her often, but when he did, she felt a zing all the way to her soul. What did it mean? Why did he affect her so?

"What's wrong? You look like you've seen a ghost."

Did she? Her hands felt clammy, which was why she didn't reach up and remove his hand when it lingered on her cheek. She must look pale and queasy because she felt the eggs and toast threatening to make an appearance.

"I'm fine." She smiled, hoping to convince him and thwart any further questions. "I usually add creamer in my coffee. I shouldn't have skipped it. Too much caffeine." She even threw in a chuckle.

He didn't look convinced. His brows were still low and his eyes filled with concern.

She placed a hand on his chest, shocked to feel his heart beating abnormally and at a high rate of speed. He was truly worried about her. How sweet.

"Not to mention, I didn't expect to see you look so handsome in a uniform. You gotta warn a girl next time."

He finally cracked a grin. His head lowered a fraction as if he were going to lean in and kiss her.

Yes, please!

Then he froze and nodded. "We should go."

Her hand slipped away from his chest as he walked around her and toward the front door. Moment was over. Which was for the best. Getting involved with someone from town, especially Bolt who'd been the kindest to her so far, would not be wise. She wasn't planning on sticking around anyway. Get to know Pepper some, plan a future time to hang out, and then hightail it out of town.

Where she'd go from there, she wasn't sure yet, but

something would come to her. It always did. She might be impulsive, but it also gave her adventure in life. Because life shouldn't be dull and boring. It was meant to be lived to the fullest extent.

The drive to town was quick, and he parked in the lot next to the sheriff's department like last time.

"Not a lot open until eight. You can hang in the office until then if you want."

Cherry pushed her lips to the side, contemplating it. "Does the meanie behind the desk work today?"

Bolt chuckled. "Charlotte? Yeah, she works there every day. She's nice once she lets her guard down." He frowned. "Be careful today. Pepper doesn't rub everyone the right way, but she's a part of the town."

"And I'm not."

He tilted his head, offering an encouraging smile. "We can be protective of our own. A lot of stuff went down with the Cheetahs. It will take a while for that to disappear. People won't be unkind..."

"But they won't be welcoming. I got it. I'm a big girl, Bolt. No need to worry about me."

His lips tilted downward again. "I find I can't help myself. You should get a phone. If you need me, I want you to be able to call me."

"I'm fine."

His frown remained. "You say that a lot."

"Because I am."

But she could tell by the agitation in his gaze that he didn't believe her. Didn't trust her.

This time she reached out to him, grazing his cheek. "Fine. If it'll make you feel better, I'll check out a prepaid phone. Something cheap, so that if I need to call you I can."

He nodded. "Thank you."

His gaze held strong to her eyes until they ventured lower to her mouth. She wanted to reach out again and grab him around the neck and pull him closer. Take charge and demand the kiss that he seemed to want to give her.

Instead, he turned away and opened his door. "Let's go. I'll introduce you to Charlotte properly. She won't bite, I promise."

She rounded the truck and looked around. For a Sunday, it was quiet, although it was also super early in the morning.

"Another time. I want to walk around for a while. I told you, I want to explore."

That darn frown was still plastered on his face. Then he checked his watch. "Meet me back here at noon. We can have lunch together. I can get your phone number."

Right. From the phone he insisted that she get. He was not going to give up on that.

"Deal. I'll see you then."

She turned around and walked in the opposite direction before he could argue with her and convince her to stick by him. She was a big girl. She'd been taking care of herself for as long as she could remember. Her mother sure didn't take care of her like she was supposed to. Some of her mom's co-workers, other dancers, had been more maternal than her mother had ever been. Her mom didn't even know what that word meant.

Walking along Main Street was quiet. Like Bolt said, the places weren't open. Not that she had a reason to go into the hardware store when she passed it. The boutique she would've dipped into. When it opened, she would. She turned the corner once she got to the end of the street and saw a diner down the way. She already ate, but it would kill some time while she waited for the stores to open. She needed to buy a phone—for Bolt. Another cup of coffee would be nice too.

She took a seat in a booth away from the door in the way back. This place definitely wasn't quiet. She didn't take the booth in the deep dark corner on purpose. She just didn't have anywhere else to sit. The place was packed.

"Hi. Welcome to Lucky. I'm Callie. What can I get ya?"

What was Bolt talking about? This woman with pretty, long blonde hair seemed friendly enough.

"Uh, a coffee, for now. Thanks."

While the doughnuts on the counter in the clear display looked tempting, she had to watch every penny she spent. Even having this coffee was splurging.

Callie nodded with a gentle smile and walked away, bringing her coffee within less than a minute.

The soft sounds surrounded her. People spoke quietly, darting lots of glances her way. She met every person who peeked at her with a solid stare. She wasn't going to cower away from them. She hadn't done anything wrong, so why should she? They always looked away first.

The bell above the door rang with merry. Callie greeted the young, handsome man with a cheery hello.

Seth.

Pepper's Seth?

When he looked around the diner, checking out where to take a seat, his eyes pinned on her. As he moved her way and stopped at her booth, she figured, yep, Pepper's Seth.

"Cherry?"

She nodded and waved a hand at the empty side across from her.

"So you know who I am?" he asked with a scowl.

Cherry shrugged. "I heard Callie call you Seth. Bolt mentioned a Seth was dating Pepper. So unless there's more than one Seth in town, I can only assume you're Pepper's Seth. That's all I know."

His maddened expression softened as his shoulders loosened and he leaned back into his seat. "Your deductions are correct."

Callie swung by and put a coffee in front of Seth. "The usual?"

He nodded, and she left as quickly as she appeared.

"What's the usual for you?" Cherry was only curious because making idle talk was better than the icky silence filling the space.

"Eggs, over-hard, toast, and lots of bacon. I don't always come in on the mornings, but when I do, I get the usual."

"And why are you here this morning?"

He leaned forward, propping his elbows on the table. "I should be the one interrogating you."

She forced herself not to fiddle with her coffee mug and smiled as if his words didn't affect her. "Interrogate away. I have nothing to hide."

Seth leaned even closer, lowering his voice. "I won't let anyone hurt Pepper. I don't care if my brother is the sheriff."

Well, that wasn't a subtle threat at all. Not that Cherry minded. Pepper was lucky to have someone who cared about her so much. She'd never had that a day in her life.

"Do you like having a brother and sister?" Bolt had given her the rundown last night on everyone in their circle. The people she'd most likely have to deal with the most. Springing these unexpected visits on her.

Seth's eyes narrowed, silent for a beat as if trying to dig deeper into a simple question. She wasn't trying to play games here.

"Yeah, I do. I won't let anyone hurt them either."

She looked away, staring out the window. The parking

lot was full of cars. The sun was shining. The day already proved it was going to be a hot one by the temps that stifled her as they walked out of the house this morning.

"I always dreamed of having a brother or sister. I figured with as loose as my mom is, I would've gotten one eventually. Guess she was only careless when it came to me."

Her gaze swiveled back to Seth, who looked confused and startled by her candidness.

"When I found out I had a sister, you have no idea how excited I was."

"Sisters. Or did you forget about the evil twin?"

Cherry nodded. "Oh, yeah, I totally dismissed her when I read that article. I don't need that kind of crazy in my life." *I already have enough I can handle.* Though he didn't need to know that.

"You should stay away—"

"Don't warn me away from her. She said she'd give me a chance." Well, Pepper said she'd meet her for lunch or something one day. That was saying she was giving her a small chance.

He surprised her by smiling. Not a devious or cunning one, but with a touch of kindness lingering in it. "I was going to say, you should stay away from Evan."

"Yes, Bolt has already told me that. What's the story there?"

Seth leaned back, taking a sip of his coffee before speaking. "It's a long one."

She spread her arms wide. "I got all the time in the world."

"How are you doing?" Bolt asked Pepper as they chatted in the break room. It was close to his shift being done, and Pepper had been on duty for a few hours and would finish the night out.

She shrugged. "Fine, I guess. How was Cherry last night?"

Bolt shuffled through the entire evening on fast-forward, then let out a breath. "I honestly don't think she's here to do anything bad. She swears she didn't stuff the rag in her pipe and doesn't know who could've. Although, I do think she was holding back about knowing who could've."

Pepper frowned. "Why would she do that?"

"She doesn't know us. She doesn't trust us yet."

It felt better for him to say 'us' instead of 'me' because it pained him to think Cherry didn't trust him. But he figured if she didn't trust him, she didn't trust anyone else yet either. Despite that, he was happy to know she did what she said she'd do. At lunch, she showed him the prepaid phone she bought and gave him her number. Although she didn't get a lot of minutes, so she made it clear to only call her if it was very important.

"Seth had breakfast with her."

Bolt nodded. He already knew that because Cherry told him at lunch. She had only nice things to say about Seth. She also told him she would stay away from Evan. When she settled her car, she'd make sure he was with her. Seth had told her the whole story of what went down with Evan. Bolt was thankful she was starting to see why she needed to keep her distance from Evan.

"Are you mad at him?"

"No. He was gathering intel is what he said." Pepper grinned. "He's not going to listen, even if I told him to stay away from her."

No, Seth didn't listen to many people, even his brother who had arrested him before to teach him how to grow up and that consequences came with actions. But Bolt figured if Pepper asked him to, Seth would try hard to respect her wishes.

"He wants to invite her over for supper."

"Well, the results should be in soon. That's what you told her you'd do. Chat over food."

Bolt didn't want to take sides. Of course, if it came down to it, he'd take Pepper's side, but he also felt bad for Cherry. All she wanted to do was get to know her sister, and Pepper was pushing her away.

"Yeah, I know. I will. I'm glad he didn't do it before the results came in." Pepper huffed out a large breath. "Everyone likes her. They hate me and I've been here how many months now. She hasn't even been here a full day and they all like her. I stopped at the gas station and Greg had nothing but wonderful things to say about her."

Bolt laughed. "He's also a guy who can't help but look. Cherry's a beautiful woman."

Pepper's eyes narrowed. "Don't tell me you have the hots for my sister, Bolt."

He stiffened, his tongue stuck in his throat. Perhaps he should've worded that differently.

"I would never...she's pretty, but I...you're my friend. You come first."

Pepper laughed, surprising him. "You should see your face right now. It's so red. So unlike you. She is pretty." Pepper's smile died. "She obviously knows how to get under people's skin. How to fool them. How to make them like her with ease. Greg wasn't the only one who had nice things to say about her."

Bolt wanted to tread lightly here. Sure, he saw Pepper's

side of things that Cherry had a master plan and the first part was to get everyone to like her and on her side. But he also spent the most time with Cherry so far. He knew her upbringing had molded her in certain ways, made it easy for her to chat with people. Pepper, on the other hand, did not endear anyone to her side with ease.

Plain fact was, Cherry was more likable, and Pepper wanted to see the nefarious part of it instead of the truth.

Bolt had been wrong this morning warning Cherry the townsfolk wouldn't like her. He figured they'd be on Pepper's side because she was part of the town. Oh, how wrong he'd been. He felt bad for Pepper that they hadn't.

"It's okay. I get it. You don't have to figure out how to protect my feelings. It's nothing new, people liking my sister over me. Doesn't even matter it's a different sister. I can see you like her, even though you think you shouldn't."

Bolt put his hand on her shoulder. "I would never do anything to hurt you. I won't cross that line with her."

"The fact that you have to say that means you want to." Pepper patted his hand before removing it. "I would never ask you to hold yourself back if you want something. I'll only say be careful."

Bolt frowned. How did this conversation turn so wild, so quickly? Who said he wanted Cherry? One stupid comment about how beautiful she was and Pepper assumed... well, to be fair, he did think she was beautiful. His cock had jumped to attention too many times last night, which confirmed it as well. But that didn't mean he'd think with his dick over his head.

"I don't sleep with women because I think they're beautiful. I want more than just sex from a relationship." He looked away. "In fact, I don't sleep with women often. If you haven't noticed, I'm not that smooth when it comes to women."

"If Seth hadn't stolen my heart first, you definitely would've."

He snapped his head at her. "Seriously?"

Pepper chuckled. "Yes, seriously. You were the only person to treat me normal when you first met me, even when I wasn't that friendly. You were kind and patient. You're, like, the perfect guy. My sister would be lucky to have you. Any woman would be."

He could feel his cheeks flaming again. "Thanks, Pepper. You don't have to say that, but it means a lot. Also, you keep calling her your sister. It's like you've accepted it before it's been confirmed."

"I don't know what to say. I felt it in my gut this morning that she wasn't lying. I also saw a bit of my dad in her." Pepper looked at the floor and rubbed her foot against it. "I always wanted a good relationship with Lillian. I wanted that sisterly connection others have. Maybe now's my chance for a re-do. Does it make me dumb I want to trust her?"

She raised her eyes until they hit his.

"No, it doesn't. Because then it makes me dumb too."

Pepper patted his shoulder. "Well, neither of us are dumb, so..."

"So, we're trusting her?" Bolt wasn't sure where this conversation was going now. It'd been an odd one since the beginning.

"I think so."

He winced, then grinned. "I need you to sound more confident than that."

"What does your gut say?"

Oh, man. He didn't want to answer that question. His gut

had failed him before. The scar on his stomach proved that. He'd thought he'd been cautious and smart in the woods how many months ago. One bad move and Wayne Barten proved him wrong.

"Bolt, I trust you and your instincts."

Pepper would never know how much that meant to him. Nobody—not even the sheriff—had ever had that much faith in him.

"She's hiding something, but I don't think it has anything to do with you. I truly think she wants a good relationship with you, but I also think she's running from something. I can't get her to tell me what it is."

"Well, if anyone can, it's you. I say we trust her." Pepper's brows dipped low, her eyes full of concentration. "And if my sister is in trouble, then we fix it. Because that's what family does."

He knew Pepper wasn't just talking about biological family, but the people who became your family in other ways. Like their small, tight-knit group. They were family. They'd been through so much together, and he would always consider them family.

"We'll get to the bottom of it."

He would get to the bottom of it. Nothing would stop him.

6

CHERRY FLINCHED when she heard Bolt walk into the kitchen, yet she didn't turn around. She stared at the silly origami rose she created out of a napkin and hesitated.

A rose?

Well, it was better than a heart, but not by much.

She knew how to do a few other shapes and animals, but the rose hit her mind first and she went with it. Now she was unsure.

"Thanks for making coffee," Bolt rumbled behind her.

Deciding she couldn't change it now, she threw the napkin in the paper bag and rolled it shut, then turned to him.

"You're welcome. I made your lunch too."

Bolt frowned, blowing on his coffee. "You didn't have to do that."

She shrugged like it wasn't a big deal—because it totally wasn't.

"I made myself a lunch, so why not yours too."

His lean body—so defined in all the right places—rested

against the counter as he took a sip of coffee. "I appreciate it. You know you don't have to keep coming into town with me. You can chill around here."

And be home all alone? No, thanks. She didn't want to risk it. Nothing had happened in the week she'd been here, but that didn't mean something couldn't if she suddenly put herself in a vulnerable position.

The week had gone faster than she realized it would. It's like she blinked and it was over. Every morning—on the days Bolt worked—she went into town with him and hung around, stopping into the stores and chatting, saying hi. She walked around, getting her exercise in, but always made sure to be around people. Never alone. It wasn't official or anything, but she helped Mrs. Dunburry at the boutique most days. She had the coolest outfits and accessories that Cherry loved to organize and reorganize, finding new ways to make them look pretty in the displays. Mrs. Dunburry seemed to enjoy the company. If Cherry wanted to know about something—or someone—in town, Mrs. Dunburry was full of information. She was the worst gossip in town. Not that she hadn't gotten the story from Seth, but Mrs. Dunburry gave *her* version of everything that went down with the Cheetahs, Evan, and everyone else.

Two days ago, the results came in. She and Pepper were half-sisters. There was no denying DNA. She'd yet to actually sit down with Pepper and talk about it. Act like sisters. Hopefully soon. Because one of these days, Bolt was going to ask her when she planned to leave, and she didn't know what to tell him.

Because she didn't want to leave.

The people seemed to like her, and she liked them. The town was growing on her. The intricacies of it. The gossip. The closeness the residents had.

Even Bolt himself.

He was the utmost gentleman that she'd ever met. Honestly, she hadn't met many nice men in her life. Not hanging around her mother as long as she had. He gave her a roof over her head. He fed her. He chauffeured her around. He took care of her. So making his lunch was nothing compared to how much he helped her.

"Cherry?"

She blinked, realizing she'd zoned out on him.

"I enjoy going into town. I'm pretty sure Mrs. Dunburry is expecting me." It was as good an excuse as any.

She wasn't ready to admit her problems and why she didn't want to be alone. Surprisingly, Bolt hadn't inquired more about the rag in the pipe. It's as if it never happened. Oh, how she wished she could pretend it never happened.

He nodded, though a slight frown still marred his handsome face. "Umm...so, the sheriff is having everyone over tonight for supper. You're invited, of course."

"Really?" Her first official invite to a party. How exciting.

A short grin appeared. "Yeah. You're Pepper's sister. She'll be there. It'll be a good time for you two to get to know one another."

In a neutral space with others around. Very smart. She didn't mind at all because Bolt made her feel more centered and sure of herself. It wouldn't be as scary knowing he'd be there in case things got out of hand. Not that they should, but Cherry had come to learn things always had a way of turning for the worst.

"Who will be on duty if all of you are there?"

Bolt had the craziest schedule. He'd had Saturday off the day she first met him. Then he had Tuesday off, and worked through until today, Saturday, again. He told her last night when she asked that he had tomorrow and Monday off. No days were ever the same he informed her. It's as if the sheriff wanted to keep people on their toes, making no set schedule. Worried the Cheetahs could do something if they knew the routine? Cherry wasn't sure and she didn't want to ask. She didn't want to do anything to rock the boat.

"I'll be on-call if something happens. Pepper, the sheriff, and I rotate. We're a small county. Nothing crazy usually happens."

Until the Cheetahs came along, though neither of them voiced it.

It made sense. Not to mention, according to Bolt, the other three towns in the county had their own police force. Most calls went to them before the sheriff's department.

"Thanks for the invite."

Then silence filled the room. Weird, awkward silence. Which didn't normally happen between them. She could talk to Bolt about anything and everything and it never turned odd. She felt safe and comfortable with him. Maybe one of these days she'd spill her secrets. Her problems.

"Well, you ready?" He stood up and downed the rest of his coffee.

"Yep."

He nodded, then shuffled past her, brushing her shoulder with his as he put his cup in the sink. She turned, grabbed his lunch bag, and twisted back around, flinching when she realized he had moved closer into her space. A breath away.

"Your lunch."

He took the bag and smiled. "Thanks."

His gaze dropped to her lips, snapping back up to her eyes. She wanted so badly for him to give in, stop resisting. Just kiss her already. Although, she also knew why he hesitated. Pepper would always come first between them. She was only someone passing through. Pepper was a good friend.

It sucked, but it was nothing new in her life. Always being looked over for someone else. Never important enough. Never loved like everyone else.

He nodded again as if she had said all of that out loud, agreeing with her. She wasn't lovable.

She followed him out of the house, her lunch bag in hand and her purse strapped over her shoulder.

The ride was mostly quiet, except for the radio filtering through the speakers. Country, which wasn't a genre she had enjoyed before. She found she was starting to like it. Bolt only listened to country music.

He parked the truck and looked at her. "Let me know when you're ready to take care of your car. Have you gotten the title for it yet?"

Nope. While it should be easy enough, she didn't want to make the call.

"Working on it. I'll get it soon."

"Then you'll be gone?"

Ouch. What a way to tell her she was losing her welcome status in his life.

His cheeks flamed a bright red as he reached out yet didn't quite touch her. "I didn't mean it to sound the way it came out. You're welcome to stay with me as long as you need. I was only curious if...when...how long..." He sighed. "None of that is coming out right."

"I shouldn't be in your hair too much longer. As soon as I get the title and buy a new car, get to know Pepper some, I'll be on my way. I promise."

His lips turned down, his eyes flashing a bit of pain. "I

didn't mean it the way it sounded. You don't have to leave. I mean, so soon. I wasn't trying to rush it. That isn't what I meant."

She believed him, yet her heart still ached from the way he said it. The way he blurted it out as if he didn't want her around anymore. Again, nothing new. Everyone always got sick of her sooner or later.

"It's okay, Bolt. I'm not offended." Just hurt. Gutted to the core. Not that she'd ever admit it.

She threw a smile out, picked up his lunch, and handed it to him. "Have a good day. I'll see you around five."

He took the bag, brushing his fingers with hers. She hated the spark of heat she felt from the gentle touch.

"Yeah, you too. Call me if you need anything."

She wouldn't, but she nodded to appease him, then hopped out of the truck and waved her hand. She didn't even look to see if he watched her walk away. Most likely, he didn't. She was nobody to him. Pepper's half-sister who didn't have her shit together. Broke and homeless. Yeah. She wasn't surprised he wanted her out of his house—his life. She was mooching off him and taking advantage of his kindness. She'd be living in the woods if it weren't for his kindness.

She did her usual rounds, popping into different stores, saying hi and chatting about the weather and mundane things. They seemed to enjoy her visits as much as she did. Sure, part of it was to be around people and stay safe. The other part was simply because she enjoyed conversing with others. She was definitely an extrovert.

When she sat in the park at one of the picnic tables to have her lunch, she smiled thinking about what Bolt thought of his rose origami she made him. The smile died quickly as images rolled through her mind. Disgust and irritation that she would do something so...romantic. She should've gone with a swan or dumb shape that didn't say 'Hey, I like you. Kiss me already.'

Although her appetite disappeared as her mood turned sour, she forced herself to eat. In a few days, she wouldn't be eating so well, so she had to take advantage of it while she could.

She pulled her phone out of her purse and fiddled with it. It was time.

Considering she didn't have enough money to maintain a regular cell phone bill, she didn't know many numbers. Only two she knew by heart. Her mom's and the club where she worked. She dialed the club first.

Peggy answered, and her heart rate slowed down a fraction.

"Hey, Peggy. How are you?"

"Girl! Where are you? I haven't seen you in, like, two weeks. You okay?"

The concern in her tone startled Cherry, but only for a second. Peggy was the closest thing to a friend she had. While Peggy was twenty years older than her, she understood her more than her mom ever would.

"Yeah, just went on a road trip. Came to meet my...half-sister." Keeping a secret wasn't a big deal anymore. She knew he had found her and was bidding his time. Not to mention her mom—if she cared to wonder where she disappeared to—would figure out she sought Pepper out.

"You should've told me you were leaving. I've been worrying like crazy about you. Your mom said you were fine. I guess I should've listened to her."

Cherry could've been lying dead in a ditch and her mom

would say she was fine. The woman didn't care about anything but herself.

"Sorry. I didn't mean to worry you. I have a favor to ask. Kind of a big one."

"You got it, girl. What do you need?"

This was where it got tricky.

"I need the title to my car. It's beyond repair, and the mechanic here is willing to buy it from me."

She heard Peggy release a short breath.

"Yeah, I know. I don't have a key to give you to get in. I know where he hides one."

Peggy lowered her voice as if someone were near her. "He finds out I went into his house without asking, there's gonna be hell to pay. He's been looking for you. He's been as worried as me that you aren't around."

No, Cherry wouldn't say he'd been worried about her. More like pissed she ran away. Of course, he had no reason to be. He kicked her out of the house after accusing her of cheating on him. The man was certifiable. Another guy looked at her—for even a second—he got insanely jealous. Their last fight had been a doozy. Yelling so loud the neighbors had called the cops. He had raised his voice more than she had. All she wanted to do was leave and never come back. Just like he told her to. "Get out, you cheating whore." Then as quickly as he said it, he was trying to apologize and beg his way back into her good graces. It had always been hot and cold with him.

"I didn't take much with me. Some clothes. So, unless he threw the rest of my stuff out, it's in his bedroom in the closet. He keeps it in a fire safe. I know where he keeps the keys. In his tackling box in the garage. Thinks it's the safest spot. I think it's dumb."

Not that she had ever said that to him. She'd always had

to be careful what she said to him, how she said it. It had been like walking on eggshells the entire time she'd been with him. If her mother hadn't—

Nope. No use laying blame on someone else. She played a part in it as well. She could only blame herself.

"He hides a house key under the tenth brick around the pathway to the front door."

"Once I get it, where am I sending it?"

This was why she loved Peggy—trusted her the most out of everyone in her life.

"Minnesota. I'll give you the address to the sheriff's department here." He knew she was staying with Bolt, but on the off-chance it wasn't him who stuffed the rag in her tailpipe, no need to give him the information.

She trusted Peggy to get her what she needed, but she wouldn't put it past him to find out anyway.

"The sheriff's department? You locked up?" Peggy nearly shrieked.

"No! My sister is a deputy. It's the best place to send it."

"Are you safe?"

Cherry thought of Bolt and his kind eyes, his generous heart. For now, yes, she was. As soon as she left him, she'd be a sitting duck.

"I am. You don't have to worry about me."

"Well, if I need to call you, I just call this number?"

"Yep. It's a prepaid phone, so I should go. I don't have a lot of minutes. I appreciate this, Peggy. I'll text you the address."

"Keep in touch, girl. Take care of yourself."

She hung up with Peggy, feeling better she'd have the title in her hand soon.

But also feeling the dread filling her up.

Because as soon as she had the title, she had to leave.

Bolt didn't seem like he wanted her around much longer. She understood that.

BOLT STARED at the rose origami and felt even worse than he had this morning.

Then you'll be gone?

What an idiot! He had made it sound as if he wanted her gone—now. So far from the truth. The past week had been one of the best weeks of his life. She made it so much brighter and livelier. When she left, his house would feel so empty. So, no, he was not ready for her to leave at all. The only reason he had brought it up was so he could prepare—get his heart ready—for when she left. Like the moron he was when it came to women, he said it all wrong.

What did this rose mean?

Well, it obviously didn't matter now because she had fled as fast as she could this morning after his bumbling. If she had a thing for him, it was over. He'd made sure of that.

"What's that?" Danny asked, walking into the break room.

Bolt glanced up, shoving the rose back into the lunch bag. Which was dumb after he thought about it, especially by the way Danny's brow rose.

"Just a napkin."

"That you felt the need to hide after I already saw it."

Bolt stood up from the table and grabbed his bag to throw it away since he was done eating, yet he stopped himself before letting it go above the trash can. He didn't want to throw the rose away. Now if he pulled it back out, he'd look like even more of an idiot in front of Danny.

"I didn't mean to surprise you, Bolt."

He sighed, figuring it didn't matter now anyway. She was leaving soon and glad to get out of his house. The bag dropped from his hand, the rose disappearing into the trash can.

"You didn't. Although what are you doing here? When did you guys get back?"

Danny poured a cup of coffee and leaned against the counter. "Late last night. I was chatting with Logan in his office. I wanted a cup before I left."

"Everything okay?" Bolt knew the sheriff had come in this morning for a little bit, but he didn't work Saturdays often. Only when there was trouble. If Danny was popping in, since he worked for the FBI, that meant there was trouble.

"It's all good. We chatted a bit about Cherry. Odd name."

"It suits her. I like it. What's there to chat about? She isn't here to hurt Pepper." He believed that way down to the bottom of his gut. There was no way it was wrong. Not this time.

Danny held up a hand as if warding him off. "I didn't say she was. You like her."

"She's my friend." Like Pepper was.

Well, except for the part where he wanted to kiss Cherry and a whole lot more he shouldn't even fantasize about. He'd never had those kind of thoughts about Pepper before.

"Logan said you were a bit touchy about Cherry. Nobody can say a bad thing about her if you're around."

"He said that?" Was he that obvious about his feelings concerning her? Could she see it too?

Duh. No. Because she wouldn't have run as fast as she could away from him this morning if she could.

"He did. Not in a bad way. Just that..." Danny smirked. "You like her."

Bolt looked away, staring hard at the trash can that now held something special. He shouldn't have thrown away the rose.

"She's different. She's always happy and vibrant. Talks a lot, not that it bothers me. She has a soothing voice." He sighed, dropping his head in defeat. "I didn't know it was so obvious."

"Everyone around town seems to like her too. So Kat said. Hell, even Kat didn't have anything bad to say about her, and you know how difficult Kat can be."

Bolt snickered. "Oh, I know. Charlotte hasn't warmed up to her though."

"Give it time. I'm sure she will. How long is she sticking around?"

Bolt didn't even want to think about it. "Don't know. She didn't say. Her car is busted, and she has no way out of town."

"Logan told me. Nothing on the rag bit, uh?"

"Nope. I haven't come right out again asking her about it, but I have an inkling she knows who did it. She likes to talk, just not about herself. I mean, she's mentioned her mom here and there, but not much else."

"Be careful."

Bolt's brows puckered low. "I always am."

Danny held up his hands again after setting down his mug. "I meant watch your heart. Don't get too attached because she'll eventually leave." Then Danny grinned deviously. "There's nothing wrong with having a little fun though."

Fun?

As in sex?

Bolt didn't know if he had it in him to have sex with her.

That wouldn't be protecting his heart. He wanted more than just a romp between the sheets.

"She deserves better than that." *And I want more than that.*

He didn't say it out loud, but he knew Danny saw it in his eyes.

"Can't wait to meet her tonight."

Bolt wasn't sure how he felt about the get-together tonight, but he knew Cherry had been wanting to spend time with Pepper, and now was her chance.

The rest of the day went by quickly. Cherry was in the parking lot waiting by his truck when he came outside. The ride home was quiet, besides the part where he asked her how her day went and vice versa. She wanted to change after getting some paint on her shirt. She said she had some fun in the hardware store looking at paint samples. He wanted to know why she had been looking at something like that but didn't ask. Fighting—or arguing—this morning hadn't been pleasant. He'd like to avoid it if he could.

As soon as she changed, they headed to Logan's. He pulled into the driveway at the same time as Deke and Charlotte. Introductions were made between her and Deke. Charlotte even seemed slightly less frosty toward her. Perhaps she was starting to like Cherry as well. It didn't shock Bolt one bit. The entire town adored Cherry. She was very easy to like.

Danny and Kat arrived a few minutes later, and Bolt had to look away when Danny gave him a goofy grin after meeting Cherry. Seth and Pepper arrived last. Logan was grilling tonight. Bolt was happy to see Cherry and Pepper take a seat next to each other by the bonfire Logan had started before heating up the grill.

Seth appeared by him holding an extra beer. He took it

and nodded in thanks. Though he didn't open it. He was on-call, so he had to be levelheaded if he had to leave abruptly. Seth didn't know he was on duty.

"So, how's it going?"

"Good."

Seth cocked a brow. "I meant with Cherry. You getting sick of her yet?"

Never.

"She's fine. Why?"

"Pepper's been struggling all week about this. Whether to put herself out there. Whether to push Cherry away. She's thinking about asking her if she wants to spend a few days with us. We wanted to see if you're okay with it?"

Bolt jerked back. "I don't have any say about it. It's not like...we're together or anything. I'm being nice."

He couldn't suppress a groan when Seth looked at him like Danny had this afternoon.

"Does everyone know I have a dumb crush on her?" Everyone but her, apparently.

"It's not dumb, Bolt." Seth took a gulp of beer. "She's beautiful. Any man can see that."

"Does Pepper know you think that?"

They chuckled together.

"Pepper knows I love her. I'd be lost without her."

A sharp pain hit his chest. He almost reached up to rub across his heart but stopped himself.

Would he be lost without Cherry? His house would definitely be a lot quieter, and he wasn't sure he'd like that.

"You don't have to run anything by me, Seth. If Cherry wants to stay with you two, that's fine."

"You find anything more about that rag business?"

Bolt shook his head. "She doesn't open up about everything. Trust me, I've tried. Maybe she'll confide in Pepper."

They both sought out the women sitting close to the fire. Not that it was chilly out, but there was something about a bonfire that enticed a person to sit close. The heat washing over your body. The smells. The sound of wood cracking and spitting.

He wished like hell she'd tell him everything. Every little secret inside her.

7

"YOU DIDN'T MISS MUCH NOT MEETING our dad. He gambled too much, and my mom enabled it. Grew up with a sister I never got along with. My childhood sucked."

Cherry laughed, then threw a hand over her mouth, her eyes widening. She didn't mean to laugh at what Pepper said because it wasn't funny. It was just the way she said the last part that made her giggle.

"I didn't mean to laugh. I wasn't laughing at you."

"Oh, I get it. It's good to laugh sometimes."

"My childhood wasn't any better." Cherry looked at the flames dancing before them. "My mom is a stripper. Has been all my life. I'm kind of jealous of how tone her body is and everything. She still commands the stage, and guys can't keep their eyes off her."

That garnered a chuckle out of Pepper, making Cherry feel even better and less like a fool.

"She's always been more concerned about herself than me. Despite her lack of attention, I made it through to adulthood."

Pepper tilted her head. "You're twenty-four. You didn't go

to college. Or anywhere local, like a community college. Why not?"

Cherry decided to ignore the fact she didn't tell Pepper any of it, meaning Pepper had a deep background check done on her. There was no point in being offended. Not when Pepper had a twin sister who tried to kill her. Pepper had to be cautious, Cherry could respect that. She understood being wary and watching her step.

"Never had the money. My mom tried to get me to join her. She said we'd make a good duo up on stage." Cherry stuck out her tongue and shoved a finger in her mouth as if she wanted to gag. "The money enticed me, but then I thought of all those disgusting men ogling me and it was easy to say no."

"Yeah, I could never do that. I can't even dance." Pepper glanced behind her. Cherry figured to seek out Seth, making her think Pepper might not know how to dance but she wanted to. At least, with one guy.

Maybe she'd teach her someday. Cherry never joined her mother on the stage, but that didn't mean she didn't have the moves.

"I read the article you saw in Florida. It was very thorough. I'm glad I didn't see anything like that here. I want to forget it ever happened and move on." Pepper jerked her attention Cherry's way, her eyes widening in large circles. "I didn't mean that I want you to leave. This might take me a while to get used to, but..." She looked at the ground, then back at her. "But it'd be nice to have at least one family member that I'm close to. It'll help me think there's nothing wrong with me."

"I'd like that too. That's all I wanted when I came here. A chance at getting to know my sister."

Another tentative smile graced Pepper's lips. "How long do you intend to stay?"

"I called my friend Peggy. She works with my mom. She's always been like a second mom to me. Well, more like an actual mom than my real mom. Anyway, she said she's going to grab the title to my car, and then I can get a new one. Be on my way and out of Bolt's hair. I think I'm overextending my stay." Cherry reached out and touched her arm. "But I would love to stay in touch. Visit now and again."

"I'd like that." Pepper eyed her funnily, glancing behind them again, her eyes narrowing when she met her gaze. "Did Bolt say he wanted you to leave?"

Cherry shrugged. "In so many words, yes. It's okay. I can be a handful. My mom's said it plenty of times. Still does."

Pepper nodded as if she understood how much those simple words could hurt.

"Bolt would never kick you out like that. Maybe you misunderstood him."

"I don't think so. He basically asked me when I'll be gone. He tried to backpedal, but words don't lie."

Pepper swallowed hard. "No, but they can come out sounding the wrong way and not being what you meant. I should know. I suck with words. People always take what I say the wrong way. I'm not a big people person. Hell, everyone in town loves you and you've been here a week. I've been here months and they still haven't warmed up to me."

"They like you. I haven't met one person who said something bad about you. Or unkind."

Hope filled Pepper's eyes. "Really? Are you sure?"

Cherry giggled. "I swear. I would never lie to you." She frowned. "I know how it feels to be lied to."

"Where will you go from here? Back to Florida?"

"No, there's nothing there for me."

And what was there wasn't something she wanted to go back to. Ever.

This time Pepper reached out and touched her arm lightly. "Are you running from something? Because not only am I your sister, I'm a deputy. I can help. I also used to work for the FBI. I have contacts and resources."

"Why would you ask that? There's nothing wrong."

Pepper frowned, her brows drawing low. "There's the business with the rag in your tailpipe. There's also the fact I can read people well, even if I suck at getting along with them. Bolt even thinks you're hiding something."

He did?

He never gave her that impression. Wow, the man sure knew how to fool her.

"Just like he wants to help, so do I." Pepper looked at the fire, putting her hands out as if she wanted to touch the flames. "I made the mistake when I got here to keep my secrets close to my chest. To lie and figure it out on my own. I nearly paid with my life. Seth didn't only save me from death, he saved me from missing out on a life I didn't know I needed."

Pepper dropped her hands and returned her gaze to her. "You can trust me. You can trust Bolt. He's a good guy."

"I don't know who..." Cherry let out a large breath. "Damn it. I said I'd never lie to you."

Pepper's lips turned up into a wide grin. "That's right, you did."

"Maybe I have an inkling. But it's nothing. He wouldn't hurt me." She didn't want to say that was a lie, but it felt false as it left her lips.

The fierce look that snapped onto Pepper's features frightened her. "But he did try to hurt you. Something seriously bad could've happened messing with your car like that. Who is this guy?"

"A mistake. It's fine."

"You're not going to give me a name, are you?"

Cherry smiled, resting her elbows on her knees. "How about a compromise? If he does something else, I'll tell you. Otherwise, I'd rather just let it go. I've been here a week, and he hasn't shown his face. That makes me think it wasn't even him."

She might not have seen any sign of him, but she'd felt the hair on her arms stand up on numerous occasions throughout the week. Felt eyes on her, even when she saw nothing out of the ordinary. If he was watching her, he was doing a damn good job staying in the shadows.

Pepper stared hard at her, not loosening her intense expression at all. Cherry did not want to get on her bad side. It was scary.

"Fine. One thing, even if it's something super-duper tiny, you tell me his name. Promise?"

Pepper stuck out her hand.

Cherry reached over and shook it.

"Promise."

"Now about Bolt."

Cherry flinched, retreating her hand from Pepper's strong grip. "What about him?"

"He'd never hurt you, Cherry. He's a good man."

"I know. You said that already. But, like I said, I'm a lot to handle and get on everyone's nerves."

"As my sister, I'm going to give you my first sisterly advice."

Cherry chuckled, her heart swelling with joy that they even got to this point so fast. With the way Pepper had greeted her in the very beginning and ignored her all week, she didn't think they'd get this close so quickly.

"Okay. What's your sisterly advice?"

"Open those big green eyes of yours. Really look at that man. Think about how he's treated you this week. Do you think he wants you out of his house?"

Well, before this morning, she would've said no. They got along so well. Laughing at silly jokes. Talking about nothing and the space not getting awkward. Making sure she was always comfortable and not needing anything. Looking at her in a way that set her body on fire. His gaze always lowering to her mouth as if he wanted to kiss her breathless and not stop until they were both gasping for air.

Yet, he sounded so...distraught this morning.

Maybe she read him all wrong. Heard it incorrectly.

"Hmm, mmm. That's what I thought." Pepper picked up her beer from the ground and took a sip. "That man doesn't want you leaving. He just plain wants you." Another intense stare came at her. "Sister or not, if you hurt him, I'll have to hurt you."

Seemed fair. Not that she planned to hurt him.

BOLT SHUT and locked the door behind him. Cherry glanced over her shoulder when she heard the lock click.

"Umm...I guess I'll see you in the morning. Maybe we can check out the lake."

He'd love that. After he screwed up earlier this morning making her think he wanted her to leave, he was elated she wanted to hang out on his day off. Driving wouldn't take that long, since it was only a short distance from his house, but he'd love to run there if she was up to it.

"Sounds like a plan. Do you run?"

Her eyes bulged as a silly grin touched her lips. "Only when I have to. But if you want to make it a workout, I'm game."

"It's not that far..." he trailed off, not adding *not far* to him was a lot different from her. "About a mile..."

By the way her lips twisted in a wicked jest, he knew his instincts were right. His definition of *not far* was nowhere close to hers.

"I can do that. No problem."

That's one of the things he enjoyed most about Cherry. Her willingness to try anything. Her upbeat attitude and positive thinking. She didn't want to do it, but she would.

"We don't have to run the entire way."

"You worry too much, Bolt. It's all good. I'm going to get ready for bed."

Then she left the foyer before he could say anything else. Like an apology for earlier and making her think he wanted her gone. She didn't bring it up all night, so he wouldn't either.

She hadn't said anything to him on the way home from Logan's about spending time at Pepper's, so either Pepper didn't ask her, or she didn't want to say anything yet.

The kitchen brightened as he flipped the switch up. The counters were clean, the dishes put away. A towel hung through the loop on the oven handle, something Cherry did, not him. His place looked homey with little touches here and there for the first time since he moved in a year ago. All it needed was a woman's touch. Not that he was a super messy guy, but he didn't think about things like folding the blanket and putting it over the back of the couch until it was time to use it. Doing laundry before the basket became overflowing and annoying to look at. Picking wildflowers from the woods and putting them in a glass in the middle of the table. He'd have to buy a vase so the next time Cherry did that, it'd look even lovelier sitting in the room, giving off a nice aroma.

He'd miss her when she left.

Hell, he didn't want her leaving at all.

Ignoring the ache deep inside to knock on her bedroom door, he got ready for bed himself. And what would he do when he knocked anyway? Kiss her? Get an invite inside? Tell her how beautiful she looked tonight? Like she did every day and night.

After brushing his teeth and using the bathroom, he tossed off his shirt and pants and slid under the covers. His eyes glided to the wide-open curtains, letting in the sliver of moonlight that filtered through the trees. He didn't feel like getting up and closing them. Sleep wouldn't come easily regardless, and now he had a reason to get up early. More time to spend with Cherry.

It was a little past eleven and he didn't feel an ounce of tiredness in his body. More like revved and raring to go. For what? He had no idea.

He closed his eyes, pretending to sleep, as if that would actually make it happen.

He jerked upright when he heard a muffled scream. *Cherry!* He swung out of bed, glancing at the clock.

1:33 AM.

He swung the door open and silently chastised himself for not knocking. Until he saw her sitting up in bed, her arms wrapped around her knees with a frightened expression on her face.

"Hey, what's wrong? What happened?" Bolt sat on the edge of the bed, placing a hand on her arm.

The panic in her eyes decreased a fraction when she met his gaze.

"Cherry?"

"I...it's nothing. I must've had a bad dream."

She shifted, making him loosen his grip and drop his hand from her arm. Okay, she didn't want him touching her. He could respect that.

But he wouldn't stand for lying.

"It's not nothing. I heard you scream."

She shivered. "I'm sorry I woke you."

He hadn't been sleeping. Sure, he'd closed his eyes, trying to find that elusive sleep, but he hadn't dozed off since his back hit the bed. Nothing new.

"Maybe it'd help to talk about it."

Another tremble rippled across her body. "I don't think it would."

His hand lifted. She jerked. Sensing she wasn't afraid of him, even though she shifted away, he kept going until his hand hit her cheek, smoothing across in a gentle caress. She leaned into his hand, closing her eyes. His instincts had been correct. She was spooked, but not by him.

"I can help you if only you'd let me."

Her eyes opened, the fear still present.

"Was it really a dream?"

She shook her head slowly.

"Then what was it?"

"You'll think I'm seeing things."

He frowned, sensing there was more to that statement. As if he wouldn't be the first person to tell her she was going out of her mind.

"I won't."

She glanced at the window. He followed her gaze. The wind had picked up since they arrived home. It had been relatively quiet this evening, making it a nice night for a bonfire. With the way it howled and moaned now, it would've been dangerous to start a fire. A small tree close to his house knocked and scrapped occasionally at the window.

"Cherry?" he whispered her name, putting pressure on her cheek for her to look at him.

Her gaze swiveled back to him, the fear intensifying.

"I thought I heard something, which woke me up. When I looked at the window, I swore I saw someone standing outside." She chuckled, though no humor mingled with it. Then she grasped his hand and removed it from her cheek, dropping it to the bed and letting go. "It was obviously the wind and the tree banging on the window. I feel so silly now. It was nothing. I'm sorry for waking you. Truly, I am."

Bolt looked at the window again and the tree swaying heavily to and fro as the wind whipped around. Not good signs for their run tomorrow to the lake. A sign it planned to rain soon?

"I'll go check it out."

He stood up and she reached out, grabbing his hand, holding on tighter than was necessary. Her panic was filtering out in waves.

"It's fine. It was nothing. Don't go out there."

Because she didn't think he could handle it? Because, damn it, he could.

Or because she didn't want to be alone? That reasoning would work much better for him. For his pride.

He leaned in, brushing her cheek one more time, dying to swoop in and kiss her. He resisted, but barely.

"Let me make sure it was nothing."

He had to practically rip his hand out of hers, telling him she was a lot more frightened than she wanted to admit. He threw on a pair of pants and a shirt and grabbed his weapon from the nightstand. He never slept too far from his service weapon. He grabbed a flashlight he kept in his closet.

She was in the hallway when he stepped out of his room. "Stay inside."

"You don't have to go outside. It's the wind. It was nothing," she begged as she followed him to the front door.

He slipped on his shoes, ignoring her pleas, because frankly, they were starting to piss him off. It was easy to hear the fear in her voice, but it also made it feel like she didn't trust him enough to keep her safe. He could do this, and he was so sick of trying to prove himself to everyone.

"Bolt—"

"Enough, Cherry!" he snapped, hating the way she jolted back a step and the terror in her gaze that increased as if he had hurt her. He sighed, turned, deactivated the alarm, and then unlocked the door. "I can handle this."

Then he walked outside and shut the door. The wind whipped around, slapping him in the face, neck—his entire body. It felt sticky out, the air charged, as if waiting for something to happen. Definitely rain on the way.

As soon as he stepped off the porch, his security lights popped on, making it easier to see. His vehicle looked undisturbed. With the wind making a ruckus, it was hard to hear anything out of the ordinary. He started to circle the property, taking his time, looking for anything odd or that didn't belong. When he neared her window, he paused, staring at the ferns nestled against the side of the house.

Crushed.

As if someone had stepped on them to get closer to the window.

She hadn't been imagining it.

Sure, the branches could've been the thing that woke her, but the silhouette she saw against the window hadn't been fake.

His heart pounded as the rage inside built.

Who the hell was messing with her? Trying to hurt her? Scare her?

He turned around, glancing around, staring at the woods, the darkness that lay before him. His eyes had adjusted to this side of the house where he didn't have motion sensor lights, something he needed to rectify. Nothing looked off. No animals. No person hiding. That he could see anyway.

Was someone still out there hiding behind a tree? Waiting? For what? What was this person's endgame?

He continued walking around the house, looking for other clues. Besides the area around her window, nothing else looked disturbed. When he entered the house, Cherry wasn't in the area. He locked up and slipped off his shoes. She wasn't in the living room or the kitchen, and the bathroom door was wide open with the lights off. He found her in her room, huddled in the middle of the bed, same position as he had originally found her.

He sat down and set his gun and flashlight on the nightstand. She jerked, her eyes pinned to the gun. A shiver wracked her body. He shifted until she couldn't see it, sensing she wasn't a fan of the gun.

"I'm sorry for yelling. I didn't mean to."

Her mouth was turned down, her eyes filled with pain more than panic. At least the fear had started to ebb away, although he didn't like to see the pain either.

"I'm sorry for making it difficult on you. I didn't mean to make you think you couldn't handle it. I just didn't want you going outside because I have an overactive imagination."

"How many times has someone told you that?" He ached to reach out, but he stopped himself. Now was not the time for distractions. They needed to have a serious conversation and he couldn't distract himself from it.

She bit her bottom lip and shrugged.

Avoiding the question. Fine, he wouldn't pry it out of her yet.

"I think it's time you told me who wants to hurt you."

Her arms tightened around her knees. "I don't know what you're—"

His finger over her lips stopped the rest of the lie from leaving. "Don't treat me like an idiot because I'm not one."

"I'd never do that."

"You were about to lie to me, saying you don't know."

She looked away, her eyes turned down as if she were staring at her feet, which started to wiggle under the blankets. "Did you find something out there? Is that why I'm getting the third degree?"

"First the rag in your tailpipe. Now someone's peeping into your window."

Her head whipped to his. "It was the branches."

"The branches didn't crush my ferns underneath the window. You didn't imagine anything." Damn it. He scooted farther onto the bed, grabbing her by the shoulders when she started to shake. "I'm not trying to scare you, but I won't lie to you. So, please, don't lie to me either."

"Oh, Bolt." Then she bent her head, leaning into his chest.

He wrapped her securely into his arms, vowing silently he'd protect her with his life. It wouldn't be easy, not with the way she held certain parts of herself back, but he wouldn't let that stop him.

He'd never forgive himself if something bad happened to her.

"Cherry, you need to tell—"

Her arms slid around him, squeezing his shirt tight. "Not tonight. Please, Bolt. I promise I'll tell you everything tomorrow. With Pepper. I promised her if something else happened, I'd tell her. But please, not tonight. Just hold me."

How could he argue with that? The plea in her tone. The tremble in her touch. The terror in the way she clung to him. He couldn't deny her anything.

8

IN THE LIGHT of the day, things didn't seem so scary. She acted like a frightened child scared of the dark, and she wanted to scream at her idiocy. Bolt had to think her the biggest moron in the world. Clinging to him as if she couldn't solve her own problems.

Well, she could. She did. She was not a weak woman in need of saving.

Yet his arms around her had made her feel safe. Made her feel like nothing could touch her.

Like the gentleman he was, he offered to stay in her room last night, and she let him like a pathetic fool. He slept above the covers and nothing sexual happened. That should've been her only regret last night, except it wasn't. It wasn't even the worst regret she had.

Never again would she act like a scaredy cat. Nobody would frighten her to the point she begged for anything.

She watched as Bolt cleaned up the kitchen from breakfast, then her attention turned to the window where the rain beat against it. So much for running and enjoying the time at the lake on his day off.

Now this whole day would suck.

When a knock sounded on the door, she gripped the coffee mug tighter and wished she could magically disappear from the room. Hell, the town altogether.

Bolt came back into the room with Pepper in tow. She was dressed in her uniform, officially on duty. Cherry would've liked it much better if she were here as her sister, not a deputy.

Pepper took a seat at the table. Bolt sat on the other side, scooting his chair a fraction closer to her.

"Morning."

Though she sounded chipper, she knew she hadn't fooled either one of them.

"Bolt tells me you had an interesting night."

Well, that was one way to put it. Made it seem as if she hadn't acted like a frightened child.

"Did you ever try to tell someone, like a teacher, parent, or friend about something that was going on and they didn't believe you? Or say they did believe you, and yet, nothing ever happened or changed?"

They both looked at her oddly. If she was going to tell them everything, they had to understand. Maybe her question was dumb, but she had a point to it.

"I remember telling my mom one time that Lillian was stealing my chore money. Not that we earned a lot for doing chores. But I worked hard for that money. She didn't believe me. And I had no proof. She said I didn't put it in the same place or spent it without realizing how much I spent."

So Pepper understood. She knew the feeling Cherry experienced more times than she cared to count.

Bolt didn't say anything.

"Remember how I told you I didn't go into my mom's line of work?"

Pepper nodded.

Cherry fiddled with her mug, staring at the dark substance inside. "Well, I didn't get on stage, but I waitressed for a bit. Started dating the manager and, like an idiot, moved in with him. I hate to say I was taking advantage of the situation or anything, but money was tight and he offered a place to stay and I took it. I figured I'd have a better chance to save money and find a place of my own with him helping me out."

Ugh. How familiar did that sound with what Bolt was doing? Helping her out because she was broke. At least she wasn't sleeping with Bolt. Then the stories would sound way too similar.

Of course, she *wanted* to sleep with him. How sad and pathetic was that?

"So this guy...he followed you here," Pepper stated when Cherry didn't continue.

Cherry looked up and shook her head. "I don't think so. He does have a possessive streak. Always getting in my business, asking where I was going and who I was going with. Getting a little too testy with guys when they'd make lewd remarks at the club. He thought I was his, and I told him I was my own person. We fought too much. All the time."

Pepper frowned. "It doesn't sound like someone who's going to give up easily."

"Yeah, well, I can take care of myself. He knows I'm not afraid of him."

"What's his name?" Pepper drew out a notepad with a pen, poised and ready.

"Dean Anchor. But it's not him."

"You just said he was possessive," Bolt said tightly.

Cherry twisted his way, noting the tension in his shoulders, his jaw clenched and a muscle jumping in his cheek.

"He would drive me to and from the club. I mean, you've seen my shitty car. It's not always reliable. I let him up until I told him I wouldn't take his possessiveness anymore." Cherry shivered, gripping her mug harder. "That's when I started to get the feeling someone was following me. Watching me. About three weeks before I left."

"Dean?" Pepper prodded lightly.

"No, it couldn't be him. He'd still be at the club when I would leave sometimes, and I'd get the feeling. I never saw anyone in particular. Just this...weird feeling."

Pepper tilted her head. "Who'd you try to tell?"

Her sister was no dummy. Of course, her odd question in the beginning was starting to make sense to her now.

"My mom. My friend Peggy. Dean. They all told me I was being silly. Nobody was following me. Why would they?"

"Did this person," Pepper said, hesitating on the word person, "ever do anything? Approach you? Or you've always had the sense someone was watching?"

"No one's ever approached me. No flowers or anything, like a secret admirer, if that's what you're asking. Just" – Cherry couldn't hold back another tremble— "this sense someone is always watching me. I don't have anything to prove it. And you're thinking—"

Bolt's hand covered hers, cutting her off and settling her emotions because she'd been shaking so hard the coffee in her mug almost spilled over the edge.

"I believe you."

Her bottom lip wobbled at the sincerity in his voice. Nobody had ever believed her before. And she didn't blame them. It seemed crazy to think someone would follow her. She wasn't anything special. They'd never done anything to her. No contact. No jumping out at her. No leaving things behind. Stalkers—if that's what she wanted to call this person—usually made their presence known in some sort of way.

"It could be anybody, especially working at a strip club. Creepos coming in and out," Pepper said with disgust. "You're sure you don't think it could be Dean that followed you here?"

"He kicked me out after a big fight, then retracted his words, begging me to stay. I told him I was moving out still and we were done. He laughed at me and didn't believe me. Always thinking he has the control like I'm his little puppet. Though I saw him flirting with a new waitress the same day. I hate to admit he was right, I didn't move out that day. A few days later, I saw the old article about you and I thought now was as good of a time as any to meet you. I was getting ready for work, planning to tell Dean I wanted vacation time—and that I was officially moving out—and I swore someone was in the house with me. I heard the front door open. I know I did. I crawled out of the window and went to the club. Dean was there. It wasn't him. I mean, I didn't check out the house. I could've been hearing things. I told him I needed some time. He denied me. So I told him I quit and he had no say what I do. I hit the road without looking back. Half my shit is still in his house."

Cherry stared hard at Pepper, pleading with her eyes for her to believe her. Like Bolt did. His strong, confident words 'I believe you' washed over her again with such elation. Nobody—nobody—ever believed her. His hand was still holding hers. She had let one hand go from the mug, which allowed him to slide his fingers through hers. She didn't know how much she needed that support until he showed her.

"I know you want to think it's Dean because he can be a real jackass, but it's not him. He's an asshole, but he's not a psycho asshole. He was possessive, sure, but he never hit me. He wasn't physical with me. I was an idiot for sleeping with him, but I'm one woman in a long line of women he takes to bed."

At that confession, she wanted to slip her hand out of Bolt's, but his grip tightened as if telling her it didn't matter. That her past didn't define her in that way.

Ha! Who was she kidding? Bolt didn't want her that way. If he did, he would've made a move last night. They slept in the same bed all night long.

Pepper finally nodded, her eyes trailing to their locked hands, then back to her face. "That doesn't help us then. It could be anybody."

"But we live in a small town," Bolt said with confidence. "We start asking around about people who've been in town. Outsiders stick out like a sore thumb."

"It's the summer. Lots of tourists come through town," Pepper replied, sighing.

"Yeah, but in the past week, which ones have been around town—a lot." Bolt squeezed her hand. "Cherry's been in town all week. If this guy is following her around, makes sense he'd be in town too."

"I'll start asking around. I'll have Logan help me."

Bolt nodded. Cherry figured they didn't want to leave her alone, and she was totally a-okay with that.

"When the rain lets up, I'm going to add motion sensor lights all around the house. Nobody is creeping up that close again without me knowing." Bolt frowned. "I'll call my brother Carson. He might help."

Cherry appreciated everything these two were doing for her. But they didn't need to.

"I'm sure this is nothing. I'll be fine. I hate for you two to go through all this trouble for nothing."

She jerked when Bolt reached out with his other hand, putting it behind her neck and pulling her closer. His hot breath hit her lips, enticing her to move even closer. Pepper's short chuckle had her stopping a stupid impulse that would make her look like a complete fool when Bolt rejected her.

"Stop saying you're fine. It's not fine. Nothing is fine when someone is terrorizing you. Scaring you. You might think I can't solve this, but I can. Pepper and I will. This person is not going to get away with hurting you. Got it?"

She inhaled deeply, her heart skipping a beat at the way his eyes slid to her lips. *Yes, kiss me.*

His fingers tightened around her neck. He leaned even closer, his lips getting precariously close to hers. "Got it?" he whispered, his breath like a kiss upon her lips.

"I got it."

Then he loosened his hold and let her go, breathing as heavily as she was.

Damn him.

Why couldn't he kiss her and get it over with?

It was for the best. She wouldn't be sticking around much longer anyway.

"I APPRECIATE YOUR HELP." Bolt didn't look up at Carson as he said it. No doubt he'd see nothing but indifference.

If it wasn't that, it was anger and irritation. Bolt still had no idea why his brother shut him out. Cut off communication and acted like he hated him for some reason. Though it hadn't been just him, but the entire family. Carson rarely came around anymore. He didn't call their parents to say hi. He didn't attend holidays. One day, it's as if his brother died and this man who looked like his brother showed up. Bolt wouldn't say they had been super close growing up. Carson was older by nearly five years. By the time he came, Carson didn't want a baby following him around. He played with him on occasion, but for the most part, Carson merely tolerated him. Now, he acted like a stranger.

Carson nodded as he stepped off the ladder. "Who is this woman again?"

"Pepper's half-sister. We're not sure what's going on, but I don't want someone sneaking up on the house again."

A short nod answered him, then Carson tossed his head toward the woods. "I can set up some surveillance cameras too if you want."

"I don't want to take up much more of your time. You sounded busy when I called."

That was Bolt's polite way of saying Carson didn't sound happy to hear from him.

"I'll do it."

Then Carson picked up the big black duffel bag he had and headed for the woods.

End of conversation, apparently.

"You can help."

The clipped words had Bolt jumping. He hadn't expected that. While he had stood by while Carson installed the motion sensor lights to the house, he hadn't done anything. Despite offering his help twice. With one sharp no, and after an annoyed grunt, he stopped offering.

They worked in silence setting up three cameras. Two in the back that hit the sides of the house and part of the backyard. Coverage to get angles of both sides of the house and backyard together. One camera that gave a nice view of the front yard. Carson didn't say anything aside from asking for certain things from his bag or calling out for a tool. Bolt didn't know what to say anyway so the silence didn't bother him.

When they were finished, they went back inside the house where Carson told him to grab his computer.

Cherry popped out of the kitchen when they arrived and announced with a merry voice she made coffee. Walking back into the dining room with his computer, he found Cherry sitting next to Carson chatting away, both holding a cup of coffee. For the first time in the longest time, Carson had a smile on his face. Not a full-blown one, but a half grin that looked so foreign. He couldn't even remember the last time he had seen his brother show an ounce of happiness.

All because of Cherry.

Why was he surprised? She could light up a room with ease. Any man who saw her stopped what they were doing and gawked. She was a beautiful woman. It didn't take much to shower her with attention.

She'd won the town's approval in a day. Hell, she'd won over their tight-knit group in only a week. After everything that happened, they didn't trust easily, especially Pepper, and she had decided Cherry was here to do no harm. Of course, his gut had said that from the beginning.

"Here you go." Bolt set the computer down on the table a little harder than he meant to.

Carson eyed him but didn't say anything.

"Let me go grab your coffee. Be right back."

Cherry darted out of the room.

Carson started clicking away on the keyboard. Bolt didn't speak. Nothing friendly would come out anyway. Because, even though they weren't on the best of terms, he didn't want to get on Carson's even worse side. And heaven help him, but he wanted to warn his brother off Cherry. To stay the hell away from her. To not smile at her. To not even talk to her.

Damn.

He'd never gotten this jealous about a woman before. One he wasn't even dating.

Getting in his brother's face would be the dumbest thing on the planet. The man was a Navy SEAL. He could crush him in two without breaking a sweat. It'd be signing his death warrant if he said one word, brother or not.

Cherry bounced back into the room, holding out a steaming cup of coffee. He smiled, forcing himself to calm the hell down. He should be happy she was able to elicit a smile out of his brother. Not jealous.

"Thanks."

A jarring ring sounded from another room.

Cherry frowned. "I think that's my phone. It's probably Peggy." Then she left the room again.

"Give me your phone," Carson demanded.

Bolt didn't even argue. There was no use. In the beginning, when he started being so abrupt and rude, Bolt called him out on it. Now, he just went with it. There was no point in arguing because it never swayed Carson.

Carson tapped around on his phone, then waved him to stand in front of the computer. "This is the system where you'll monitor the cameras outside. It's all on the app on your phone too. If something steps in front of the frame, a beeping sound will go off. This is low-key, nothing high-tech like I have at my cabin, so if you need to use it, it's yours."

Yeah, his cabin had come in handy for Deke and Charlotte. The bad guys had still breached the house, but at least Deke and Charlotte had warning and made it out of there alive.

Carson handed his phone back and stood up, gesturing for him to take a look at everything.

The screen was lit up with all three cameras. They were in black and white, nothing fancy, but they were clear. Bolt messed around with the program, making sure he knew how everything worked before his brother left. He didn't want to have to bother him again. These interactions were stressful. It killed him inside his brother was so standoffish.

"I like Cherry. She seems nice."

Bolt whipped his head at his brother. No expression littered Carson's face.

"You don't have to look at me like I'm going to steal your woman. I would never do that to you."

Bolt stood up, surprised Carson was using so many words with him for once. They never had actual conversations. And about women—forget it.

"I don't know what you're talking about."

"I know the look of murder when I see it, Bolt. You weren't happy when you walked into the room and saw us chatting."

Bolt gritted his teeth, remembering the smile on his face.

"That look there," Carson said, pointing at him.

Bolt shrugged. "I haven't seen you smile in years. First time you do it's with her. I wish you could smile with me."

Boy, that sounded sappy even to his ears. But hell, as kids, even though he could annoy Carson with his begging to play with him, he'd still laugh and give in. He'd smile and play, then threaten to throw his toys away if he didn't give him some peace for a while.

"Na, that's not why." Then Carson's lips curled halfway into a grin. A shit-eating grin that said he was laughing at Bolt. "See, I can smile at my brother."

"You're mocking me now. We both know she'd pick you over me any day. They always do."

Carson frowned. "I've never stolen one of your women before."

"Yeah, okay. Fine, I'm talking in general. I always come out the loser. You know I don't have *women*. They glance at me and see an idiot."

"Do you even know what we were talking about? Did you hear anything?"

"No."

"Well, then you should shut your mouth because you're completely wrong about what you saw. I've never known you to be jealous."

Bolt clenched his teeth again. "I'm not jealous. And you don't know me at all. You don't take the time anymore to know me. You don't even care about me or Mom or Dad. I don't know what happened to you, but I wish I had my brother back."

"No, you don't. He wasn't a good guy." Carson grabbed his duffel bag from the table.

"This guy sucks. The old Carson I could at least talk to."

"I know you can keep her safe. But don't get shot again, Bolt. I didn't like seeing you in a hospital."

Then Carson turned and walked out.

Well, that was news to him. Because he didn't remember Carson visiting him once. Even his parents didn't mention that he had shown up to check on him. It had bothered him more than he cared to admit. Not that he'd ever tell Carson that. Of course, everything he just said to him was new as well. He never pushed back at his brother. Today he had.

It felt damn good.

"You were shot before? How badly? I thought Mrs. Dunburry had told me everything. She didn't tell me that."

Bolt swiveled toward Cherry, hating the distraught look on her face.

Odd Mrs. Dunburry would leave that out, but obviously, his near-death wasn't exciting news. Because he was a big fat nobody in this town.

"Last fall. It wasn't a big deal."

Only almost died, but she didn't need to know that. He didn't like her expression and wanted to change it back to a smile.

"Who called?"

"Who shot you? What happened? Why have you never mentioned this before?" She took a few steps closer. "Why is he worried someone might shoot you again? If he was talking about Dean, he won't hurt anybody."

"Do you believe that? You said he was possessive. That kind of thing never leads to anything good. Did he hit you?"

"No, I told you, he never hit me. He wouldn't dare." Cherry crossed her arms. "Now stop avoiding my question. Who shot you?"

She had a look of determination on her face, so he gave her the short version. Very, very short version. Left out all the parts that made him look like the idiot he had been. He needed her to have faith in his abilities, that he could keep her safe. So far, he felt like he was nowhere close to having that.

"Are you sure all this Cheetah business is over? They hurt a lot of people." She moved closer, within arm's reach. He swore she was going to touch him, but she didn't. "I don't want to see you get hurt."

"I won't."

He'd never let someone get the drop on him like that again. Never be painted the idiot again. Once was more than enough.

"You can trust me, Cherry. I can help you. I can keep you safe."

She smiled—finally. "I know that."

Then why didn't he believe her?

"Now you answer my question. Who called?"

Not that it was his business, but he wanted to know. If it was Peggy, he had to know. Because as soon as she got the title to her car, she'd get paid and then be out of his life. The thought was more than depressing. It was devastating.

"Peggy."

She hesitated.

His heart stopped.

"She couldn't find the title. It wasn't in the safe."

Like a shock to the heart, it was beating again.

"That's...sorry to hear that."

Jumping for joy couldn't happen, but what came out of his mouth was dumb too.

He had no idea what to say. All he wanted to tell her was how wonderful that was to hear. How sad he'd be when she left. How much she brightened his world, never fully realizing how dull it had been before she walked into his life.

It was insane how he felt.

They barely knew each other.

Maybe it was time they really got to know each other. Maybe if he showed her the kind of guy he could be—the right guy for her—she wouldn't leave.

Except he didn't know how to do that.

Not being the lame guy he was.

———

THE LIE SLIPPED OUT EASIER than she thought it would. She honestly had no intention of keeping the truth from him.

But the thought of leaving, of never seeing him again was too much.

So she lied.

Told him Peggy couldn't find the title when it was safely in her possession waiting to be mailed. She'd have to call Peggy and tell her to wait. Give her some excuse for why because Peggy put herself on the line for her, breaking into Dean's house to get the thing. She'd want to know why Cherry wanted her to wait.

Or she could come clean right now.

But then he'd hate her for lying.

"So Dean took it and hid it. That guy..." Bolt shook his head. "I'm glad you got away from him."

So was she. Dean had his mean side, but she felt bad for him taking the fall for her lie. Not enough to confess—yet.

"It has to be somewhere in the house. I'm sure I can get Peggy to go look again. Maybe I didn't put it in the safe. The house is a mess, and my memory is terrible. I could have put it anywhere."

And she should stop talking before he figured out she was lying. He was good at detecting that from her. He could even think she was lying right now.

"You'll be safe here until she finds it. I promise."

She frowned. Why did he keep telling her that? She didn't doubt it. Not once since she met him.

If anything, she was more worried about him than she was about herself. The thought of him getting hurt...it was unbearable.

She finally found the courage to follow through on her urge to touch him and placed a hand on his chest. His heart was beating wildly, almost in the same galloping rhythm as hers.

"I've never doubted I'm safe with you. You can stop reassuring me."

He nodded, then his eyes glided to her hand pressed to his chest.

"Your heart is racing." Well, duh, she didn't have to point it out.

"Because the thought of you getting hurt worries me."

She picked up his hand and placed it over her heart. "I worry about the same thing. I hate knowing you got shot before."

His jaw tensed and he jerked. "It's not a big deal."

"Seems like a big deal to me."

"So does this business with your ex. Yet you keep telling me it's fine."

Because she didn't think it was Dean. Whoever was out there watching her, it wasn't him. She could handle Dean. She *did* handle him. But this unknown person frightened her. She didn't like the unknown.

"I'm sure I'm imagining things."

"Those crushed ferns tell me differently."

She almost giggled at the intense conversation they were having holding their hands to each other's chests. What a picture it made.

"What's funny?"

Maybe a short chortle slipped out.

"Nothing. None of it's funny. It's just...the way we're standing...talking about it."

His eyes glided to his hand pressed against her chest. "Your heart is still beating like crazy."

"So is yours."

This time his eyes made a path to her lips.

Yes.

She wanted him to kiss her. Break the tension that had been simmering between them since the moment they met. Pepper and everyone else—Bolt—obviously trusted her. Took her word for what it was. That she was here to meet Pepper and get to know her. Do her no harm. Otherwise, Pepper wouldn't be helping her. Bolt wouldn't be acting so protective.

Right?

Or were they all acting, waiting for her to make a move? Something she had no intention of doing. It wouldn't be the first time she was played by people she thought had cared about her.

"Cherry..." His breaths were heavy, his heart still racing. His eyes were dilated with pleasure. She could see what he didn't want to say.

"Yes."

She made sure to answer with a firmness that he couldn't interpret. She wasn't asking him to continue with whatever he wanted to say. She was telling him to devour her.

He leaned in.

The loud ringing of the doorbell made them jump apart.

Bolt looked at her with regret, then frowned at his phone. "My phone should've beeped."

Then he walked out of the room to answer the door. She followed, happy to see Pepper return. A bit apprehensive about it as well. Because Pepper didn't look happy.

Maybe getting involved with Bolt was a bad idea. Well, of course, it was a bad idea. She was always only good for one thing. A roll in the hay. Men saw her and thought 'oh, she's good in bed. Let's do it.' They didn't see the woman behind the beauty her mother bestowed upon her. While Bolt was one of the kindest guys she had met, he wouldn't want her sticking around. All she'd been doing since she arrived was mooch off him. Nobody liked a moocher.

"What's wrong?" Pepper asked Bolt, noting his frustration.

God, Cherry hoped he didn't tell Pepper how they almost kissed. Even though Pepper seemed to have given her blessing to...to explore her friendship further with Bolt, it didn't mean she wanted to talk about it with him in the room.

"Carson and I installed motion cameras around my house and my phone didn't beep that you drove in the driveway. I thought I had it working right. I guess I didn't."

His expression, like someone had just killed his puppy, broke her deep inside. She knew that feeling well. That feeling of failure. Like she could never do anything right no matter how hard she tried.

"What happened?" Bolt asked, trying to mask his irritation and failing. Cherry could still see the desolation in his eyes.

"Look at the cameras first. I don't have much. It pisses me off."

Well, that sucked to hear. But Cherry didn't expect anything different. Whoever was out there knew what they were doing. Knew how to stay in the shadows and out of the view of any prying eyes.

"Nothing? Nobody noticed anything around town?" Bolt asked as they both followed him into the dining room.

"No. Nothing out of the ordinary. Of course, now that I was asking questions, they all said they'd keep an eye out." Pepper looked at her and smiled. "You made friends real quick around here. Sorry about it, but people are going to bombard you with questions when you go into town next time. I tried to be discreet about it, but I don't know how she does it, but Mrs. Dunburry got a bit out of me that I couldn't hold back."

Cherry matched her smile. "That's why she's the queen of gossip in town. She knows how to interrogate on the sly. I'm learning so much from her."

Everybody laughed at that, which had been Cherry's intention. Though Bolt's smile didn't last long.

"What's wrong? Do you need Carson to come back?" she asked, hating the deep frown returning on his face.

"No!"

She flinched at the way he barked the simple word. Even Pepper jumped.

"I mean, there's nothing wrong with it. It shows an alert." Bolt held up his phone but refused to look either of them in the eyes. "My phone was on silent. That's why we didn't hear it go off. It won't happen again." For that, he met her gaze.

He was too hard on himself. She didn't know how to reassure him she trusted him with her life, especially with Pepper in the room. So she didn't do anything but nod.

"Well, having the cameras is a huge help. Whoever was snooping around last night, if they do it again, we'll get them on camera." Pepper said it so confidently, Cherry could feel the tears pricking the back of her eyelids.

Nobody believed her. Not even her mother. Now, her half-sister, who was still weary of her, believed her. She was awestruck by it all.

"I should get out of your hair." Pepper glanced between them, lingering on her longer than Bolt. "Can I have a word, Cherry? Walk me to the door. I'll talk to you later, Bolt."

He jerked his head he heard but didn't look at either of them.

Cherry followed Pepper to the front door, her brows

drawing low when Pepper kept looking behind her shoulder as if making sure Bolt didn't follow.

"Is something wrong?" Had Cherry missed something? She wasn't a dumb blonde, clueless and full of air, but she also wasn't a trained law enforcement officer like the two of them. She didn't see what they saw.

"Go easy on Bolt. He's harder on himself than he should be."

"I'm not mad at him. Does it seem like I am?"

"No, but..." Pepper hesitated. "It was awkward in there." A half-hearted laugh escaped. "Anything you want to share with me?"

Like how they almost kissed before she rang the doorbell? No, she didn't want to talk about that.

"Bolt's a great guy, but he's not the one for me." *He's so much better than I am.* Put together and going places in life. What was she other than drifting through life going from one guy to the next mooching off them? So damn pathetic. Bolt deserved better than her.

"We're friends," Cherry continued when Pepper said nothing. "He's so kind to me. I don't know what I'd do without him. I'd be living on the streets, that's for sure."

Pepper cleared her throat. "Umm...so, like, Seth and I chatted, and if you want to stay with us a few days, that's fine. We don't mind."

The pounding of her heart rushed to her ears, drowning her in the loud sounds. Her sister was welcoming her into her home. After the way she greeted her at the first meeting, she never expected to be to this point so soon.

"I'd love that. So much."

It didn't mean leaving Bolt would be easy. She'd miss him. But she'd also love getting to spend more time with her sister.

"Cool. How about Tuesday? It's my next day off."

"Great. I can't wait."

They said good-bye and Pepper left. The excitement was coursing through her system—right along with the dread.

How did she tell Bolt she'd be leaving soon? Even after she lied about the title. She was still leaving.

9

Bolt's entire body sizzled with desire the moment he heard her walk into the kitchen. Her steps were quiet, but the energy that'd been generating between them from the beginning was like a live wire. Gaining power by the second every time she got close. He didn't turn around because he didn't trust himself not to get as close as he could to her and kiss her.

"Pepper left."

Yeah, he heard the door close. Despite the yearning to go listen in on their conversation, he ignored the impulse. Eavesdropping wouldn't be respectful, especially when Pepper had asked to speak to her in private. He'd never disrespect his friend like that.

"Did you lock the door?"

Might seem like a dumb question to some, but he couldn't drop his guard at all. Not like he had with his phone, having it on silent, making the camera alert virtually useless. Some kind of protector he was.

"I did."

He inhaled, then exhaled slowly as his body trembled when her voice sounded closer. They should keep their distance. He had to keep her safe, and any distraction could be their downfall. *His* downfall.

Another shiver coated his body when her hand landed on his shoulder.

"Bolt?"

He finally turned around from the kitchen sink where he had been putting his empty coffee mug. Her hand fell to her side.

"Are you okay? Don't be upset about the camera thing. Everything turned out fine. It was only Pepper."

"This time it turned out fine. It won't happen again."

He swore it wouldn't.

She nodded, a bright smile on her face and confidence in her eyes. How could she have so much confidence in him? It was amazing.

"It's kind of late to go for that run. What do you want to do for the rest of the day?"

Make you laugh. Make you happy. Make you forget all about your worries.

"Whatever you want to do."

It's not like he could actually say what was on his mind. How embarrassing would that be?

"Do you have any board games? Or we could watch a movie? Or I saw you have a gaming system. I'm not too bad at video games. Whatever you want to do."

Well, that wasn't helpful. Too many options and they all sounded like fun because he'd get to do them with her.

"Let's start with the first one and go from there."

Her smile brightened even more. "Name the board game. Let's do it."

Yes, they should do it.

But until her problem was solved, he had to keep his head in the game—the survival game. Any distractions that messed with that would have to wait.

The evening, despite how the morning and afternoon had gone, was pleasant. They laughed, they played, they acted like they'd been friends since childhood. Things with her felt perfect and right.

When it came time for bed, the awkwardness returned.

"Umm...if you need me, just holler. I'm not too far away. Don't forget the cameras are working and the motion sensor lights will go off. I don't have my phone on silent."

"I'll be okay. You worry too much, Bolt. It's going to be fine."

And she said *that* too much. Nothing was fine, and pretending like it was wouldn't make the bad disappear.

They both hesitated before turning to their respective rooms.

He didn't get much sleep. No surprise there. It rained all day the next day, so they still couldn't go for their run to the lake. It consisted of another day of games and movies and so much fun and laughter, it hurt to think about her leaving.

When it was time for them to leave for work the next morning, he didn't think it was possible, but his heart shattered. Her words cut him so deep, he didn't think he'd ever recover.

"I forgot to tell you I'm staying with Pepper for a while. It's her day off. So no need to worry about me when you get off. I'll be with her."

And how long had she known this? Since Sunday when Pepper asked to speak with her? No doubt that's when she had asked. He should've listened in on the conversation. Because then he wouldn't be blindsided like he was right now.

"Yeah, okay."

Cherry bit her bottom lip. "Thank you for letting me stay here."

So she was never coming back? This was it.

"Of course."

They stared at each other for the longest time. He couldn't stand the awkwardness.

"Do you have your bag packed?"

She nodded, then snatched the brown paper bag from the counter. "I made your lunch today too. Have a good day at work."

He took the bag from her hand, careful not to touch her. The slightest contact would send him over the edge. "Thanks. Appreciate it."

Then they were off. The good-bye in the parking lot was stilted as well. She walked away without turning around once, and he stood there like a lost little puppy watching her leave him for good.

The day dragged on. When lunchtime rolled around, he opened his lunch bag, disappointed she hadn't made his napkin into origami this time.

So that was that.

It was for the best.

No matter how many times he tried to remind himself of that, he failed to get it to sink in.

He didn't have much to say to Charlotte, and she must've sensed his dark mood because she didn't try to pry anything out of him. He was polite but short with the sheriff as well. He nodded and said hello to people when he was out on patrol, but his mind was everywhere but where it should be.

When it came time to head home, he waited in his truck as if Cherry would be coming soon and realized how pathetic he was acting. He put the truck in gear and went home. The house was silent and depressing.

That night he didn't get an ounce of sleep. Not even an hour. His eyes might've been closed, but nothing happened. No peace. No serenity.

No Cherry.

The sheriff stopped him three days later before he headed out on his route, calling him into his office.

"You okay, Bolt? You look tired."

Yeah, he'd seen the shadows around his eyes. He knew it didn't look good. But there wasn't anything he could do about that. If he couldn't sleep, he couldn't sleep. Not one night since Cherry had left had he gotten any shut-eye. It was impossible to focus on the simple act because all that ran through his mind was worry.

How was she doing? Was she having fun with Pepper? Most likely. Was she missing him? Probably not.

Not like he missed her. Like a part of him had been stolen, snatched away in the blink of an eye.

She'd barely been in his life, and it felt like she'd been there forever. It was as if she had taken a piece of him when she left.

"I'm fine."

Logan nodded but didn't look convinced. "You'd tell me if something was bothering you, right?"

Meaning he couldn't have a deputy on the streets like some loose cannon. He was capable of doing his job despite his exhaustion.

"Of course."

Logan dismissed him, though Bolt didn't think Logan believed a word he said. Before he could escape, Charlotte stopped him as well.

"Cherry got something in the mail. Thought you might

want to drop it off to her." Charlotte held out a long white envelope addressed to her, postmarked from Florida.

Return address: Peggy.

What the hell?

The title to her car?

He thought Peggy couldn't find it.

Cherry lied to him. Straight to his face. Why? And how come he hadn't picked up on her lie? Because he'd been too distracted by other things, namely his attraction to her.

Well, it didn't matter. She didn't matter.

He stared at the outstretched hand but didn't take the envelope.

"You should call Cherry to come get it. Or Pepper. That's where she's staying now."

He'd had yesterday off, and Pepper had worked and still Cherry was with her sister. Rightly so. That's why she had come to town. As far as he knew, because Pepper had filled him in, no more signs someone was following her. It didn't mean the person went away. Pepper had some of her contacts in Florida check on Dean and do a full background on him. He had priors for a few assaults and resisting arrest. The man had a violent history, which wasn't good. The fact he'd been out of town for the past week—according to the stand-in manager at the strip club—was even worse. He could be the culprit causing havoc in Cherry's life. She could deny it all she wanted, but he was the most likely suspect.

But again, not his problem anymore.

The pity on Charlotte's face pissed him off. Like she felt sorry for him. Proving once again he was the loser in the situation. And wasn't he for not seeing her blatant lie?

"You haven't seen Cherry all week. I'm sure she'd enjoy a

visit." Charlotte's hand refused to lower, taking the envelope with her.

"Like I said, call her or Pepper."

"Take the damn envelope, Bolt."

"Don't tell me what to do, Charlotte. I'm not your damn puppet."

With that, he left.

Screw Charlotte, and screw Cherry.

───────

CHERRY SMILED as she took the envelope from Charlotte. Whoops. She forgot to call Peggy back and tell her not to mail the title. Well, at least, Bolt didn't know she had it. She wouldn't have to admit she lied.

"Have you talked to Bolt this week?" Charlotte asked with a sweet voice, but she saw the devil dancing in her eyes. Charlotte still hadn't fully warmed up to her yet. She saw the distrust in her eyes every time they spoke.

"No, I haven't. It's been so busy, and the week went so fast."

And it really had. One day she was with Bolt and the next, the days zoomed by. She'd been having such a great time with Pepper and Seth. They were both so wonderful. Sure, there were awkward moments with Pepper, but only because they didn't know each other that well yet. But in the last few days, they'd gotten to know each other. Spoke about their childhood and the things they wished happened differently. As the days went on, things between them got easier.

Seth was amazing. He loved Pepper so much, it made Cherry positively blissful inside to see her sister so happy. It also made her insanely jealous. She wanted what Pepper had. That one person who spoke to her soul. Oh, and Seth spoke to Pepper's soul like they'd been meant to be together before they were even born.

"I don't like to meddle in other people's affairs. I hate it when people do it to me," Charlotte started. "But you should see him. I can tell he misses you, and he's been such a bear the last few days. I tried to get him to give you this, but he wouldn't."

The way Charlotte eyed her, it's as if she knew Cherry had lied to Bolt. But that was impossible, unless he told her.

If he had, then Charlotte wouldn't have said she thought he missed her. Did he? Because she missed him like crazy. While Seth lived on the outskirts of town like Bolt, he had more houses around him than Bolt. It didn't make her feel safer. Not like she had at Bolt's. It was odd, considering more people were around her.

"Thanks. He's working today, right?" Cherry knew Pepper was. Seth was at work. She was on her own today.

She planned to do her daily rounds around town and hang out with Mrs. Dunburry like she normally did. After that, she'd wait for Pepper to get off work like she used to do with Bolt. Then they'd go home together.

Though she was starting to feel like she was cramping Pepper and Seth's style. Not that they said anything to her, or even acted like it. She felt it in the air like an incoming storm. Brewing and rattling the sky that trouble was coming. *She* was the trouble.

The envelope felt heavy in her hands.

It was time to leave. Officially leave town.

She'd overstayed her welcome.

"He is. Though I'm sure if you call him, he'd drop by. I can even call him on the radio for you."

No, he wouldn't like that. He wouldn't come. Not if he

knew about the letter, which meant he figured out she lied to him. He'd hate her for that.

"It's okay. You have a great day, Charlotte. Thanks for this."

She left the sheriff's office and started her day like usual. By lunchtime, the envelope was burning a hole in her purse. It was time.

She told Mrs. Dunburry she had to run an errand and she'd be back soon. The walk wouldn't be pleasant, but she couldn't exactly ask anybody for a ride to Evan's garage. Nobody liked him. She had promised not to go there alone, but she'd be fine. It was a beautiful afternoon day. The sun was shining. People were out and about. Nothing would happen.

Knowing how mad Bolt was at her, it wouldn't help to call him. He wouldn't come to her rescue. He wouldn't even deliver the envelope to her. That said enough.

The garage was empty when she got there, besides Evan, who rolled out from underneath a car and looked at her with a smooth smile. She wished there would've been a customer or two, but too late for that.

"Afternoon, Cherry. It's nice to see you again."

She waved the envelope in the air. "I have the title. That is if you still want to buy my deadbeat car."

"A deal is a deal. Let's go into my office."

Cherry watched him walk away toward the same area the bathroom was located. She breathed a sigh of relief when she saw his office had a large window you could see through. So if someone walked into the garage they'd be able to see both of them. Not much security, but better than nothing.

Evan looked over the title, nodding as if everything looked to be in order.

"So about that dinner?"

Men liked to come on to her, but she had perfected how to turn them down with ease. Something her mother taught her. She had been good for some things. "As much as I'd love to, I'll be leaving soon."

Not much disappointment entered his expression, telling Cherry he was only asking her out to get on Bolt's nerves. Interesting.

"How soon?"

Why did he want to know?

"Soon enough I won't be able to have dinner with you. But thank you for asking."

Evan chuckled and got to work on the papers in front of him. Not long after, she was walking out of his office with a check for a thousand dollars. She felt rich. She normally didn't have this much money at one time. The sad reality was it would be gone shortly. Hopefully, it was enough to buy a bus ticket out of here and...yeah, she didn't know where she'd go, but it would get her out of this town.

The walk back to Main Street wasn't as fun as the walk to the garage. Everything weighed on her. How she'd tell Pepper she was leaving. How she'd tell Bolt.

Well, maybe not Bolt. He hated her now. He wouldn't want to talk to her again.

She jumped when she heard tires crunching on the gravel behind her. It startled her so much, she tripped, tumbling down the ditch.

A car door slammed.

Her ankle writhed in pain. She was a goner now. Whoever it was would get her with ease. She couldn't run for her life.

She closed her eyes, hoping the end was quick.

"Cherry!"

Her eyes popped open to see Bolt rushing down the ditch to her side. The full-blown panic on his face surprised her.

"I'm so sorry. This is all my fault."

What was his fault?

Because, for the first time that day, her world felt like it was back on its correct axis.

10

———

HE COULDN'T BELIEVE he did this. Scaring her so badly she had fallen and injured herself. He hadn't meant to peel to the side of the road so abruptly, but seeing her by herself sent him into a panic.

"I'm okay, Bolt. It's fine." She sat up, scooting her legs up, wincing.

"You're not fine. What hurts?"

She pointed to her right ankle. "I think I twisted it. It's throbbing, but give me a few minutes and I'm sure it'll be fine."

He gritted his teeth, hating how she used the word *fine* so loosely all the time. Damn it! None of this was fine.

"Why are you out here by yourself?"

It didn't take a genius to know where she had been coming from. Evan's garage was nearby. She had gotten the title from Charlotte. Now she had the money to leave town.

Well, good.

Maybe if she left, he'd get some peace. Find the energy to sleep.

Ha!

What delusional thinking. He couldn't even sleep before he met her.

She wouldn't look him in the eye.

"I know you went to see Evan. I can figure that out myself. I guess it was a dumb question. I thought you said you wouldn't go there alone. Not the first thing you lied about then."

Her eyes whipped to his. "I'm sorry. I didn't mean to lie to you. You have to believe me, Bolt."

He had believed her. With so many things. He wasn't sure he had it in him to continue to do so if she was only going to keep lying to him.

"You shouldn't have gone by yourself. I don't trust, Evan."

"I didn't think you'd want to hear from me."

So far from the truth. All day he'd been frustrated knowing she lied to him, but it hadn't stopped his feelings. He still wanted her. Still cared about her, despite trying to tell himself he didn't.

"You should've at least called Pepper."

She looked crestfallen that he hadn't disputed what she said. Why give her more ammunition to hurt him? It was better if she thought he was mad. It would keep her safe. Because until they knew where Dean had disappeared, she wasn't safe. Any kind of distraction could cause him to make a mistake. He felt like he'd been doing nothing but make mistakes with her. Hell, he'd just made her sprain her ankle.

"I didn't want to bother her. I have it all taken care of now, and I don't have to go back there again."

She tried to stand up, slumping back onto her butt when she couldn't handle the pain in her ankle. A cry of agony escaped, and he sensed by the shame in her eyes she hadn't meant for it to come out.

"I got you."

Then he scooped her up into his arms before she could protest. Her arms wound around his neck, startled at first, but then giving in and sinking into his embrace.

"I can walk."

"No, you can't. You couldn't even stand on your own. Why can't you accept help when it's offered?"

"Because no one ever offers it. I'm not used to people caring so much."

His entire body went rigid at her words. The pain and suffering he heard in her voice were too much. It broke his heart to think how alone she was in the world. At least he had his family. His parents tended to hover too much at times. His brother, though they didn't talk often, would still help out if he asked.

He set her down gently near the hood so she could use it to balance while he opened the passenger-side door. His arm wrapped around her waist to help guide her into the seat. When he got into the driver's side, he realized the vehicle was still running. Seeing her fall had sent him into a full-blown panic. He was lucky he even got the vehicle into park before jumping out.

"I'll take you to Dr. Matthews."

"No, that's not necessary. I'll be fine."

"You should get it checked out." He clenched his jaw, holding back more words that would only start an argument. She needed to stop saying the damn word fine.

"I'll ice it when I get home. It's not broken or anything. It's a slight twist."

"Fine, I'll take you home." His hands tightened on the wheel. "To Pepper's."

Not his house. Because it certainly wasn't her home. She made sure of that. He hadn't expected to not hear from her all week once she left his house. Yet that's what happened. Radio silence. That hurt worse than her keeping it from him to the very last moment she'd be gone.

"I don't have a key."

He looked at her. "Then I'll call Pepper. She'll meet us there."

"No, it's okay. Drop me off at Mrs. Dunburry's. I'll make sure to keep off of it."

That he highly doubted. She was giving him a line. He could sense it.

"I don't believe you."

She flinched, cowering away from him. "Bolt..."

He shook his head, partly to stop her from saying whatever she wanted to say, and partly from irritation that he let that slip. That he hurt her. His words had come out harsher than he intended, and for the first time, she was afraid of him. As if he'd hurt her. Never. No matter how angry he got at her, he never wanted to hurt her.

He put the vehicle in drive and pulled onto the road.

"Where are we going?"

"If you don't want to see the doctor or for me to call Pepper, then you can relax at my place until Pepper gets off of work. You shouldn't be on that ankle, and you know as well as I do, it'll be hard to do at Mrs. Dunburry's."

She didn't respond, and he took that as an agreement that he was right.

They drove in silence, not that it took too long to get to his house.

Her door opened before he could round the vehicle, but he scooped her into his arms before she could stand up.

"I can walk, you know."

He pressed his lips together, needing to stay silent.

Nothing good would come out of his lips right now. Anger filled him up. Half at her, and half at himself.

Somehow, he managed to get the door unlocked without putting her down. She disarmed the alarm for him. He went straight to her room—the spare bedroom he couldn't think of as a spare anymore—and set her down on the bed.

"Bolt—"

She didn't finish whatever she was going to say because he walked away, refusing to let her. He took a sandwich bag and threw some ice in it, grabbed a bottle of water, and then a washcloth from the closet. When he walked back into the room, he saw she had set her purse on the nightstand and adjusted the pillow better behind her back.

He set the water bottle on the nightstand and grabbed the other pillow she wasn't using and lifted her leg gently, hating the wince he saw cross over her face. Then he laid the washcloth over her ankle and set the ice on top of it. He was no doctor, but he always remembered his mom putting a rag or cloth of some kind between the skin and the ice.

"Do you have your phone on you?"

She nodded.

"Call me if you need me. Or call Pepper. Whatever. Call someone. But don't leave this bed for anything."

Then he walked out, set the alarm, locked the door, and left.

Left with his heart back in the house, sitting in the palm of her hands just waiting for her to crush the rest of it.

"HEY, YOU WANTED TO SEE ME?" Pepper asked him as she walked into the break room.

Bolt turned around from the sink where he had been dumping out the cold cup of coffee he hadn't finished this morning. Charlotte always kept the break room in order, but he figured that was her way of saying she didn't appreciate him hollering at her. That he could clean up his own shit. He didn't mind. He forgot he had left it sitting on the counter anyway.

"Cherry's at my house."

Pepper's eyes lit up with happiness, surprising him. "She didn't tell me she was moving back in with you, but that's fine." There was relief in her eyes. "I was starting to feel a bit claustrophobic. I mean, don't get me wrong, I've been enjoying getting to know her, but..." She sighed. "It's a lot, you know. It's some heavy shit, and I need time to process it. Some space."

Well, now he felt like shit because that was not the reason she was at his house.

"Umm...Well, that's not exactly why she's there."

Pepper frowned.

"She sprained her ankle this afternoon. I found her walking from Evan's—"

"That bastard hurt her!"

Bolt rushed forward and grabbed Pepper's arm to stop her from leaving. "No, no, he didn't do anything. I did."

Pepper tensed. "What in the hell are you talking about, Bolt?"

He quickly told her everything that happened and how she ended up at his house.

"I've been checking my phone like crazy. No one's been near the house. If I didn't have the camera system, I would've never left her alone."

Pepper stepped closer and touched his shoulder. "You didn't hurt her. I know she's safe with you, and I know she's safe at your house. We'll find Dean and everything will be back to normal."

What did that even mean? What normal? Where Cherry left town and it was like she never existed in their lives? He didn't want to go back to that normal. In a short amount of time, she had come to mean a lot to him. But none of that mattered. Cherry didn't seem to feel the same way in return. How could she? She lied to him about the title and didn't keep her promise to call him when she was ready to deal with Evan. She went on her own, meaning she hadn't trusted him to help her take care of it. To help keep her safe.

"I'm sorry for dumping all that on you." Pepper's cheeks bloomed a bright red.

"It's okay. That's what friends are for. I'm not saying she can't stay at my house. I don't know why she didn't want to call you. She doesn't want to stay with me anymore."

"Why? Because of this delusion you hurt her. She tripped and fell. It was an accident."

"If I hadn't scared her, it wouldn't have happened."

"Can I borrow your house key?" Pepper asked, holding out her hand. "I get off first. I'll go pick her up. This way I can lock your door when we leave."

Bolt didn't know what he expected, but it wasn't Pepper giving in so easily. After confessing she was ready for a break from Cherry, he sort of expected her to convince him to take Cherry in again. Honestly, it wouldn't have taken much convincing.

His keys jangled as he removed them from his pocket. He unhooked the key from the chain and placed it into her waiting palm.

"Thanks for taking care of my sister, Bolt. I can always trust you."

It was nice to know one of the Chapman sisters could

because it didn't seem like Cherry trusted him. Otherwise, she wouldn't have lied.

───────

PEPPER PULLED into the driveway and parked the car. The light breeze blew through her hair as she exited the vehicle and walked to the door. The key twisted with ease, and thankfully she didn't forget the code to the alarm Bolt had given her.

Silence greeted her.

"Cherry? It's Pepper."

No lights were on in the living room to her left, and she didn't expect there to be any on as it was still light out. The sun wouldn't start setting for another few hours. The TV wasn't on either. Bolt had said he'd brought her to the spare room to rest. Maybe she was sleeping.

The first moment of panic hit her when she found the room empty.

"Cherry!"

Racing out of the room, she told herself to remain calm. Bolt had said he monitored the app all day long. If someone had stepped into view on the property, the alarm would've gone off. The same went if Cherry tried to leave.

The bathroom was empty, as was the dining room. When she entered the kitchen, her heart pounded at the sight.

The sink was full of dishwater, and a plate and fork were sitting inside the dirty water. She dipped her finger, shivering at the coldness that hit her. The water had been sitting for quite a while. The dish rack had a few clean dishes as if Cherry had started them and stopped midway, evident by the two glasses and a dirty bowl still sitting on the counter.

Why would she stop doing dishes in the middle of them? Why was she doing the dishes in the first place? She hurt her ankle. Bolt had to carry her into the house.

Well, according to him, anyway. Had Cherry lied that she hurt herself? Was her ankle really sprained?

If she left the house, why hadn't the camera alarms gone off? Why would she leave? She had no reason to run. Unless someone tried to get in the house.

Pepper made another round through the house, finding every room empty. She even peeked into Bolt's bedroom, thinking maybe Cherry decided to lie down in there for some reason. Nothing. Nada.

Cherry's purse was still on the nightstand in the spare room. Her shoes were sitting on the floor next to the bed. Nothing looked disturbed in the house. The door had been locked and the alarm had been set. If someone had come to grab her, there would be signs of a struggle.

How could someone disappear out of thin air?

She felt her heart being ripped from her chest.

For the first time in her life, she thought she had the chance at having a real family connection. She had a sister. She had a second chance at being a sister.

Now that was being threatened. Because that chance was wavering on the edge of destruction. Where was her sister? How could she have disappeared from a locked house?

Her hands trembled as she pulled her phone out.

Her finger wobbled as she swiped at the screen and hit dial.

Bolt answered on the first ring.

"Cherry's missing. My sister's gone, Bolt."

11

He vividly remembered the last time he felt this kind of full-blown panic coursing through his veins. When Deke and Charlotte had been pinned down in Carson's cabin waiting for reinforcements to arrive. *He* had been the first reinforcement to make it there. The feeling then had almost crushed him to the point of passing out, and he could feel that same boiling energy hitting his system.

What happened if they couldn't find her? Why had he left her alone? Why didn't the cameras pick anything up?

Question after question pelted his brain and the panic increased in steady increments. His hands were shaking as he gripped the steering wheel hard. His vision went in and out from focused to blurry as he drove like a bat out of hell. His entire body vibrated with intensity until he swerved into his driveway and slammed on the brakes. For one brief moment, he froze.

The thought of walking into his house and seeing the evidence for himself—that she was truly gone—brought him so close to desolation, he had the urge to back up and drive in the opposite direction.

Except Pepper needed him. And he had sworn to himself he'd never screw up again. That he'd be the hero for once.

No matter how hard he tried, he always screwed up. Every single time.

First, she got hurt today because of him. Now, she was missing because of him.

He slammed his door and rushed inside the house, nearly colliding with Pepper who was pacing in the foyer.

"I called Logan. I didn't know what to do. Last time I didn't call him, he was so mad at me."

Bolt knew she was referencing going off on her own to check out the cabin Evan had been hiding in when the Cheetahs had been after him. That had resulted in her evil sister, Lillian, knocking her out and stealing her identity for a short time.

"We'll find her. She has to be here. I swear the camera didn't send one alert."

His phone had been glued to his hand the moment he left her alone. Constantly checking it, his hand hurt from gripping it so hard for so long.

"I looked in every room. She's not in this house. The sink is full of water like she was doing the dishes and stopped in the middle of it. The water is cold. She's been gone a while."

He frowned. "She shouldn't have been on her feet."

His eyes trailed to his living room that looked cleaner than when he left. The blanket was folded and sitting nicely on the back of it instead of sprawled half on the cushion and half on the floor like he had left it. The stack of movies he had piled on the floor in front of the DVD player was back on the shelf, stacked in a straight row. The dirty cups he had sitting on the coffee table were gone.

Cherry had cleaned up his house.

Something he had let get dirtier than he normally lived. It'd been a rough week. A very long week of missing a woman who he'd gotten used to having in his space. He hadn't cared about things like doing the dishes every day, keeping things looking tidy, or even putting his clothes away. They still sat in the laundry basket on the floor in his room. Unless she had put those away too.

He walked away to double-check the house.

The dining room was empty as was the kitchen. His eyes glazed over as he stared at the dirty dishwater. Why had she been on her feet? He had told her to stay in bed resting. She hurt herself.

He hurt her.

Damn it!

A shiver wracked his body as he dipped his hand in the cold water and removed the plug. The slurping sound of the water rushing down the drain kept him in a trance until nothing was left but the few dishes she had been washing.

He turned around, hating himself for wasting the time on something so trivial. Her bedroom was empty, not that he had doubted Pepper. Her purse sat on the nightstand, her shoes by the bed. The covers looked rumpled as if she had dipped under them for a while. Both pillows were against the headboard. The bag of ice and washcloth he had given her was gone. He checked the closet for extra measure. Empty.

The bathroom was empty as well. He even checked behind the shower curtain. Because why not? It couldn't hurt.

His laundry room was nothing more than a tiny closet that held the washer and dryer with no room for anything else to fit in there. His house hadn't been built with a basement for some reason. He ended in his room. Nothing looked disturbed. She didn't venture into his room to clean up—or she hadn't gotten to it yet. The laundry basket sat in the spot he last left it. His blankets on the bed were rumpled as he left them. His curtains were wide open.

But his closet doors were closed.

He didn't remember closing his closet doors.

The door rattled as he shoved it to the left. A loud thump echoed in the corner from the opposite side. He grabbed hold of the door, shoving it back to the right, along with the other one.

He crouched, shoving his pants to the side, releasing a heavy sigh.

"Cherry." His voice slid out in a whisper. He was afraid his eyes were playing tricks on him.

Why was she hiding in his closet?

She blinked a few times, moaning, then she finally focused on him.

"Bolt!"

She lunged up and into his arms, crashing into him. He wasn't prepared and he tumbled backward with her in his arms. He made sure he took the brunt of the fall. By the way she clung to him, he didn't think she would've registered anything anyway.

Quiet tears hit his shirt.

Shit.

What happened to her?

"Pepper," he croaked. He cleared his throat and tried again. "Pepper! In my room."

He slowly sat up, albeit awkwardly as Cherry refused to let go of him, attached to him like a crab to a net.

A short sob had him looking up at Pepper when she entered the room, halting near the door.

He nodded toward the closet.

"I didn't think to look in the closets. Why..." Pepper's voice trailed off, noting how Cherry was still silently crying into his chest.

It took a few minutes for Cherry to calm down, wipe her eyes, and lean away, noticing Pepper in the room.

"Hey, are you okay? What happened?" Pepper asked, deciding to sit down so she was level with them.

"I thought someone was outside."

Bolt felt her tense and knew she was holding back.

"My phone didn't alert the cameras picked up movement."

He wasn't claiming she was lying, but proof said otherwise.

She swallowed and refused to look at him. She even tried to twist to stand up, but he tightened his grip. He wasn't ready to let her go. She might be ready to get up, but he wasn't feeling quite steady. His heart rate had yet to settle down.

"Cherry, why were you doing the dishes? What exactly happened?" Pepper asked with a firm tone, brokering no argument. She was using her cop voice.

Cherry trembled in his arms, telling him she didn't like it.

"I got sick of sitting on the bed. My ankle wasn't throbbing anymore. I tried standing on it and it felt okay. I got up and walked around to stretch it out some. Picked up the living room. I saw the dirty dishes and thought I'd help Bolt out a bit."

Pepper nodded. "Why did you stop midway doing them? What happened? I called out to you when I got here. Why didn't you answer me? I was worried about you."

The last sentence held a touch of accusation as if Pepper

thought she had heard her but chose not to come out. But that didn't make any sense.

None of this did, and it wouldn't until Cherry told them everything.

"I thought I saw someone outside in the woods." She tensed again. His fingers brushed her hip lightly, to calm her, to offer comfort that he had her in his arms. She was safe. "Just behind the cameras, as if he knew once he crossed that threshold, he'd lose the advantage."

Bolt frowned. Carson had hidden the cameras well. They weren't visible unless the person looking knew where to look. Or the person had watched them install them.

At least the cameras had hindered the person from getting closer.

"Why didn't you call me?" He hated the hurt in his voice. "Or Pepper? I told you to call if there was trouble."

Someone. Anyone. It was just like her going to see Evan on her own. Ignoring help that was right in front of her.

She bit her bottom lip, daring a look at him. She looked so frightened, he wanted to pull her closer and chase all her fears away. But he knew that wouldn't do a damn thing but make it harder for him when she left and give Pepper a show she didn't need to see.

"You'll be mad at me. Even more than you already are," she whispered, dropping her gaze.

"I'm not mad at you."

He was hurt she didn't trust him enough, but he wasn't mad at her. He could never hate her. She might not make the best decisions, but he didn't think she did it out of cruelty. She was one of the sweetest, kindest women he'd ever met. She was so damn lovable. He'd yet to meet someone who didn't like her in town.

"I grabbed my phone and hid in your closet." She bit her

lip again, hesitating. "But my phone wouldn't work. I ran out of minutes. I didn't realize I had until that moment." She looked up at Pepper. "I must've fallen asleep hiding. I don't even know what time it is. I guess I didn't hear you call my name. Bolt opening the door startled me awake."

Pepper flipped her wrist up. "It's almost six o'clock."

Cherry's eyes widened. "I ran in here around three."

She'd hidden in his closet for almost three full hours. Scared and alone. Without help in her reach. No escape.

It was all his fault for leaving her in the first place.

CHERRY SAT CURLED on the couch with a blanket over her legs. Pepper had called Logan, which in turn had made the entire gang show up at Bolt's house. Aubrey was in the kitchen cooking food for everyone, with Charlotte and Kat helping. Bolt, Logan, Danny, Seth, and Deke were in the dining room sitting around the table talking about their next options concerning her case. She was curious about what they'd come up with. How did you fight an unknown entity? Someone who lurked in the shadows but never stepped out? Who was always there, watching, waiting, never making a move?

She did nothing but sit in the silent living room staring at the blank TV. Bolt had offered to turn it on, but she declined. It wouldn't help distract her or pull her from her turbulent thoughts.

No doubt he had to think she was such an idiot for how she reacted. She felt like one.

Who knew what would've happened if she hadn't left the bed? Maybe she would've never seen the person and this would've never gotten as out of hand as it was now. But her

ankle had only been bothering her a little bit. A slight throb
that she had ignored when she stood up from the bed. She
hadn't been able to lay there anymore. She had thought
about Bolt and his kindness, even though he'd been so mad
at her, and she had wanted to show him some kindness in
return. Not just tell him how sorry she was, but also show
him. That's why she started cleaning the house and putting
things where they belonged.

The moment she saw the figure standing by a tree, not
quite hiding behind it, but not fully revealing themselves,
she went into a panic. She acted like a scared child rather
than the grown-ass woman she was.

How pathetic.

To fall asleep while hiding. Who did that? Only a dumb
blonde waiting to be killed. Yep, that was her, apparently.
Nothing but a dumb blonde.

The couch jostled when Pepper sat down next to her.

"You okay? You can join us in the kitchen if you'd like.
Sit on a stool. Aubrey's not letting us help. She's just giving
the appearance like she's letting us, but really doing all the
work."

Cherry could hear how hard Pepper was trying to sound
normal and like nothing was wrong, but she was terrible at
it. All she heard was the concern. The edge to her tone that
was impossible to hide.

"I'm okay. I don't want to bother anyone. Everyone didn't
have to rush over here. I could've been seeing stuff."

She knew she hadn't, but she didn't want all this fuss
happening because of her.

"Do you believe you imagined it?"

For the first time, Cherry heard a hint of doubt from
Pepper. Did Pepper think she was lying? Trying to do...
what? What did she think she was trying to do?

"I saw something. Maybe it was a deer. It's been a stressful day."

Pepper sighed. "Cherry, you don't have to be afraid. We're here to help."

That was the thing. She wasn't used to help. To people stepping up to the plate for her. She'd been knocked down so much in her life, all this attention was foreign. It made her feel like she wasn't worthy of it.

"And on that note, I wanted to talk to you about something."

Cherry turned her attention to Pepper and tried to force herself to stop twisting the blanket and giving away how agitated she was.

"Okay. Yeah, sure. Let's talk."

Whatever it was, it couldn't be good. Not by the tone of her voice or the forlorn expression on her face.

"I want to start by saying, this suggestion has nothing to do with me not wanting you around. It's more to do with your safety."

This didn't sound good. Pepper wanted her to leave town. She had the money to do so, and now Pepper wanted her out of her life. Until the trouble went away.

Well, she could do her one better. She'd never return.

"Yeah, okay. I understand. I'll leave. I'll get out of your hair. It makes the most sense."

Pepper frowned. "And you'll come stay with Bolt?"

Cherry's lips matched Pepper's to the point she almost laughed at how much they looked alike—like sisters. "I'll leave town. Bolt doesn't want me here."

Pepper burst out laughing. Then she slammed a hand to her mouth as if she could hold it in that way. It took her less than three seconds to remove all traces of humor from her face.

"I didn't mean to laugh. I think it's funny how you don't see it."

"See what?"

Pepper cocked a brow. "I'm not going to point it out. You have to figure it out on your own. I am saying this all wrong." Pepper released a heavy breath. "I'm not telling you to leave town. I'm trying to say Seth's house doesn't have the security like Bolt's. One of us can't always be home with you. At least at Bolt's, you have the security. I'm saying you should stay with him for a while until we figure this out."

She didn't feel so secure this afternoon hiding in that closet until she fell asleep from exhaustion. Waiting and praying Bolt would return and crying to the point her chest hurt that he never did. She'd never felt so alone and afraid in her life. Not even growing up and her mother would be gone most nights spending it with a new man.

"Maybe it's better if I leave. I have the title now. Well, I had the title, and now I have the money to get out of here."

Pepper pressed her lips into a thin line, an expression Cherry imagined mothers used with their children when they weren't happy with them. She wouldn't know. Her mom never actually acted like a real mother. Just another human being raising a child, bumbling her way through, not even caring she screwed up left and right.

"That's another thing we should talk about. You said you wouldn't see Evan alone and what do you do? Exactly that. Why didn't you call someone?"

Cherry was grateful she didn't say "why didn't you call Bolt?" because then she'd have to confess she lied to him. Hurt him without meaning to.

"Well, we know now I wouldn't have been able to. No more minutes left. I didn't want to bother anyone. It was broad daylight. People were around. I didn't think it would be a big deal."

"It is. It's a huge deal. We can't trust him. We did once and it almost got most of us killed. I'm trying here, Cherry. I'm trying to open myself up and let you in, but if I can't trust you, then we're not gonna go far in developing a relationship. If we say—if *I* say—don't do something, you don't do it. If you agree to listen, then you can't go behind our backs and do the opposite."

Cherry nodded, her bottom lip wobbling. She forced the tears to remain inside. She would not break down in front of Pepper. Or anyone else again. Embarrassment still washed over her she had cried in Bolt's arms. That painted the picture of how much of a scared child she truly was.

"Say it. Tell me you won't do something like that again."

"I'll keep my word next time. I promise. I won't put myself in that kind of situation again. You can trust me, Pepper."

Pepper's expression was neutral, but Cherry sensed she didn't have her full trust. Not yet. Maybe not ever.

"So about staying at Bolt's?"

Cherry swallowed hard, twisting the blanket once again. "I don't think he's going to agree to that. I hurt him. I lied to him. I don't think he'll forgive me for it."

"He's already agreed to it, and he's more forgiving than you give him credit for."

She met Pepper's gaze, too afraid to see the lie in her eyes. There was no way Bolt would forgive her. Yet nothing but honesty shined brightly.

Pepper chuckled. "We are sisters. That's for sure."

"What does that mean?"

"I lied to the guy I liked too. Even when I knew I

shouldn't, and I did it anyway. We're more alike than I realized."

"You mean Seth?"

Pepper nodded. "We all make mistakes. I know Bolt doesn't hold grudges. I'd like to think whatever you lied about you had a good reason for it. If not..." Pepper's expression turned severe. "You better hope it doesn't happen again."

She heard the unveiled threat. Don't hurt Bolt. She wouldn't if she could help it.

"Okay, I'll stay a little while longer. But I won't be a nuisance. I'll be leaving soon because I can't stay forever. This isn't my home, it's yours. I would never smother you. I'll give it another week."

Pepper didn't look happy about her decision, which surprised Cherry. She figured Pepper would be happy once she left. While they had a nice time getting to know each other this past week, half the moments were stilted with awkwardness.

Then Pepper nodded. "Okay, one week."

12
———

ONE WEEK! That's all Cherry planned to stay. Bolt's heart started racing at all the implications. How much he'd missed her. How sad and lonely his life would be once again. How, if they didn't find the culprit messing with her, she'd be on her own. She'd be in more danger without them to protect her.

"Are you sure you're comfortable with her staying here, Bolt?"

He darted his attention to Deke, surprised by the question. Deke had been quiet while they talked about everything that happened. Danny had piped in, as usual. Trying to dominate the conversation. Logan offered his opinions when needed. Seth never said anything unless it had to deal with Pepper in the equation.

"Of course I am. Why wouldn't I be?"

He hadn't told any of them she had lied about not finding the title. He wasn't sure why she lied about it in the first place, and until he did, he'd keep it to himself.

"Why did she go see Evan after she said she wouldn't go alone? Why was she walking around on a supposed sprained ankle? Did she even hurt herself?" Deke questioned for the first time that night.

The suspicion from Deke surprised him. He'd been neutral so far, but maybe Charlotte had been harping in his ear about Cherry and he was finally taking what she was saying seriously.

"She said she didn't want to bother us, but," Pepper said, holding up a finger, "she promised not to do it again. She knows she messed up. Look, she's used to being on her own. Fighting her own battles. She's not used to having a whole group of people looking out for her and wanting to help. Give her some slack."

Bolt smiled at the way Pepper came to Cherry's defense. Only a week and Cherry had won her over. That couldn't have been easy. Pepper was a hard one to crack.

"So we trust her?" Deke kept prodding.

The table went silent. Despite the way Cherry had been acting with him lately, his gut said he could trust her. He did trust her.

If only she trusted him.

"I trust her." He was the first to speak.

Pepper shared a look with him before nodding. "I do too. But she also knows one more slip and my trust is gone. We have a week to figure out where Dean is and stop him from terrorizing her."

"She claims it isn't Dean," Logan said. "While evidence does point that way with him being off the radar, I think she'd know him the best. What happens if it's not him? We're directing all our attention on the wrong man then."

Bolt was inclined to agree with Logan. But if it wasn't Dean, they were even less close to finding out who it was.

Danny chuckled. "We should hope it is him. We got shit if it isn't. She worked at a strip club. Any wacko in there could've fixated on her. She's a beautiful woman. Men take notice."

Bolt gritted his teeth thinking how men ogled her. Danny was correct in his assessment.

"Well, then, we find Dean ASAP and eliminate him or arrest him. Until we do, we have nothing," Logan pointed out.

"Do you have a spare gun, Bolt?" Pepper asked.

He jerked, not liking the question. "Why?"

"Because if Cherry knows how to use it, she should have one. Just in case."

A muscle in his cheek twitched, he clenched his jaw so hard. Cherry didn't like guns. He could tell by the way she always averted her gaze when his was on his hip. She definitely had shied away and shivered when he slept with her in her room with his gun on the nightstand. She wouldn't take a gun even if she did know how to use it.

He wondered how well she could handle a knife. Because after he helped her up from the floor and Pepper walked out of the room with her, he had gone to fix his clothes hanging and to shut the closet door. He'd found the large kitchen knife lying near one of his black dress shoes. She'd been so scared, she grabbed a weapon. Thank goodness for that. Because if the person had broken in, she could've defended herself.

He certainly hadn't been around to do so.

"I don't think she likes guns."

"I'll talk to her about it." Pepper said it as if it didn't matter anymore if he had a spare. She'd find one for her if Cherry wanted it.

From there, the conversation moved on to other things until Aubrey informed everyone it was time to eat. They crowded around the table, and Bolt tried not to let it hurt that Cherry, despite a chair open next to him, moved passed it and took a seat next to Pepper. She was her sister after all. It only made sense. Except that the seat open by him was next to Pepper's left side and she chose to bypass him and take the other empty seat on Pepper's right side.

Supper was lively, everyone chatting and keeping the talk light. Cherry still looked pale and a bit shaken up from the day, so he was grateful his friends understood talking about what happened wouldn't help her.

After supper, everyone left at the same time. Pepper told him—in front of Cherry—that she was staying with him. Cherry didn't say anything, and he wasn't sure what to say so he nodded.

When the door shut and he turned the lock with a loud click, he felt her jump behind him. The alarm pad beeped as he punched in the code. He turned around to see her staring at the floor.

"You shouldn't be on your ankle too much."

She nodded and walked into the living room. He noticed the slight limp. Just what he thought. It pained her still, yet she was trying to play it off like it wasn't too bad.

He went to the kitchen and grabbed another bag of ice and a washcloth. When he entered the living room, she didn't look at him. She didn't react until he threw a throw pillow on the coffee table and grabbed her leg without asking.

"What are you doing?" she asked as if it wasn't clear.

He placed the washcloth and ice on her ankle that was slightly swollen. She should not have been on it at all this afternoon. Proof she wasn't faking her injury either. Not that he thought she had been. He had seen the pain in her eyes when it happened. He had heard the agony in her voice when he moved it. Damn it, he should've had Kat look at it.

Hell, Kat should've offered to look at it. Maybe she had thought Cherry lied about the injury as well.

"Please stay off your ankle. I have to work tomorrow." Something he dreaded. He didn't want to leave her alone again.

By the terror that flashed in her eyes, she didn't want him leaving either.

"I'll check in on you, I promise."

She nodded but again didn't say anything.

"What do you want on TV?" He stood up, grabbing the remote from the stand.

"Whatever you want. I'm not in the mood for much."

He took a spot on the couch, careful not to get too close to her. The easy camaraderie they had created in the beginning was gone. It felt like they were strangers. He hated it.

"Do you need anything? Something to drink? Pain medication?"

She shook her head, her eyes glued to the baseball game that flashed as soon as he turned on the TV. He left it on the channel, not in the mood for much either. All he wanted was to go back to the way things were before she left. Of course, she was leaving in a week, so what did it matter?

"I'm sorry, Bolt."

His eyes took their time turning her way. She looked like she was on the verge of tears.

"I'm sorry I lied about the title. I didn't mean to."

"Why did you?"

She grimaced, turning her attention to the blanket she'd placed over her lap. "It doesn't matter."

He scooted over and grabbed one of her hands that she had been twisting the blanket with. "It matters to me. I'm not mad. I can't say I wasn't hurt. You can trust me, Cherry."

Her teeth grabbed her bottom lip as she looked at him,

her eyes glossy with unshed tears. "I wasn't ready to leave yet. I lied because I wasn't ready to leave."

"But you're still leaving."

SHE DIDN'T EXPECT to hear the disappointment in his voice. She thought he'd be happy she'd be out of his hair. Since the moment she arrived, she'd been nothing but a nuisance. He wouldn't admit it, but it was true. She always was wherever she went.

"I—"

"You don't have to leave." Bolt squeezed her hand. "I don't want you to leave."

Her heart skipped a beat.

"Until you figure this out, you mean. Find the man bothering me."

That had to be what he meant.

"Partly, yes. What are you going to do once you leave? You'll be all alone."

She shrugged. It wasn't anything new for her. It crushed her she'd been right about why he didn't want her to leave.

"I'm used to being alone. I'll be fine."

His jaw tightened.

"I promise. I'll be fin—"

Before she could finish repeating herself, his lips were drowning it out. They were warm and soft, and she could feel the emotions he was holding back. He had said he wasn't angry at her, but she could tell by the fiery kiss he lied.

He let go of her hand and pressed it against her neck, pulling her closer and deepening the kiss. The sensations from it were something she'd never felt before. His simple, yet intense kiss was creating a reaction in her body that was making it hard to keep herself in check. If this went any further, it'd be like what she just left. Mooching off a man and sleeping with him.

She didn't want that. She wanted more. For once in her life, she wanted more.

He pulled away first, despite her wanting to do it. Unfortunately, she didn't have the willpower. If Bolt suggested they go further, she wouldn't be able to deny him. She'd soak up what she could and hate herself later for her lack of control.

"I'm sorry," he whispered, his lips still close to hers. "I don't know what came over me. I don't like it when you keep saying it's fine, everything's fine, you're fine, when it's not. Nothing is fine."

"I won't say it again."

"Thank you."

He didn't move away or let go of her neck. She wanted him to kiss her again.

"Bolt?"

"Yes?" His eyes trailed to her lips.

"Are you sorry you kissed me?"

Why did she ask such a dumb question? Of course, he was. He'd done it to shut her up.

"Not even one bit. I've wanted to kiss you since the moment I saw you leaning over the engine of your car. That makes me as bad as the other men that gawk at you."

So the attraction she'd felt between them had been real from the beginning. He felt what she felt.

"You've never looked at me like other men do. I like the way you look at me."

"So if I want to kiss you again, I can?"

They were headed into dangerous territory, and this

kind of territory didn't scare her. The only thing that frightened her was the thought of her departure. She'd miss him like crazy. Throwing sex into the mix would make it hurt even worse.

She'd felt pain before. She knew how to endure it.

"I won't stop you." She curled her hands into the front of his shirt, pulling him closer until his lips were devouring hers once again.

This kiss was more tender, gentler, as if he were memorizing the feel and texture of her lips. It spoke to her heart, a language she'd never heard before. Tenderness never entered. Only release, which didn't usually consist of affection.

Time slowed and came to a stop as they made out on his couch. She wanted to turn and straddle his lap, but she sensed he wouldn't allow that. The way he held onto her neck said he was in control of the situation. She didn't want to argue because then the kissing would stop.

The night went faster than she wanted. They watched baseball, kissed off and on—more on than off—until she noticed the game had ended. He had to get up early for work. She didn't want him to be tired on her account.

"We should go to bed. You need your sleep."

He frowned. "I'm not tired yet." Then he looked stricken. "But you probably are. It's been a rough day. I'll carry you. A good night's rest off your ankle will help."

It felt natural when he stood up and scooped her up into his arms. When he got to her room, she put her hand out on the doorframe, stopping him.

Her eyes trailed to his lips, then up to his soulful eyes that looked as hopeful as she felt. "Can I sleep with you? I mean, sleep. Not...sex. I don't think I'll get a moment of sleep by myself."

She didn't point out she would've had to sleep alone at Pepper's. But she wasn't at Pepper's, and they'd been honest with each other tonight. They kissed! She felt comfortable being honest with him about this. Her fear of being alone at night.

"Of course."

He switched courses and deposited her on his bed. Then he grimaced. "You don't have any of your things. You can borrow one of my shirts tonight. I'll grab your stuff from Pepper's tomorrow. I have a spare toothbrush underneath the sink."

"Is it okay if I walk to the bathroom on my own?" she asked with a silly grin, though she did enjoy being carried around by him. The strength in his arms was soothing. She knew she was safe with him, even if he didn't believe it himself.

"Yeah, just don't put all your weight on it." He grabbed a shirt from his closet and tossed it to her. "I'm going to make sure everything is locked up while you get ready."

She felt the loss of his presence the moment he walked out of the room. The thought she wouldn't be alone tonight shoved her panic down some. She would've been so tense all night long, and now she'd sleep like a baby knowing Bolt was right next to her.

Her ankle still throbbed, but it was more of a dull throb, barely there, but still making its presence known. Hopefully, she'd wake up tomorrow and it would be gone altogether. She found the toothbrush and brushed her teeth. His comb did the job to smooth out her hair, though it wasn't gentle getting some of the snarls that had occurred throughout the day. She undressed to her underwear and slid his shirt on. It came just past her butt. Nothing she could do about it not covering her completely. She wasn't wearing her shorts to bed.

If all went well, they would have sex. The kisses on the couch said the chemistry was on fire between them. Of course, sex would be had.

He still hadn't returned by the time she walked into the bedroom. No worries. He was in the house. She hadn't heard him disarm the alarm. She shuffled under the covers and scooted more toward the middle, giving him no choice once he came in but to cuddle with her. She could be wicked when she wanted to be.

A few minutes later, he came in with a bit of hesitation in his gaze. But it didn't stop him from pulling his pants off and tossing his shirt to the floor. He climbed in with only his boxers on, and unlike the last time he slept in the same bed as her, he crawled under the covers this time.

Her plan worked. He adjusted himself until he was right next to her. Then one of his warm hands touched her hip, pulling her closer.

"The alarm is set. The cameras are working. We're secure. You're safe." His hand brushed up her side, then down to her thigh. "I'm here. I won't let anything happen to you."

"You reassure me of that a lot. I already know that. So there's no need to tell me unless it's for yourself. I have complete faith in you. I wish you had more faith in yourself."

"I...I just want you to trust me."

Not what he wanted to say, she sensed. But she also didn't want to argue semantics.

"I do."

"Then promise me you won't see Evan alone again. That you won't go anywhere alone."

Meaning she hadn't trusted him earlier today when she visited Evan on her own.

"I promise."

His hand made another path up and down her side. The sweet caress sent shivers of anticipation through her.

"I want to kiss you." He followed through on his wants, softly pressing his lips to hers. It was short-lived. "I want to do more than kiss you."

"I'm not stopping you."

This time he pressed a kiss to her forehead.

"But not tonight. Not until you feel better. I don't know what's happening between us, but we should take whatever it is slow."

Because she was leaving. Because it would be as hard for him as it would be for her when she did? Hope filled her inside that was the reason.

"I trust you, Bolt. If you want to wait, then I can wait." Her hand found his cheek and smoothed up into his hair. "But just know, it's going to be the hardest wait of my life."

With that confession, he smiled and kissed her.

And kissed her until she thought she'd die from the pleasure building between them.

When he kissed her for the last time for the night, she didn't think she'd be able to fall asleep.

She was out like a light a few minutes later.

13

HIS HAND CUPPED HER HIP, though he didn't move for fear he'd wake her up. There was no need for both of them to be up in the middle of the night. The last time he checked, his clock had read 2:02 AM. He thought, for a brief moment, when he closed his eyes that he'd fall asleep because she was next to him. She'd bring him that peace he'd been searching for the past few months.

But nope.

Sleep still eluded him. He couldn't toss and turn like he usually did because he didn't want to wake up Cherry. She looked so serene asleep. As if nothing in her world was bothering her.

His fingers tightened on her hip, and he didn't realize what he was doing until she moaned lightly and shifted. He snatched his hand away before he did something stupid like that again. Thankfully, it hadn't woken her up. She needed her sleep. She'd had a rough day yesterday.

Twisting, he glanced at the clock again.

2:32 AM.

Not much time had passed.

It was going to be a long, endless night. Lying next to her, aching for something he couldn't have wasn't going to help the Zzzs hit him.

Carefully, so he didn't wake her, he crawled out of bed, grabbing his phone and gun from the nightstand before leaving the bedroom.

Maybe he'd been an idiot for denying her what they both wanted. Sex. An intense explosion of two bodies that ached for each other.

Yeah, no doubt about it, he was an idiot.

He should've kissed her and kissed her, then kissed her some more before giving over to the pleasure that had been plaguing him since the first time he saw her.

So what she was leaving? There wasn't anything wrong with a little harmless sex. It'd been a while for him. He could use some. Cherry was a beautiful woman, ready and waiting.

Except he'd never had that kind of sex. The one-night stand, forget 'em and leave 'em kind. One, she was leaving him. Two, he knew he'd never forget her. She was the kind of woman who appeared only once in a lifetime. Full of life and energy and everything good in the world. She brightened a room with one joyous smile. It wasn't surprising she'd won over the town with ease—and their group. Well, most of the group. Charlotte still had her reservations, and Deke seemed to have jumped on her bandwagon.

He got it. He understood. Too many things had happened in the past year, and they couldn't afford to let their guard down. They shouldn't.

Yet his gut screamed, clenched with an intensity that said he could trust her. That she wasn't here to do harm. Though harm was in the air. Harm was out to get her.

While he'd mucked up several times this week, he wouldn't fail her again. Not if he could help it.

He poured a cup of water and downed it in one swallow. It did nothing to soothe his rattled nerves. Nothing would. Not until he knew Cherry was safe and out of harm's way.

The cup made a short clinking sound when he set it in the sink. His kitchen was back to being cleaned and organized. The towel he'd taken down from the oven handle and hadn't replaced when she left was back in its spot, hanging with merry. The little touches he tried to erase when she left were back.

But for how long?

Because he knew the moment she left again, he'd erase it all. Make it appear like she'd never been here in the first place. The memories would be too much. He wouldn't want to remember a moment of it. He'd forget them all. Because thinking about her, letting the memories in would only send him further down the hell he'd already found himself in.

What was he doing?

Falling for a woman who was not meant to be. If he had the crazy urge, or the courage, to ask her to stay, she wouldn't. She might be enjoying the small-town life right now, but not many people could stand it long term. It took a lot of patience to get used to the slow lifestyle, to other people being in your business no matter how much you tried to keep things to yourself.

It wouldn't matter how hard he fought, she'd leave.

Hell, in a week she planned to leave.

He didn't have much time left with her.

He should soak up all the time he could, then erase all the memories forever.

A shiver wracked his body.

His gaze jumped to the window. His eyes darted around

the yard, looking at the shadows, the cracks of light from the moon peeking in between the trees.

Nothing appeared out of place. His phone resting on the counter hadn't lit up with an alert or sounded with a short ping that something had crossed paths in front of the cameras.

Yet his senses tingled. His gut screamed.

Something was out there.

Someone.

He grabbed his phone, his gun in his hand as he walked to the dining room window, which was larger than the kitchen's.

Still, nothing looked out of place. No figure lurking behind a tree. No lights illuminated the yard. No alerts making his phone alive.

Was this how Cherry felt all the time? The sense someone was watching her, yet not seeing anything.

It was disturbing. Not much frightened him. Not after getting shot. Nothing could be scarier than almost losing your life.

But this scared him. The thought some unknown enemy was out there, waiting, watching, just biding their time to strike. To hurt the woman he was coming to care about way too much.

He jumped, then laughed when Cherry's hands wound around his stomach.

"I didn't mean to startle you," she whispered, her head pressed against his back, her hands tightening on his stomach.

"I didn't expect you to wake up. I hope I didn't wake you."

"I don't know what woke me, but I didn't like seeing you not in bed." Her hands felt icy cold as her nails dug into his stomach. "Did your phone alert go off? Is someone out there?"

Yes, he felt a presence. Someone was in the woods, hiding.

"No, nothing went off. I got up to get a glass of water."

He might sense something was out there, but he didn't want to frighten her more than she already was.

"Come on," he said, twisting around so he could see her face. "Let's go back to bed."

If he didn't have his gun and phone with him, he would've carried her back to the room. She didn't appear to be limping as badly as she had when they went to bed. Such a good sign to see.

As soon as they were cuddled underneath the blankets once more, he put his hand back where it had been in the beginning. On her hip. This time, he didn't fight the urge to keep it still. He drew it up and down her skin, reveling in the tiny trembles that coated her body.

"Bolt..."

He stared into her eyes, waiting for her to finish whatever was on her mind. Though he sensed what she wanted to say.

Why was he holding back?

He'd already had this argument with himself in the kitchen. There was no sense in fighting it anymore. There was no sense in holding back. For once in his life, he needed to live in the moment.

He pressed his lips to hers in answer to her unspoken question. Her hands were finally starting to warm up as they wound around him, clinging to his back. The kiss turned intense, all their frenzied need popping to the surface, waiting to explode.

Her hands trailed down to the edge of his boxers, dragging them down. He helped her along, snagging her shirt as well, tossing it across the room. Then he claimed a nipple, relishing in the way her low moans filled the room.

"Yes, Bolt. Love me."

He tensed for a moment, so brief he hoped she didn't notice. Her hands hadn't stopped swerving a path across his back so he could only assume she hadn't.

Love me?

Did that mean more than what was happening right now? Love her? Or just her body?

Because damn it, he could fall in love with her with ease. Hell, it might've already happened. But right now wasn't the time to ponder it.

Her panties disappeared, then his lips were trailing down her body until they found the perfect spot. She was wet and ready for him. He'd show her the pleasure first. His tongue dove in, pulling the bliss out in small increments. Enjoying the way her hands fiddled with his hair, occasionally pulling when he hit a spot she really liked. Her low moans gradually got louder and louder until a tiny cry rented the air.

"Yes, Bolt! Yes."

He never knew he could love hearing his name screamed out loud like that. He wanted to hear it again.

He slid up her body, pausing before kissing her. "Is it okay if I kiss you still?"

She bit her lip with a coy smile hiding. Then she flicked a finger across his lip. "It was a bit wet there. Now you can kiss me."

He chuckled, then dipped in to devour her lips as he had down below until she pushed on his shoulders. His smile didn't die but the confusion was written in his eyes.

"Lay on your back. It's my turn."

He'd had sex before. Three girlfriends that didn't go very far. Maybe it was him. Maybe it was the fact they didn't want to live in a small town anymore.

But he'd never had a woman go down on him. It wasn't something his old girlfriends had ever offered, and he didn't ask.

She licked her lips, the anticipation growing in her velvety-green eyes.

Hell, he wasn't going to say no.

He rolled off her and rested into the bed, shivering when she straddled him and her hands slid down his chest.

She palmed his hard cock, biting her lip, that teasing, coy smile reappearing.

His breaths were heavy, his body taut with tension. Her devilish looks, her hand stroking him was putting him on the verge of exploding.

"You might..." he croaked with need. "You might want to go slow. I don't think I'm going to last long."

"Slow it is," she whispered before her mouth wrapped around his cock, taking him deep.

He arched off the bed, groaning with desire.

She pulled out slowly, her tongue swirling and doing things he didn't know it was capable of. Then back down. With controlled patience.

Shit.

Maybe slow wasn't better. He could feel the pleasure building and it was almost painful to hold back.

"Cherry..." her name barely came out in a whisper.

She either didn't hear him or she refused to respond. Her ministrations continued with aching patience until he couldn't take it any longer. He tried to push her away, but her mouth clamped around him like a suction cup. She downed every drop that left his body.

His entire body felt more relaxed and depleted than it had in a very long time. She slid up his body in almost the same way he had hers.

A crafty smile lit her face. "Is it okay if I kiss you still?"

He chuckled at the question.

"Hell, yes."

Then their lips were locked once more. He rolled until she was under him, then because he could feel the ecstasy building again, he plunged deep inside her. He captured her moan that would've escaped, their tongues dueling as their bodies started a battle of their own.

Her legs wound around him, holding on tight. His hands slid through her tangled hair, gripping hard, but not enough to pull.

In and out. Thrust after thrust. Until he felt her tense beneath him. The same chaotic energy pulsed through his veins and he came with her.

His hot breath hit her neck as he rested his head on her pillow.

"That would've been a tragedy if we never did that." She giggled, blowing out a relieved sigh.

A damn tragedy indeed.

He wouldn't be able to keep his hands off her now. Once definitely was not enough.

Her leaving...that would be the worst tragedy of all.

CHERRY STRETCHED like a cat when Bolt slid out of bed, her body sore in all the right places. "I didn't hear the alarm going off."

He shook his head. "It didn't. But it is time to get up. My

body's internal alarm kind of knows when it's time to get up. You should stay in bed. Stay home."

Like that, the fear jumped back inside her like it had never left. For a brief moment in time, it had disappeared.

"No, I'll come into town with you."

"Mrs. Dunburry doesn't keep her shop open as long on Saturdays."

"Please, Bolt. I can't stay here by myself. Not yet. I need a few more days."

He nodded, understanding.

"You can use the shower first. I'll go make some coffee." He smiled and headed for the door.

Her words stopped him. "Or we shower together."

He turned around with a mischievous smile. "Or we could do that."

She'd never showered with a guy before. Dean wasn't that kind of guy. He liked quick, rough sex, and that was that. No fun. No teasing. No foreplay. Not like Bolt who'd treasured and cherished her, in and out of the bed.

They had fun soaping each other up, touching and playing until Bolt groaned with regret they couldn't be late. They dressed, her in yesterday's clothes, and him in his uniform that had him looking so dashing. He made coffee while she fried up some eggs.

"You should try to keep off your ankle today as much as you can. I'm sure Mrs. Dunburry will understand."

She kissed him on the cheek, grabbing the salt near the coffee pot. "It's feeling better. But I'll be careful."

The drive into town was short, like usual. He parked, and instead of doing her daily walk around town before joining Mrs. Dunburry, she joined him at the station. Charlotte was friendly, but she didn't hang out with her while she waited for the boutique to open. Bolt left to start his shift. She missed him the moment he left her view.

Mrs. Dunburry fussed over her, making her sit on a stool at the register, coddling her like a baby. It was odd. Lovely, but odd. Even her mother had never treated her like this. Like she was something precious and shouldn't ever feel pain.

Bolt came into the shop a few hours later, smiling at Mrs. Dunburry with a look she didn't understand. Until Mrs. Dunburry excused herself to see if the customer in one of the aisles needed help. Something she had already done before Bolt came in.

"I know when I'm not wanted," she said with a hearty chortle and walked away.

"Are you trying to steal a kiss?" Cherry teased.

"No, but I will." Bolt swooped in and kissed her lightly before anyone saw them.

Not that it mattered. Mrs. Dunburry was sure to interrogate her once he left, and Cherry didn't know if she'd be able to keep the stars out of her eyes, or the feeling of new love out of her voice. What she felt for Bolt was something she'd never felt before. She never wanted the feeling to disappear. She came here looking for her half-sister and she found more than she could've ever hoped for.

Bolt set a phone on the counter, pushing it closer to her. "For you."

She eyed it but didn't pick it up. "What do you mean? I can't take that."

It was a smartphone, not anywhere close to the cheap flip phone she had bought for emergency use only.

"You can and you will." He picked it up and punched in the lock code. "You open the phone up with the same passcode as my house alarm. I already put the camera app on here, so if you happen to be at the house by yourself, you have access to the cameras as well."

He showed her everything and held out the phone as if she'd take it from him. She absolutely would not.

"I can't afford that. I can't accept it."

"You don't have to pay me for it. I want you to have it."

She shoved it away, shaking her head. "It's too expensive."

Bolt leaned forward, cupping his hand behind her neck, pulling her closer until his forehead was against hers. "I need you to take it. I need to know you can call me if something like what happened yesterday ever happens again. It better not, but you need a safety net, and this will help. Please, Cherry. Don't argue with me on this. When you..." He swallowed, his hand tightening on her neck. "When you leave, I'll take it back. No big deal."

When she left.

But she didn't want to leave. That week timeframe she had given Pepper, she wanted to take it back. Retract her words as if she never said them.

"You know Mrs. Dunburry won't even interrogate me now for answers. She's going to assume something is going on between us."

Bolt's eyes shimmered with desire. "Well, there is. So why hide it? It's impossible to hide anything in this town."

Except for the person stalking her. They hid very well. She wouldn't admit it, not yet anyway, but she'd felt eyes on her all morning. All the customers who entered had been familiar, no new faces. She'd never seen anyone staring at her from outside. Whoever was out there watching her hid well. Stayed in the shadows and out of view.

"Okay, I'll take the phone. For now."

He kissed her, more desperately this time, but kept it

short. Then he placed the phone in her hand. "Keep it on you at all times. Not in your purse, but in your pocket."

She nodded.

"When Mrs. Dunburry locks up, be sure to go back to the station until I get off."

She nodded again.

"How's the ankle?"

She patted the side of the stool. "Totally great. Mrs. Dunburry hasn't let me stand at all. I'm getting better every second. Gaining more energy every minute." Her eyes trailed from his eyes down his chest, landing on his pants.

He got the meaning. His cheeks bloomed a deep red, and his lips curled up into a boyish grin that said he was shy for some reason. Maybe because they were in public and she was undressing him with her eyes.

"That's good to know. I foresee you needing your energy tonight." He leaned in. "I have the day off tomorrow. So we can sleep in."

"I look forward to it."

He snatched another kiss before turning around to leave.

"Hey, Bolt?"

He twisted her way.

"If I...umm...if you want me to cook tonight, I will. You cooked last time I was there."

He frowned, then it morphed into a smile. "We'll see how your ankle is." Then he turned around and left.

He knew. He knew she changed her words at the last second. Because she had really meant to ask if she wanted to stay longer, would he mind?

He might not admit it, but eventually he'd get sick of her. They always did. She'd see how the week went and reevaluate the situation then.

14

CHERRY KEPT a smile on her face as she held one end of the pink streamer while Charlotte attached the other end to the wall. She couldn't let anyone see how much getting ready for this baby shower was killing her. Because the news she found out this morning couldn't be happening.

Yet, it was. She knew the exact moment it happened. One month ago when Bolt took her with such passion neither remembered to grab a condom. She was pregnant because they both lost their minds in lust.

Of course, that's all it was.

One week had passed, and instead of asking if she could stay, she pretended like she never made the deadline. He didn't bring it up either. Life went on. Even Pepper didn't make a mention that she hadn't left. One week turned into two, which ultimately had turned into a month. Here she was, helping the women set up Kat's baby shower. She was thirty-two and half weeks along, due around the end of October, with a baby girl on the way.

She ached to press a hand to her belly, wondering what she was having, but stopped herself before the impulse took over. She couldn't let anyone know. Not until she told Bolt. But first, she had to process the news herself. It didn't occur to her she skipped her period. No, the sign she should take a test had been the nausea she had experienced the past two days in a row. She managed to hide it from Bolt because he worried about her too much already. She thought it'd been a stomach bug, not wanting him to go all mother hen on her. Then her boobs started to tingle, and that's when the light bulb went off. She bought a pregnancy test, giving Julia who rang her up a look to keep it to herself. Hopefully, the young teen gave her that much. She used Mrs. Dunburry's bathroom, nearly cried from the results, and took the evidence with her. The trash can on Main Street now held her secret.

This was the worst news ever. A baby! What did she know about raising a baby? Nothing. Her mother didn't teach her anything but how to dance on stage, seduce a man, and drop them like a hot potato.

When Bolt found out, he'd think she seduced him just to keep staying with him. She had it made right now. A roof over her, food in her belly, a man who made her feel safe. A job. Mrs. Dunburry had shocked her when she handed over that first paycheck.

"You show up every day and help me more than you know. Of course, you should get paid for your efforts. I never realized how much help I needed until you showed up. I would be lost without you now, Cherry."

But would she? Would she really be lost without her? Nobody ever needed her. She screwed up more times than not.

When she told Bolt she was pregnant, he'd see through her. He'd see how scared she was to be on her own again. To be thrust into the world with no one to have her back, with no one who cared about her. He'd tell her to stay out of pity.

She never wanted to leave. He didn't want her to stay forever.

"Cherry?"

She blinked, shaking her head clear of the turmoil raging a war in her mind. Charlotte was looking at her like she had lost her mind. She had. It had imploded the moment she read the word pregnant.

"Are you okay? I called your name several times."

"Yeah, of course. Sorry."

She smiled and waited for Charlotte to hand over the piece of tape so she could attach her side. Charlotte finally conceded, and she finished the task with ease, stepping off the chair with shaky legs.

Charlotte caught her around the arm, preventing her from falling and embarrassing herself further.

"When I picked you up from Mrs. Dunburry's you seemed...off. A bit shaken. You still seem that way." The concern in Charlotte's eyes surprised her.

Everyone had warmed up to her, except Charlotte and Deke. They were cordial, but she had seen the suspicion in their eyes every so often. She didn't know what else she could do to make them trust her.

"Did something happen today?"

She shook her head. Because nothing happened. At least not with what Charlotte was asking. Did her stalker finally announce himself? Did he approach her or leave a little gift? Nope and nope.

And they all knew it wasn't Dean anymore. Two days after Bolt had given her the phone—and she passed the number along to Peggy—she called telling her all about Dean's troubles. Apparently, he had left a week or so after Cherry had—purely coincidence—to help his sister in Arkansas, who was having trouble with her boyfriend. He beat her. So Dean beat him up. He sat in jail for nearly a week before his sister finally paid his bail. She had appreciated him coming to her rescue, but she hadn't liked he used his fists in the process. Dean was back in Florida, and his sister was back with her boyfriend.

The news had depressed everyone. Because if it wasn't Dean, then who was it? Cherry had no idea who it could be, but she figured Charlotte and Deke thought she had something to do with what was going on. Like she was in cahoots with whoever was following her. Why would she do something like that? What would be the point of it?

Pepper believed her. Bolt believed her. That's all she needed.

Charlotte narrowed her eyes, clearly not believing her. "You'd at least tell Bolt if something happened, I hope. I know you don't like me, but you should tell him whatever happened. I'm not an idiot. I can see you're shaken about something."

Cherry frowned. "You're the one who doesn't like me. I've done everything I can do to prove to you I'm not here to hurt Pepper, and yet, you still don't believe me."

"It's hard to when you hide stuff. Like whatever's bothering you now."

"Nothing's bothering me. I didn't sense anyone watching me today. He took the day off, I guess."

Charlotte's eyes narrowed even further into tiny slits, not appreciating Cherry's sense of humor. Well, it was the truth. She hadn't sensed anyone watching her. Most days, her skin crawled with unease because she could feel eyes on her. Every time, she tried to ignore it. Every time, she failed. But some days—rare days—she didn't feel anything. Those days were so rare, it's as if she dreamed them.

"Everything okay in here?" Aubrey popped into the room.

"Yeah, it's all good," Charlotte snapped and walked out of the room.

Aubrey moved closer with one of her gentle smiles she always wore. She was the quietest, yet nicest one in the group. Cherry felt so bad about everything that had happened to her, though never let Aubrey see it. She knew Aubrey wouldn't want that kind of pity from anyone. She knew she wouldn't.

"Give her time. She'll warm up to you." Aubrey's eyes filled with concern. "She's right, though. If something happened, you should say so."

Cherry brightened her smile as much as she could, removing all the fakeness behind it. Well, most of it. "Nothing happened, I swear. It's been a good day."

Besides the terror of finding out I'm pregnant. Very good day.

Aubrey looked as if she believed her. Honestly, she wasn't lying. They didn't need to know about the baby. Not yet. This was Kat's day anyway.

An hour later, people started arriving. Friends and family of Kat's. The house was filled with happiness and joy. Laughter filled the rooms. Even Kat, who had very up-and-down moods during her pregnancy, didn't look sad once. Cherry found it difficult to keep a smile on her face, but she made it through the party without showing a frown once. She knew most people, as most of them were from town. It wasn't hard to join in conversations or feel like the oddball in any of the games. She'd shown up almost two months ago and inserted herself into this small town like she'd been born here. The thought of leaving now felt like her heart was being ripped from her chest. She didn't know if she could do it.

Not just leaving Bolt either, but Pepper too. While their relationship blossomed every day, she saw Pepper's hesitation at times. Cherry sensed she was still smothering her even though she lived with Bolt. As if she were intruding on Pepper's town and would soon wear out her welcome.

Eventually, Bolt would feel the same. Hell, he could already feel that way and she hadn't noticed.

Kat oohed and aahed over all the baby gifts, but no amount of begging would get her to reveal the name she and Danny had picked out. They wouldn't know the sweet baby girl's name until she arrived.

When the party ended, she made her round of goodbyes a lot faster than Pepper, which said a lot. Because Pepper still felt like most people didn't like her so she didn't try to engage them in conversation like Cherry would.

The first part of the drive to Bolt's house was quiet. Halfway there, Pepper finally spoke.

"Charlotte's worried about you."

Cherry scoffed. "She hates me. I highly doubt she's worried."

"She thinks something happened today."

How many times would she have to go over this? No doubt a few more because Bolt would be on her case as well. Someone, most likely Charlotte, probably told him her worries. Just. Great.

"Nothing happened. I keep telling everyone that and no one is believing me."

It was like her life was on repeat. Same horror, new people enacting it. She thought she'd found people who trusted her, who took her at her word. Now they were slipping into her old life. Where no one ever believed what she said. Like her mother. Like Dean. Like Peggy.

Well, she was half-lying, but not about what they thought. Nothing nefarious had happened today.

Pepper pulled into the driveway and Bolt opened the front door before they even had a chance to open their car doors. The security cameras worked wonderfully.

Her hand went for the handle but Pepper's hand on her arm stopped her. Cherry met her gaze.

"I believe you. But something is bugging you." Pepper let out a harsh breath. "Are you thinking about leaving? Is that it? I know none of us has brought it up, but you had said you were leaving over three weeks ago. It's okay if you want to leave. None of us will be mad. Of course, we'll stay in contact."

Meaning, her sister didn't care if she left. Sounded like she'd even help pack her bags.

"I could tell you were forcing out a smile tonight at the party. I know your moods, Cherry. We might not have known each other long, but I know your moods. I can see a fake smile a mile away. It's something I've perfected myself."

Pepper let out another heavy breath.

"You can tell me the truth."

Perhaps, but Bolt deserved to know first.

But maybe it was better if she kept it to herself. Maybe it was better she finally left. Leave before she wore out her welcome. Before her sister started hating her and Bolt started resenting her.

He was wonderful. Took care of her in every sense. In and out of bed. Same as Dean had. It's as if she were destined to repeat the same cycles over and over. With men. With people believing her. She couldn't escape any of it.

"It's been a long month, Pepper. Leaving is on my mind every day. I don't want to overstay my welcome, and I'm afraid I might have."

Pepper glanced out the window, and she followed her gaze. Bolt stood on the porch staring at them, yet he hadn't moved toward the car. Such the gentleman, giving them the space they wanted. But she saw the tense stance, the rigidness in his face. He didn't like waiting on the porch. He didn't like keeping his distance. As soon as she walked inside the house, he'd inquire about what they were talking about, and she'd be forced to lie. He'd see it, and she'd crush his heart for doing something she swore she'd never do again.

Which meant she'd have to tell him the truth and then she'd be forced to leave.

"I said it's okay if you leave. I didn't say I wanted you to leave."

"We both know you have reservations about me, even if you don't say so. It's there."

Pepper shook her head. "No, I don't. Sometimes, I feel overwhelmed by it all, but I don't doubt you and your motives." Pepper reached out and squeezed her arm. "Do you want to leave Bolt? He'll be crushed if you leave."

So would she, but they'd both move on.

"I'm sure he's getting sick of me." Not the sex, though. The sex was intense and wild every time they came together. He'd miss the sex. No surprise there, it was one of her talents. Making men feel good.

"I think you need to open your eyes up."

If Bolt had feelings for her, she'd know. Because he would've told her. He was always honest with her, and he'd yet to tell her he loved her or that he wanted her to stay forever.

"Look, I'm not leaving yet. Nothing happened today. I'm sick of having to explain that over and over."

She wrenched open the car door and slammed it shut, stomping like a petulant child toward the house.

"Cherry—"

"I'm fine," she snapped, cutting off Bolt. She didn't need him asking—and not believing—her as well.

She slammed the front door for extra measure and proceeded to the bathroom and threw up.

Okay, so maybe she wasn't fine.

BOLT STARED AT THE DOOR, then turned his attention to Pepper who had exited the vehicle.

"What the hell happened?"

Pepper winced and shrugged. "I don't know how the conversation escalated like that. Charlotte thought something was bugging her and mentioned it to me at the beginning of the party. I kept an eye on her and it did look like something was wrong. I asked her about it in the car. She claims everything's fine. That nothing happened today."

"That looked like she's pissed. What exactly did you say to her?"

This time Pepper grimaced. "I might've...mentioned..." Pepper cleared her throat, erasing any hesitation from her gaze. "I told her we wouldn't be mad if she left. That if she's afraid to tell us she wants to leave, it's okay. I thought that might be what's bugging her."

Cherry leaving?

No.

No, no, no. That couldn't happen. He'd lose a part of himself if she left. She'd stormed into his life like a ball of energy and now he was used to having her around. Her brightness, her happiness, her joy for life and everything in it. The sex was nice too. He'd never felt so close to another person before. She'd take half his heart along with her if she left.

"And what did she say?"

Pepper twisted her lips as if bidding her time to find the right words. "That it's on her mind a lot. That she thinks she's overstayed her welcome. That you're getting sick of her."

Was that how she felt? Had he done something to make her think that? Was he too clingy? Not clingy enough? Why would she think he was getting sick of her? If anything, he wanted to spend more time with her. Take several weeks off, board themselves inside, and not come out until they were forced to.

"Well, I'm not."

"That's what I told her." Pepper crossed her arms. "Look, not much has happened in the past month. We've eliminated Dean as a suspect, which is great. But whoever is watching her hasn't made another move. Sure, she has the feeling someone's out there, but she hasn't seen anyone. Not like that day she hid in the closet. The cameras haven't picked up on anything besides the stray deer or two. It could go on forever. Or it could already be over."

What was he supposed to say to that? Because damn it, he knew all of that. He sensed the person himself sometimes. Late at night, when he couldn't sleep—still—he would walk around the house, looking out the windows. He never saw anything, but he felt the presence. The evil lurking in the woods. Waiting, watching, bidding its time. He never confessed any of that to Cherry because he didn't want to frighten her. Though she had seemed to be finding her courage in the past week. She didn't hang out in town on some of the days he worked. She helped Mrs. Dunburry Monday through Friday in the shop, and on weekends, if he worked, she stayed home. Nothing had happened like the last time she was alone.

"Bolt?"

"Pepper?"

She flinched as he snapped her name a little harsher than he intended.

"Do you love my sister? Have you told her how you felt?"

He clenched his jaw, not appreciating being put on the spot.

"I would never kick her out. She can stay as long as she wants."

Pepper frowned and moved closer, stepping on the first step, and shoved a finger into his chest. "I told Cherry she'd be sorry if she hurt you. Now I feel like it's time to give you the same warning. If you hurt my sister, you can kiss our friendship good-bye."

Wow.

That was unexpected.

He didn't confess he loved Cherry, but that didn't mean he didn't love her with every breath in his body. It wasn't fair for Pepper to hear it first. He hadn't found the courage to tell Cherry yet. To confess his feelings and beg her not to leave. Begging didn't seem like such a far-off concept anymore. Not with knowing Cherry had been thinking about leaving all month long. He should've never ignored it. He should've brought it up in the beginning when the first week passed and told her how he felt.

Pepper poked him again. "Did you hear me?"

"I heard you. I would never hurt her."

A tight jerk of her head said she understood what he wasn't saying. "Don't mess this up, Bolt." Then she turned around and left.

But he was so good at messing things up.

When he walked inside, he found Cherry in the living room, sipping on a glass of water.

He took a seat next to her.

"How was the party?"

She smiled and nodded enthusiastically, but he saw what Pepper was talking about. The forced cheeriness. The fake smile. Her skin even looked a little pale.

"Great. Kat's beautiful. Glowing and everything. She had a great turnout. I wish you could've been there."

Yeah, he was okay with the fact the guys weren't invited. Baby showers weren't his thing. Hell, he didn't even like celebrating his birthday. Having the attention on him wasn't something he cared for. It gave people more chances to see all his faults because all eyes were on him.

He didn't want to ignore the elephant in the room. The fact she stormed into the house and snapped at him. That she argued with her sister for the first time.

Yet he didn't know how to broach the subject.

"What did you and Pepper talk about out there?" she asked, surprising him that she brought it up first.

"Everything that you two talked about." His hand found hers, sliding his fingers until they were interlocked. "I've enjoyed the past month."

"Me too."

His eyes glided to her lips that he was dying to touch. He always got a hello kiss and a good-bye one. The hello kiss was missed when she got home and he felt the effects of its nonappearance.

"You don't have to leave." He pulled their locked hands to his lap. "I don't want you to leave."

"Why is that?" She frowned. "Because of that asshole out

there watching me? Because what we have is comfortable? Because I'm good in bed?"

"Seriously, Cherry!"

Was that what she thought about him? That he only wanted her for sex? Maybe she didn't feel what he felt for her. Complete and utter devotion. Love so deep it would kill him inside if she ever left. By the sounds of it, she planned on leaving.

She slid her hand out from his and stood up. "I can't do this, Bolt. Not anymore."

He didn't want to be talked down to, so he stood as well. He still didn't feel like he was on even ground with her. His world was slipping and falling apart and he had no idea how it got to this point so fast.

"Do what? What are we doing? What do you think we've been doing this past month?" Because for him, he'd been sharing a part of himself he never shared with others.

He told her things he didn't tell others. He even thought about sharing his insomnia with her but didn't want her to worry he wasn't at full power. That he could still keep her safe, even though he was so tired half the time. Hell, it was surprising she hadn't noticed.

"Pretending. We've been pretending and playing house when it's just been sex. That's all I'm good for."

He grabbed her arm when she started to walk away. The way she winced made him want to puke that he hurt her. He released her immediately.

"You're more than that. Don't ever say that again. It hasn't been just sex for me."

"I live here rent-free. You buy the food. You pay the bills. You even gave me a damn phone!" she shouted. "We have sex. It's the same thing I had with Dean. Same thing, different guy."

He didn't think she could dig a hole deeper into his heart until she said those words. She compared him to that possessive asshole.

"I told myself not to use you like that, and here I am doing it anyway."

"So that's it? That breaks it down to the T for me. What I mean to you. Nothing but a means to an end." He threw his hand at the door. "You're free to leave anytime you want. I'm not stopping you."

He would've before she broke his heart. He would've gotten down on his hands and knees and begged her to stay. But fool him only once.

Her bottom lip wobbled, telling him she was on the verge of tears. Damn it, he didn't want to see her cry. She put them in this position. She broke the happiness they'd been living in.

"It's for the best."

"Yep. For the best." If she insisted, so would he.

She moved a few steps before stopping near the threshold of the room. "Can you drive me to the bus stop in Neptune tomorrow?"

Wow. She knew where the bus stop was. She must've researched it knowing she was waiting for this day to happen. He felt blindsided. He woke up, made sweet love to her before getting ready for work, thinking they'd have a nice night in after the party, and here he was talking about her departure instead.

Where did it all go wrong?

Somewhere in between him dropping her off and her arriving to the party. Like Pepper had said, something was bothering her. Instead of telling him, she was lashing out. She was pushing him away.

That had to be it.

She was scared of something. Scared to tell him. So pushing him away was easier. Well, not for him.

"I can ask Pepper. It's fine."

He rushed forward, grabbing her hand to stop her from walking away. He turned her around and kept a hold of her hand as he walked forward, making her walk backward until her back hit the wall. He had her trapped. While he didn't want to be *that* guy, the one who appeared possessive and willing to do anything to get what he wanted, he had to be in the moment. He couldn't let her walk away. Not like this. Not lying to his face, especially when she promised not to lie ever again.

"I'm going to pretend you didn't just lie to me. I'm going to forgive you for everything you said. I'm going to erase the pain that those words hit me with. I'm going to keep you here until you tell me what's going on."

"I didn't lie."

He grabbed her other hand, trapping both as if he'd slapped handcuffs on her.

"I'm not like Dean."

She swallowed hard. He watched as her eyes widened with panic as if trying to convince him he was exactly like Dean. Acting like a maniac like he was.

"No, you're nothing like him. But it's the truth. He did everything for me like you do. I never said a word. I never tried to stop him. Same for you. I mooch like it's okay."

"I never did anything I didn't want to do, Cherry."

"It doesn't make it right, Bolt."

She tried to push him out of the way with her body. He didn't move a muscle. The movement did nothing but make him go hard and think of all the ways he could please her against the wall. She tried to shake her hands free, and he only clamped his grip tighter. He raised her hands above her head, moved in closer, pressing his body snug against hers, trapping her against the wall.

"I know what you're trying to do."

She smirked. "Get free from you. Yes, that's what I'm trying to do."

He matched her sly grin with one of his own. "If you wanted to get free, you'd use the moves I taught you. You're enticing me. You're trying to prove your point it was only sex. Of course, my body is responding because I'll always want you. It doesn't take much. But that only proves how attracted I am to you. You not fighting to get away proves how much you don't want to fight me."

Her smile died. "Let me go, Bolt."

"I will. When you tell me what happened today."

Her eyes turned down and he hated he couldn't see them. Read them.

"You'll only think it's another excuse for me to stay."

"Cherry, I don't think you've used any excuse to stay. I think you've stayed as long as you have because you want to. I haven't said anything about you leaving because I don't want you to. I just said it a few minutes ago I don't want you leaving. Whatever it is, I can handle it."

Her eyes popped up.

"I'm pregnant."

Well, shit. He didn't expect that.

15

HE DIDN'T LOOK disgusted or annoyed. He didn't look panicked or like he was going to get sick, kind of how she felt. He looked nothing but in shock.

Yeah, that's what had hit her earlier today.

Then a slow smile grew until his lips were curled so wide, she thought his face would break.

"You're serious?"

Why would she mess about something like this?

"Yes. I took the test today."

"Well, that's not bad news."

He couldn't be serious.

"It's not great news either."

His grip on her hands didn't loosen, but his body didn't feel as rigid. His smile died down some. "Why not?"

"What do I know about being a mother? I didn't exactly have one growing up."

"You'll be a wonderful mother. You brighten up a room with one sweet smile. You're great with people. You're nice and thoughtful. You care about others. It's not hard to see how wonderful of a mother you'll be."

Did he really believe that? She had a hard time seeing it.

"Why do you think I'd expect to you leave knowing you're pregnant?"

"I'm already a burden on you. To add on—"

His lips silenced her. She couldn't resist him, opening her mouth, letting him in. It was foolish, knowing nothing would last between them. He'd eventually see how much work it would be to have her underfoot *and* a baby.

"You've never been a burden. Never," he whispered against her lips. "I would've let you leave. But knowing you're pregnant, you can't leave. You just can't."

"Bolt—"

"Don't argue about this, Cherry. Please. I don't want to be the bad guy in this situation, but I will be if I have to. You can't leave now."

"You're not exactly giving me much of a choice." She shook her wrists that were still bound by his hands against the wall.

But he was right, of course. If she had wanted to get free, she could've. Or, at least, fought hard for freedom and hurt him in the process. She already hurt him. With all the lies that left her lips. Like the true gentleman he was, he would forgive her for it all.

She didn't deserve him.

But fear made her do crazy things. In the end, it would be better if she left. Why couldn't he see that? She left nothing but destruction in her wake. She'd destroy him too.

"Okay, fine." He dropped her wrists, freeing her from the shackles. "You can leave my house. But you can't leave town."

"I can do whatever I want to do."

"That's my child inside of you too. Not just yours. What

about what I want? I helped create it. I had the lapse in judgment just as much as you."

Meaning his mind had gone warp speed trying to remember when it could've happened. She knew it'd been the first time they had sex. They'd been in such a frenzy to have each other, neither thought about getting a condom. One error and it produced a huge problem.

"What do you want, Bolt? What do you want from me?"

He sighed. "I want you to trust me for once. To let me in. To let me love you as you deserve to be loved."

No.

No way he could be laying something heavy like that on her.

"Yes, Cherry, I love you. I have this weird feeling no one has ever actually said that to you. Which is why I didn't want to say it yet. I didn't want you running from me. But I can feel your body vibrating with energy as if getting ready to sprint right out my front door."

"It's because of the baby. You're saying it because of that."

A muscle in his cheek bounced, his jaw tight. "Think what you want, but that's not the truth. I think you know that deep down. Pregnant or not, I love you. I don't want you to leave. I want to figure out where we go from here together. As a team. As partners. As two people who care about each other. Because you might not want to say it, but I think you love me too."

She didn't even know what love was. What it felt like. He was right. No one had ever said those three little words to her. Not a boyfriend. Not a friend. Not even her own mother. How could she know what love felt like if no one ever said it to her before?

"Come on." He stepped away, giving her space for the

first time, but he held out his hand, waiting for her to take it. Not letting her break the rope that was holding them together. It was on the verge of snapping; she tried like hell to get it to break. He was holding it together by the threads, refusing to let it snap.

How had he seen through her bullshit? How had he seen the pain and fear she tried to hide?

The truth slapped her in the face.

Because he truly loved her.

She placed her hand in his. "Where are we going?"

"To the bedroom. I want to show you how much I love you."

She didn't need him to do that. As much as she tried to ignore it, she felt his love every night, every time he touched her. The softness in his hands. The gentleness in the way he kissed. The sensual way he moved. He'd been showing her all month long how much he loved her.

"I thought you said it wasn't just sex."

His expression tightened. "It's not. But I don't know how else to show you. To make you believe. I could keep repeating it, but I don't think you'd believe me no matter how much I say it."

Because the words were foreign to her. She knew from the first moment he touched her how much he cared. His hands spoke with such a sweet language. He was right— again. He could show her with his tender touch how much he loved her.

She grabbed the front of his shirt and pulled him closer. "Right here then. Love me against the wall and prove it."

He looked her up and down, then pressed a hand to her belly with a frown. "Will it hurt the baby?"

How could she ever doubt how this man felt about her? He didn't hide his fears. He didn't hide who he was from her.

"I don't think so. It's like the size of a sunflower seed right now or something." She chuckled.

Thankfully, she managed to make him laugh too.

"Okay, then. Let me love you."

He was asking way more from her than he realized. By the intensity in his gaze, she feared he did know what he was asking of her.

She unsnapped the button to her jeans and pushed them all the way down, shaking them off to the side. It'd gotten cooler in the past few days, and she had to buy a few pairs of pants as she had only packed shorts thinking it'd be a short trip. Early September in Minnesota was nothing like the weather in Florida.

He helped her toss off her shirt and unclasp her bra. She helped make his shirt disappear. Her panties joined the pile, and then so did his pants and boxers.

Then he lifted her and slid deep inside, trapping her against the wall once again. Like last time, she didn't mind. The whole time he held her against her will, he'd been gentle. No bruise would be found. Because Bolt would never hurt her.

His kisses were slow and sensual, just as his thrusts. She wanted him to pound into her, release the energy she knew had built from her making him go crazy with her mood tonight. But of course, he didn't give her what she wanted. He gave her the exact opposite.

Slow. Sweet. Tender.

His lips touched her everywhere on her face. Her eyes, her lips, her cheeks. They made a trail down her neck to her ear, and then down to her shoulder. All the while he pumped in and out with gentle patience while she clung to him.

"I need more, Bolt."

His hot breath ignited her senses even more as he whispered, "I need you to feel my love."

Oh, she felt it. She felt it everywhere. In her heart, body, and soul. Heaven help her, she'd take it, soak it up, and hold it hostage. He had no idea he'd never get rid of her now. He was stuck with her.

She'd never had love before and didn't want to lose it.

Maybe he felt her acceptance. Or maybe he couldn't take it any longer because his thrusts became harder, more insistent.

Soon, he was pounding into her like she had originally wanted. The moment her orgasm hit her, her teeth sunk into his shoulder. A little nibble she couldn't help. He growled in approval, thrusting a few more times, before tensing himself.

Their heavy breaths were the only sound for the first few minutes while he held her against the wall. Holding her as if he never wanted to let go.

"So that's settled. You're staying."

She giggled into his shoulder. She was.

BOLT TRIED to look relaxed as he sat in a chair in Logan's office, but he figured he wasn't fooling anyone. He knew why they called this meeting. Why Danny, Deke, Seth, and Logan all stared at him like he needed a shoulder to cry on.

Because Cherry was pregnant, and while they all claimed to have faith in her, they were all doubting it now. As if she had planned it all along and trapped him.

He didn't feel trapped. He felt elated and excited—terrified. He never imagined he'd be a father one day. Women weren't his forte, and he hadn't found the one to settle down with. At least, he hadn't before Cherry. Thirty-two wasn't old, but it was creeping up there. Most people settled down before then. Didn't they?

He'd come to terms with her age. So they had eight years' difference between them. No big deal. It didn't faze him anymore.

He'd had off Sunday and Monday, enjoying the two days all to himself with Cherry. Trying to show her in as many ways as possible that he loved her. That he wanted her to stay. That, down the road, he'd pop the question and needed to hear the answer yes. Sure, he showed her with his hands and his lips. But he also showed her in the little things he did, like cooking for her and rubbing her feet. Making sure she had everything she needed and felt safe from all harm. She couldn't doubt his love. He'd never survive the fallout if she didn't feel his love.

He knew why they were all convened in the office this early-Tuesday morning, but he wasn't going to start speaking first. They wanted to bombard him with whatever the hell they thought this was; they could start first.

Unfortunately, he wasn't even able to tell his friends and family the news first. Gossip spread around town Cherry had purchased a pregnancy test on Saturday. By Sunday afternoon, everyone had been talking about it. Pepper called first. Cherry told her the news. Then Logan called right before Danny, and Deke ended the day with his phone call. All offering congrats and 'let us know if you need anything.' His parents called wondering if the news was true, and the moment he confirmed it, his mom squealed with joy. He managed to hold her off from smothering Cherry with plans about the future, but he wouldn't be able to hold her off for long.

The only person not to call was Carson. No surprise there.

He wished he had another day off. After this painful meeting, he'd have to endure all the congrats from everyone in town as well. He hoped Cherry was doing okay. She had called out yesterday to Mrs. Dunburry, who assured her it was okay. Knowing Cherry, she was doing better than he was. Or at least faking it better than he was.

"I called this meeting for a reason," Logan started, and though he didn't look at Bolt, he knew it was about him.

"But first, I want to say congratulations in person, Bolt." This time, Logan met his eyes. His gaze was filled with happiness, but also concern.

"Thanks."

Deke cleared his throat. "Are you happy? I mean, are you excited?"

"This isn't some nefarious plan of hers, Deke. I was involved in the process. I was the idiot that didn't remember the condom one time. That's all it takes. One time. So whatever this is, you need to knock it off. I won't stand for it."

"I don't know what to say." Deke looked serious with the concern in his eyes, yet the distrust as well.

"Then don't say anything at all," Bolt snapped.

"I wish I could trust her. I really do," Deke added as if Bolt never spoke. "There's something about all of this that rubs me the wrong way. Now a baby on the way."

Bolt stood up. Logan rushed to his feet as well, which didn't take much as he had been leaning against his desk while all of them had taken a seat around the room. Deke tensed but didn't move from his spot.

"I love her, Deke. If you can't accept that, that's not my problem. That's yours. But you better keep your opinions to yourself. You and Charlotte both. She's no better. Honestly, I expected better from you. Obviously, Charlotte's rubbing off on you."

"No, almost losing the woman I love has me more wary of everything going on. The Cheetahs wreaked havoc on this town. On us! I won't let my guard down, even if you seem to be." Deke stood up when Bolt took a step forward.

Logan put a hand out as if that would stop him. If Bolt wanted to charge at him, he would. He'd get in as many punches as he could before they pulled him free.

Seth got to his feet, standing between Deke and him. Danny remained in his chair, looking relaxed and like a fight wasn't about to break out.

"We all need to calm down. Cool it, Deke. If Bolt loves her, he trusts her. Pepper trusts her." Seth's voice was firm. Telling Deke if Pepper trusted her then he should too.

"And does she love you? Is she really pregnant? Did you see the test for yourself?" Deke demanded.

No, he hadn't. But he believed her. She wouldn't lie about something like that. What would be the purpose of lying about something like that?

"What goes on between Cherry and I is just that, between us. It's none of your damn business."

"So, I'll take that as a no." Deke smirked, something so foreign on his face. Sure, he loved to laugh and joke around more than Danny, but he didn't generally smile like the devil in disguise.

Seth sighed. "You know, it's not hard to see how Pepper and Cherry are sisters. They're a lot alike in so many ways. One's stern and closed-off. Has a hard time letting people in. The other one is bubbly and friendly. Isn't shy to chat with people she doesn't know. Lets the whole world into her atmosphere. Yet they both keep you at a distance, only in a different way. It's hard to see with Cherry, but it's there. She's pretending to let you in, but she isn't. Pepper doesn't pretend. She tells you to butt out. In the end, they're alike in that respect. Interesting as they weren't raised together." Seth looked at him. "Don't give up on her, Bolt. I know you didn't say it, but I could hear it in your voice. You said it to her, but she hasn't said it back. Give her time. I have faith she will."

Seth would know. Because he'd had a battle getting Pepper to see how much he loved her. It all worked out in the end.

Bolt nodded and resumed his seat. Seth sat down as well. Deke lingered on his feet, then gave in.

"I'm sorry, Bolt. I don't mean to be the bad guy here. It can't hurt someone playing devil's advocate," Deke said quietly as if that would lessen the blow.

"Except you're playing it with the woman I love. It's okay then, huh? I'm not an idiot, despite you thinking I am. Why am I surprised? You're with Charlotte. She's always thought that of me. Always thought I was the world's worst deputy. Hell, she even thought I had something to do with Aubrey's disappearance. Wouldn't that be something if I'm in on whatever game you think Cherry's playing too? Like the bad person I am."

"Okay, enough," Danny spat, sitting up straight. "You're not an idiot, Bolt. You saved my life and Kat's. You saved Deke's and Charlotte's, even if he is forgetting that at the moment. You're a damn good deputy. We all have moments of weakness. It doesn't make us dumb." Danny turned to Deke. "Knock it off. Play devil's advocate, but don't be an ass about it."

Deke blew air out of his nose as if he were getting ready to really let it loose. Then everything seemed to deflate out of him. "I said I was sorry. I meant it. I'll stop painting her as the villain. But someone is. We don't know who. How about Evan?"

Seth perked up at that. "What about him?"

"Maybe he's the one spying on her. Maybe he's the one trying to stir up trouble."

They all contemplated that for a moment.

Danny spoke first. "Cherry said she felt eyes on her weeks before she even left Florida. It couldn't be him. He hasn't left town."

Logan cleared his throat. "Somehow this conversation got off track when all I wanted to do was offer Bolt a simple congratulations in person."

"Well?" Danny prodded.

Logan placed a hand on Seth's shoulder. "I got a call from the prison where Lillian was being held. She escaped last night."

Seth stood up so fast, he nearly knocked Logan down from the force of it. "Pepper's at home, alone. I need to go to her. Why didn't you tell her to come here too?"

Logan grabbed his arm before he could rush out of the room. "Because I knew the news coming from you would be easier to handle. Pepper's fine. It happened late in the evening, more like early morning. She couldn't have made it here yet."

"I know I think Cherry's been up to something," Deke started, "but how does it play in with Lillian? There are no records she ever visited her."

Logan shrugged. "I don't think Cherry has anything to do with Lillian breaking out. I don't even know how that would fit in with this person who's been following her. It could be two separate things. I believe it is. Nothing has happened in over a month to Cherry. No sign of anything.

This thing with Lillian has to take front and center right now."

Logan looked at him as if he'd argue with that. No arguments from him. Lillian on the loose was not good news at all. In fact, like how Seth wanted to rush out of here, so did he to make sure Cherry was okay. Did Lillian know about Cherry? Would she hurt her like she wanted to hurt Pepper? Did any of them even think that thought? Probably not as most of them were still suspicious of her.

"Bolt, I'd like you and me to have a chat with Evan. Deke's right. He could be involved somehow. He almost led us to our deaths once before. If Lillian reached out, he could fall prey once again." Logan sighed when Seth moved a step away and crossed his arms. "You think Evan's not involved?"

"I want to join you and Bolt after I chat with Pepper. If he is, I'll know." Seth swore under his breath. "Or maybe I won't. I don't know him anymore. I'd hate to think he'd help Lillian. How'd she escape?"

"She had help from a guard. He's also missing."

"My brother has his cabin if you need to use it, Seth," Bolt offered.

Seth shook his head. "We're not running. This bitch wants a fight, we'll fight."

"If that's her goal," Danny added. "We don't know what she's going to do. She's a loose cannon."

"I know exactly what she's going to do. She's going to kill Pepper. She said so the last time they spoke." The terror in Seth's eyes made Bolt shiver with unease.

Lillian could easily transfer that hatred to Cherry as well. Because she was evil incarnate and she didn't care about the destruction she caused.

"The hell she will." Deke stood up, the determination clear.

Danny took a spot next to him. "We'll call our contacts in Florida and make sure we get regular updates on the manhunt. Womanhunt. Whatever you want to call it."

"Seth, you go to Pepper," Logan added, then looked at him. "Bolt, let's chat with Evan."

He'd be happy to.

But his gut told him Evan had nothing to do with this.

And that Cherry was in terrible danger.

PEPPER SET down the notepad she'd been scribbling ideas down on when the front door slammed shut. The clock on the wall in the bedroom said Seth hadn't been gone more than an hour. She'd yet to change out of her PJs or eat breakfast. Though she did have a cup of coffee with him before he left for work. He must've forgotten something.

She didn't even get the chance to get out of bed before he was strolling in the room. One look and she knew something terrible happened.

"Is Cherry okay? What happened?"

He rushed to her side, sitting next to her, grabbing her hand. "She's fine. As far as I know, she's fine."

"As far as you know..." Pepper felt the anxious energy vibrating in his hand. "Spit it out. You're scaring me."

"Because I'm scared. I'm scared shitless for you." Seth cupped her cheek, tears gathering in his eyes. "Lillian escaped late last night. A guard helped her, and they don't have anything yet. No idea where she is."

Pepper let the words wash over her, processing them, but not. She swore she heard him correctly, but her mind wanted to change them to something else. Something less ominous.

"Pepper? Talk to me."

Seth kissed her, but she didn't kiss him back. It's as if the moment he said it, she froze. Her body was incapable of moving, of reacting, of preparing for the inevitable.

Her sister meant to kill her.

He let go of her hand, grasping both of her cheeks. "I expected shock, but not a complete shutdown. We got this. We can handle her. She won't hurt you again."

Her voice finally found release. "She did it so easily last time. So fluidly, without any mistakes. She nearly killed me. She swore she would if she got out. Not only did I thwart her plans, her boyfriend is now dead. I might've not been there, but she'll blame that on me too. She might even take it out on Deke and Charlotte."

The panic that hit Seth's eyes said he hadn't thought of that. None of them had. If Seth knew, that meant Logan did, and no doubt Bolt, Deke, and Danny. They left her out of the loop.

Why? Because they didn't trust her? She'd failed them once before, going off on her own, thinking she could solve everything by herself. Well, she'd learned from her mistakes. She'd learned a hard lesson from it.

"Why wasn't I invited to this meeting?"

Seth looked guilty as he dropped his hands. "Logan thought you'd take it better hearing it from me. It wasn't done with ill intent."

"So what's the plan?"

"Logan and Bolt are going to talk to Evan. Who knows if she reached out to him." Seth shrugged. "He'd be the weakest link in the town. Maybe she thinks he's still friendly with us. Or maybe she knows that we hate him and she'll use it to her advantage."

Pepper nodded. It was a good angle to check, but she

doubted Evan would be that dumb again. He'd learned his lesson as well. The very hard way she had.

"Deke and Danny are reaching out to their contacts in Florida to get more information. And I'm here with you." Seth hesitated for the first time since running into the room. "You do want me here, right? I didn't leave this morning knowing what Logan wanted to tell us. I would never keep that from you. I would've never left you alone."

"I know." She caressed his cheek, brushing her hand down his chest. "You also know you can't be by me twenty-four seven. I can handle it. I can handle her. Like you said."

"But I meant together."

"We will. But we can't be together all the time. I have a job. You have a job."

"Bolt offered his brother's cabin to us."

Her brow arched in a 'get real' look. She wasn't running.

Seth chuckled. "Yeah, I declined it. We're not running from her."

How did she get so lucky to meet a man who knew her so well without her speaking one word?

"I wouldn't be able to do this without you."

"You won't ever have to."

Then he leaned forward and kissed her again, and this time she responded. It didn't last long, but it was enough to calm some of her racing nerves.

"So, look, we did chat about Cherry a bit."

Pepper frowned. She knew Charlotte—and Deke because he'd support her before anyone else—still didn't fully trust Cherry. She could only imagine what was spoken.

"And?"

"And you don't think there's any possibility she knew Lillian had this plan? That she came here ahead of time.

Inserted herself into our circle. Get close and then make some sort of move."

"Do you really believe that, Seth? She's having Bolt's baby."

He didn't look away, but she could sense he wanted to, especially by the forlorn look on his normally happy face. "Do we really know if she's pregnant? Nobody saw the test, only her. It's her word only. Bolt didn't have her retake it to see it for himself."

"She wouldn't do that. She wouldn't lie like that."

"Well, as Deke put it, I'm playing devil's advocate. I had her back in the beginning of the argument, but now I'm not so sure. She inserted herself so easily into the group, into the town. Do you know who else has those kinds of skills?"

Yes, she did.

Lillian.

Born with the ability to sway anyone her way. To make men take notice. To take charge of the room with a simple smile. Lillian hadn't gotten as far as she did without knowing how to play the people closest to her.

"I let her in my life. I believed her. I wanted so badly to have a sisterly connection with her. I...I don't want to think she'd do something like that."

"I don't either, but we can't discredit it just yet. You have to be careful around her. I don't want you alone with her." Seth grabbed her hand, gripping hard. "Promise me, you won't be alone with her."

Pepper swallowed hard, hating to make that kind of promise.

"I love you, Pepper. I won't lose you again. Not like that. Not to another sister. Promise me."

She nodded. "I promise."

He wrapped his hand in her hair, pulling her closer,

kissing her forehead. "Thank you. I can't lose you again. Just thinking about last time—"

"Don't. Don't go there. It won't help. What about Bolt?"

Seth leaned away but didn't remove his hand from her hair. "He believes her. He loves her. He won't walk away quietly. He's not listening to anything anyone says that paints her in a bad light."

Heaven help her, but Pepper was grateful for that. Her own doubt was seeping in. It didn't help Seth made good points. It also didn't help her twin sister had tried to kill her. It wouldn't be that far of a stretch for a different sister to try as well. She was the oddball. Odd one out. She didn't matter, in the grand scheme of things.

Though the doubt might be creeping in, at least Cherry had one person on her side. She'd need it. These people who had become her family would be brutal. They'd stop at nothing to keep her safe. Including destroying her sister.

16

"I'D LIKE to stop and see Cherry."

Logan gripped the steering wheel and nodded. "After we speak to Evan."

"Just say it."

He knew Logan was dying to get something off his chest. The tension had been high when they got into the truck. Hell, it'd been off the charts the entire time in his office. He'd felt like the lone man out, all alone, the only one fighting for Cherry. Seth might've given him advice and made it seem like he was on his side, but deep down, he saw the truth in his eyes. Deke's words were penetrating the barrier. Slipping in and making them doubt her. Logan probably did too, despite saying the opposite.

"We don't know what's going on here. We should, as hard as it is, keep all options on the table."

Bolt clenched his fists, then unclenched, not wanting him to see how his words affected him. "Meaning Cherry could be behind this as well. Go ahead. Say it. Say her name. Stop talking around it."

"I admit, there's no record of her visiting Lillian, but a guard helped her escape."

Yeah, Bolt read between those lines as well.

"She could've had the guard erase the evidence Cherry visited her."

"It's plausible. Lillian is the most diabolical person I've ever come across. I wouldn't put anything past her. Bolt, I'm not saying any of this to hurt you. I want you to be on your guard."

He still hadn't looked at Logan. He couldn't. All he'd see was pity. Pity that he'd fallen under a spell and let a so-called evil woman play him. That's what he was insinuating. That Bolt fell right into her trap like the moron he was.

"Do you remember when Lillian switched places with Pepper?"

"Yes," Logan said with a short clip.

Of course, no one liked remembering it. They'd almost lost Pepper. Lillian almost got away with it all.

But she didn't.

Because of him.

"I'm the only one who insisted something was wrong. I'm the only one who didn't believe she was who she said she was. I'm the only one who got all of you to open your damn eyes. So excuse me if I don't want to listen to your bullshit now. You don't see what I see. You never have!"

The truck stopped at the perfect time. Bolt hopped out before Logan could respond. He didn't give a damn what he had to say. There was nothing that would change his mind.

He trusted Cherry. She might've made a few mistakes along the way with him, but he trusted her. He loved her. That wasn't a lie. What they had between them wasn't a lie.

"Bolt!"

He kept walking toward the garage. Logan could catch up with him.

Evan glared at him, wiping his hands on a rag when he walked inside.

"To what do I owe this pleasure? The deputy *and* the sheriff. Lucky me," Evan drawled.

"What happened to you, Evan? This isn't the guy I knew growing up," Logan said with regret in his tone.

Evan shrugged. "You all decided I was the bad guy. This is what you get."

"You tried to kill us. What do you expect?" Logan retorted.

"For a very good reason. And it wasn't something I wanted to do. I was scared for Stacy. I was scared for all of you. I wish I could change how I responded, but I can't."

Bolt tried to picture what he'd do in that situation. He pictured Cherry being held at gunpoint, her life on the line, and him having to make the hardest decision of his life. Save the woman he loved, or kill the people who were like family?

He shut off his brain, the decision impossible to make.

For the first time, he understood part of Evan's dilemma. How could someone make that decision? Either way, he'd been doomed.

"Lillian escaped prison." Bolt spoke first since the room had gone silent.

Evan jerked but didn't say anything for a moment. "And what, you think I had something to do with it?"

Bolt shook his head. "I don't. But the Cheetahs got to you last time. We're just seeing if they reached out again."

Evan laughed. "Reached out? Like they called me to chat." His lips turned down into an evil frown. "They called me, Stacy screaming in the background as they hit her. They didn't *reach out* to me."

"Lillian threatened to kill Pepper last time they spoke. We have reason to believe she'll come here. Has anybody in the Cheetah organization contacted you? For any reason? Threatened Stacy again?" Logan asked.

"No." Evan folded his arms. "I haven't spoken to Stacy in months. I can assure you I wouldn't try to kill anyone again for her. She wants nothing to do with me. Nobody does. I'm the town pariah."

"We had to ask."

Bolt agreed with Logan, but it still felt like a shitty thing to do. He saw that now.

Evan met his gaze. "I hear congratulations are in order. Are you sure you can trust, Cherry? She popped up at such a perfect time. Enough time to insert herself into your little group, gain your trust. Hell, she's having your baby. She couldn't possibly be involved with Lillian. Could she?"

Well, when it was said like that, it sounded damning. Like a real possibility.

But Bolt's mind filtered to every moment with her. The way she smiled at something he said. The way she moaned when he hit the spot she especially loved. The way she made a different origami napkin for his lunch bag every day for work.

She wasn't involved. No matter what anyone said, he'd never believe it.

He couldn't.

Because that meant he'd not only been a huge fool, he'd been what everyone always thought of him. The world's biggest idiot with a badge.

"If they happen to contact you, will you tell us?" Logan

asked with hope, even though they both knew Evan never would. Not after all the bad blood between them.

"Yeah, sure. I'll get right on that. Now get out."

They left, knowing they wouldn't get anything else out of him.

"Do you think he's lying?"

Bolt shrugged. "It doesn't matter what I think. Nobody seems to care what I think."

"Bolt, that's not fair. That's not what we think."

"Could have fooled me." He stared out the window, hoping Logan would get the hint he was done talking. "Drop me off at the station. I'll see Cherry by myself."

Logan continued to engage him in conversation, but Bolt wouldn't bite. There was nothing left to say. He exited without a good-bye and walked to the boutique, enjoying the light cool breeze. It did nothing to cool his anger, but it felt nice.

He walked into the store, pasting on a smile, not wanting to give away anything was wrong to Mrs. Dunburry. It'd be all around town before noon if he did.

"Hey," Cherry started with a smile, but it died quickly. "What's wrong?"

The store looked empty, even of Mrs. Dunburry, but he still leaned closer and whispered, "Can you take a walk for a few minutes?"

She nodded and stood up from the stool behind the counter. "Mrs. Dunburry is in the back. I'll be right back."

She grabbed her sweater before walking outside with him. He didn't think it was that cold, but she wasn't used to fall weather like the ones in Minnesota. Florida was still hot at this time of year.

They walked until they got to the park. He sat on the

bench far away from the playground where a few moms and their kids were playing.

"Bolt, what's wrong? You're scaring me."

He threaded his fingers through hers and smiled. "You look beautiful today."

Her hair was in a ponytail; the wind had blown a few stray strands out. Or maybe she missed them when putting it together because when they left the house, her hair had been down. Either way, up or down, she was beautiful. She wore a yellow sundress that fit her curves and showcased her lovely legs that he wanted to wrap around his waist this very minute. It was too bad they were in a public place and he had terrible news to give her.

"Thank you, but that's not why you asked me to take a walk."

"No, it's not. But I had to tell you." He smiled, though he didn't feel the force of it. He knew it was fake as much as she did. "Lillian, your other half-sister, escaped prison last night."

Her eyes bulged and trembles immediately coated her body. He knew she could put on an act, but nobody could fake shock like that.

The shivers that continued to wrack her body concerned him.

He took one hand and rubbed it up and down her arm. "Hey, it's okay. You're okay. She probably doesn't even know about you. You're safe."

"But Pepper's not. Did you even read the article? It was horrible. The things she tried to do." Her eyes rounded in shock again. "I'm an idiot. Of course, you know. You were here. You talked to her. Pepper's not safe."

"Pepper's fine. She's strong and she's smart. We're prepared."

"Of course you are. Yes, I know." She nodded and kept on nodding until he was forced to cup her chin to stop the movement.

He'd never seen her so agitated before. He didn't like it.

"You don't need to be afraid. It can't be good for the baby." He dropped his hand to her belly. "You should see Dr. Matthews and get looked at."

"You threw a huge curveball at me, but I can calm myself down. I don't need to see him. I won't overstress myself."

Bolt frowned. "Yes, you do. You're going to have a baby, Cherry. Our baby. Who do you think is going to deliver it? You need to start taking prenatal vitamins, watching what you eat. No seafood. Limit your caffeine intake, like coffee isn't good."

The gorgeous smile that rounded her lips made some of his worry disappear. "Have you been googling stuff?"

"Maybe." He matched her grin. "You know I'm going to get on your nerves baby-wise. I already worry about you. Now I have two people to worry about."

"Okay, I'll make an appointment with the doctor, as long as you come with me when it's time."

He was elated she asked.

"I'm there. Every appointment. I'm in this one hundred percent."

It was too bad his friends weren't as well. Doubting she was even pregnant.

"You're frowning again," she said, caressing his cheek.

"I'm worried about you, about Pepper."

And how he'd face his friends ever again. He couldn't look any of them in the eye without wanting the anger to rush to the surface. Anyone else they would've had faith in them and their gut instincts. But when it came to him, he was nothing but a screwup and had no idea what he was talking about.

"Can we check on Pepper later? Do you think she'd mind if we did?"

He had no clue what Pepper's thoughts were on it.

"I'd bet she'd like that."

But he'd like to think at least one person was on his side. On Cherry's side.

If her own sister didn't trust her anymore, they were in serious trouble.

———

"SHE DOESN'T WANT me here. I could hear it in her voice when I talked to her on the phone."

Bolt held her hand as they walked up to the front door of Seth's house. His comfort helped her, but not enough to hide the nerves swimming in her veins. She could feel the trembles hitting each limb, visible to everyone. Pepper would see it the moment she opened the door.

"She would've never said come over if she didn't want you here. Pepper isn't one to beat around the bush."

Very true. But Pepper had been known to lie, proof of when she first arrived in town, which meant it wasn't far off to think she'd lie to Cherry.

They were alike in so many ways. Cherry lied too, for good reasons. Just like Pepper had. Funny how that was, being sisters, not growing up together, yet having some of the same traits. She could only hope the sisterly connection they had started to create would get them through this ordeal together.

The day had gone downhill the moment Bolt broke the news about Lillian. Mrs. Dunburry had heard the news by the time she returned to the shop and knew exactly why Bolt wanted to take a walk. She had tried to interrogate her like she had more information than she had heard, but Cherry couldn't give her anything. The day had been stilted after that, as if Mrs. Dunburry thought she was lying.

She kept true to her word and called the doctor to make an appointment. Kat answered the phone. While Kat sounded pleasant enough, she heard the tinge of doubt in her voice. That conversation ended on a sour note as well. Charlotte was cold—colder than normal—when she waited in the lobby for Bolt's shift to end.

That last interaction told her she needed her own vehicle. No more relying on Bolt or someone else to get her around. She'd felt trapped, and she never wanted to feel that way again.

Bolt knocked on the door, and it opened a few seconds later. Pepper looked like nothing was pressing on her mind, as if it were another day going by with nothing bad happening.

"Come on in. You two didn't have to come over. I'm okay." Pepper shut the door after they stepped inside, then ushered them toward the dining room. "Seth popped a pizza in the oven. I figured you'd both be hungry."

"Thanks. We appreciate it," Bolt answered, tugging Cherry along.

She didn't know why she was so apprehensive about all of this. Or why she thought Pepper didn't want her here. Not that Pepper was an affectionate person—they had yet to hug —but she expected more than a 'hi, here's some food.' Her evil twin was free and wanted to kill her. Cherry thought Pepper would be a little more agitated about that. Maybe wanting to tell her how she felt. Cry on her shoulder. Something other than this indifference.

Just showed she didn't know Pepper as well as she thought.

Well, no, she knew Pepper didn't express much emotion, keeping it all inside like a coiled rope waiting to snap.

She only figured Pepper would react that way because that's how she'd react.

They all took a seat, Seth hollering from the kitchen he'd be right out with the pizza.

"You sure you're okay?" Cherry asked.

Pepper nodded and smiled. "I refuse to let Lillian ruin my day. I will not cower from her. I never have, and I'm not going to start now. Honestly, Cherry, I wouldn't worry too much about it. They'll find her. If she shows up here, we'll be ready. She won't do what she did last time."

Knocking Pepper out, taking her identity, and trying to kill Pepper.

Cherry hoped that didn't happen again.

Seth brought out the pizza, setting it in the middle of the table. "I threw another one in the oven in case this isn't enough." Then he took a seat by Pepper.

The plates and napkins were already on the table, so everyone dug in. Silence filled the room, besides the munching of the food as they ate the pizza.

Seth broke the quiet first.

"Has Lillian ever contacted you, Cherry?"

She felt Bolt tense next to her and understood why. No doubt they were all wondering if she had been a part of Lillian's escape. Perhaps that's why she showed up in town. Seth threw out the question like it wasn't a big deal, but she heard the tension in his voice. The repressed anger just wanting to let loose. Did Pepper feel the same? Did she think Cherry was in cahoots with Lillian too?

"I've never met her."

Seth dropped his napkin to his plate. "But that's not what I asked."

"Knock it off, Seth," Bolt snapped.

"No, it's okay," Cherry said, putting a hand on his arm. "I'm not offended. It was bound to happen. I'm still the unknown around here." She smiled as if it didn't hurt her, when really, she was gutted. Viscerally gutted deep inside that they still didn't believe in her.

"I've never met, talked to, or ever received any kind of correspondence from Lillian. Her escaping is as much of a surprise to me as it is to all of you."

Her eyes slowly met Pepper's. There was still no emotion swimming in her gaze. Nothing but indifference as if it were another Tuesday. How did she do that? How did she keep her emotions intact? So tightly veiled so no one could see? Cherry was jealous of that. She was so easy to read.

"I would never hurt you, Pepper. If Lillian would reach out to me, I'd tell you."

Pepper nodded. "I know you would."

But her eyes didn't portray she meant that. Cherry didn't believe a word.

"I didn't mean to upset you by coming over here."

"You didn't," Pepper reassured her. "I'm glad you did. Seth is very overprotective of me. Please don't take offense."

"I already said it's okay."

They both knew she had lied, yet Pepper had the good grace not to point it out.

"We're taking all the precautions we can. Don't worry about me." Pepper looked at Bolt, although her next words were for Cherry. "You should be cautious too."

At least, she thought they were meant for her. But it almost sounded like Pepper was warning Bolt to watch his back. Like she'd ever hurt him. Never.

Pepper returned her gaze to her. "I don't know if she knows about you, but if she does, I don't know what she'll do with that information. Be careful."

"I always am." Cherry stood up. "We should go. I'm not sure the baby is agreeing with the pizza. I'm glad you're okay."

"You don't have to go." Pepper finally looked worried as she stood as well. "I hope it's not because of us."

"No. Of course not. I'm starting to feel a little queasy."

They said their good-byes and left. Bolt tried to grab her hand while he drove the truck home, but she curled her hands together in her lap, not wanting any contact at the moment. He sighed but didn't press the issue. She was grateful he understood she didn't want to talk about what happened at the house.

She immediately went to the bathroom when they got home and promptly threw up. She liked to say it was because of the baby, but she feared it had more to do with the fact her sister thought she was the bad person. Working with the evil twin to hurt her. That burned her deep inside. She couldn't stop the retching, even when nothing but bile came out.

"Cherry, let me in." Bolt rattled the door, but it didn't budge because she had locked it.

"I'm okay. I don't look pretty right now. I'll be out in a little bit."

"You're always beautiful to me. I want to be by your side helping you through this. I caused part of this problem. That baby is inside of you because of me. I don't want you doing any of this alone."

Such a thoughtful, kind man. To think he loved such a broken woman who had no family, no money, no future.

"It's okay, really. I need to be alone right now."

He rattled the doorknob one more time, then gave up.

She rested her head on the toilet seat and let the tears flow. She had nothing left in her stomach to empty, so tears would have to take its place. They were silent, streaming down her face. The last thing she needed was Bolt breaking down the door to get in, hearing her crying.

She didn't know how much time passed before Bolt was knocking on the door.

"You're starting to worry me. Please open the door."

Her legs felt wobbly as she stood up. The mirror didn't show a pretty picture. Her eyes were red, her nose as well. The streaks down her cheeks were evidence enough of what she had done, if her eyes hadn't given it away.

"I'm going to take a shower. I'll be right out."

The water did nothing to soothe her nerves or make her feel better. The water had been hot, so it at least helped to erase the evidence because not only was her face red but so were other parts of her body. She made sure to let the steaming water hit her in every place so he'd never know what she had done.

She jumped when she opened the door, nearly dropping the towel wrapped around her. Bolt stood right outside the door, his hair on end as if he'd been running his hand through it nonstop.

"Don't ever lock me out again. Please," he begged. "Never again."

He raised his hand, brushing her cheek. "You were crying. I'm so sorry for what Seth said. I need you to know I'm on your side. You're not alone in this. So when you lock me out, that kills me inside. If you need to puke, I'll hold your hair. If you need to cry, you can use my shoulder. But what I can't do is stand outside a door and feel completely useless. I've felt that enough in my life."

"I'm sorry. I won't do it again."

And she was. Her intention hadn't been to keep him away. She had needed a moment to herself.

The towel fell to the floor. His eyes grazed up and down her body.

"Love me, Bolt. I need you to love me."

More than ever before.

He didn't hesitate to swing her into his arms and show her how much he did. He was right. She'd never lock him out again.

17

SHE ROLLED AWAY FROM BOLT, wincing at the pain below. Damn, but she had to pee. She should've never had four glasses of water before going to bed, but after throwing up the entire contents of the day, she needed something inside her. The thought of food had made her want to take residence around the toilet again. So water it had been.

The blankets barely moved as she slid out of bed. She didn't want to wake Bolt and have him hovering over her again. The night had ended on a good note. He had shown her with his hands and lips how much he loved her. Even falling asleep with his arm clutching her stomach. He'd hardly given her a moment to herself, as if afraid she'd lock him out one more time. She said she wouldn't, and she'd keep her word. She had promised never to lie again, and she knew she'd lose him if she did.

Instinctively she grabbed her phone before walking out of the room. The pee came out like a rushing waterfall, lasting forever. Of course, after she washed her hands, thirst hit her. She wanted more water.

The darkness in the kitchen sent her nerves jangling,

but she didn't turn on the light. The soft yellow glow from the refrigerator helped soothe her anxiety as she poured a glass of water. It would wake her up again in another hour or two, but she downed two glasses, feeling much better.

The glass made a soft clink when she set it in the sink. Her eyes, despite telling herself to resist, gazed out the window. The trees swayed back and forth, the wind heavy. She didn't see rain in the forecast, but it had the same feeling as the one night so long ago. When she'd been frightened by the shadow at her window.

The moon couldn't get through all the trees, only slices of light here and there. It gave the woods an ominous feeling. One that sent chills up her spine.

She shivered at the sight.

She should go back to bed.

Her phone pinged.

The button on the side when she pressed it lit up the screen. Somehow, she held in the scream that wanted to escape.

I see you.

Her eyes darted to the outside again. Flashing back and forth, searching every part of the yard and the woods she could see.

She jumped, squeezing her phone harder when she saw the figure step out from behind a tree. Just behind the camera that would've set off the sensors. This person, whoever it was, knew about the cameras.

Her phone pinged again.

Her hand shook as she turned it over to view the message.

You have a choice to make.

What? What choice? What did this madman want from her? She nearly screamed the question aloud, then clamped her lips shut. She didn't want to wake Bolt.

Or maybe she should.

No. Absolutely not. If she woke him up, he'd want to go outside and go after the person, and she couldn't bear to lose him. He was her entire world. The only person to care about her in a world filled with over a billion people, and she couldn't lose that.

She turned around from the window and went back to bed, making sure to slide in quietly so she didn't wake Bolt. He'd know something was wrong, even with the lights out. She turned her phone on silent and set it facedown on the nightstand. If the person wanted to send more messages, fine. Go ahead. It didn't mean she had to give them the time of day. If they wanted to approach the house, they would. As soon as they did, the cameras would alert the movement, and then Bolt would have no choice but to make a move. She hoped it didn't come down to that.

The remainder of the night was restless. Tossing and turning, though unobtrusively so as not to wake Bolt. It didn't matter. He must've sensed her agitation and curled his arm around her stomach once more. Though she couldn't sleep, his touch comforted her. It helped to keep the fear at bay. For the moment.

When it was time to get up, he kissed her, brushing her hair off her cheek.

"Bad night, uh? You didn't get sick did you?"

"No. I couldn't sleep. You jump in the shower, and I'll start breakfast."

He looked as if he wanted to argue, but he didn't.

She started to prepare bacon and eggs and halfway through it, she had to rush to the bathroom. Bolt was shaving, dropping the device as soon as she cupped the toilet and tried to empty her stomach. Nothing came out but the water from her late-night sipping. Bolt didn't say anything, but he held her hair, rubbing her back.

He waited patiently while she did her business and finally stood up, her legs unsteady.

"You should see Dr. Matthews today. Maybe he has something to settle your stomach."

"No, it's okay. It's all a part of being pregnant. The smell of the bacon didn't sit well with me. Now I know."

He frowned. "If it gets worse, you're going to have to call him. You have to see him regardless."

She smoothed a hand across his roughened cheek he hadn't yet shaved. "I made an appointment for next week. I told you I would, and I did."

A brilliant smile lit up his face. "That's good to hear. It's going to be a long week. You have to tell him how sick you've been getting. And no more bacon. I'll go throw it out."

"Or you eat it quickly while I hang out in the bedroom where I can't smell it."

He chuckled. "Or I can do that."

"I'm going to tell Mrs. Dunburry that I'm staying home today. I don't want to puke all day long with her in hearing distance."

Not to mention she didn't want to be bothered with questions about Lillian when she had no answers whatsoever.

"Okay." The worry was back on his face. "I'll check on you throughout the day."

She appreciated that. While she didn't want to endure

Mrs. Dunburry's nosiness, she also wasn't thrilled to be home alone.

Bolt continued to get ready for work, while she went back to the bedroom. The text messages on her phone reminded her of what happened in the middle of the night. Only the two came through. So whoever sent them gave up when she walked away. Or maybe that's all they had to say—for now.

She pasted a smile on her face when Bolt walked into the room. He saw through it right away.

"What's wrong?"

She gripped the phone in her hands so hard, she felt like she could crush it in two. Keeping secrets would put a divide between them. She needed him to continue to believe in her, to be on her side. She couldn't fight this unknown entity alone.

But he'd be mad. There was no doubt about it.

Her stomach gurgled as she leaned over to his side of the bed, pushing her phone toward him.

"I got these messages last night. I don't know what they mean."

He snatched her phone, his brows drawing low as he read them.

"This was at two in the morning. I felt you tossing and turning after that. You read them last night, didn't you?"

She nodded. "I got up to get a glass of water. The first message had me looking outside the window. I saw someone standing out there."

"Damn it, Cherry! You should've woken me up."

Mad didn't begin to describe the anger etched across his face. His outburst had her jumping, wishing she'd kept it to herself. She didn't want Bolt mad at her.

"Then you would've went out there, and I didn't want you to get hurt."

"I can handle it. I would've handled it. No matter how many times I tell you, you still don't trust me."

"I do," she cried, aching to reach out and beg on her hands and knees. But that would be embarrassing and she'd already done that enough with him. "I don't want to see you get hurt."

"I wouldn't. I—" He stopped as if remembering the time he got shot.

That's right. He couldn't say he wouldn't get hurt because it had happened before. Someone got the jump on him and almost killed him. She was so glad she didn't know him back then. It would've been hard to see him like that.

"What does this second message mean?"

She shrugged. "I have no idea. I have no clue."

He stared at her for the longest time, as if he didn't believe her. As if she knew what the person was talking about. As if she were lying once again.

His frown deepened as he stared at her phone. "It came from an unknown number. Probably untraceable. I'll see what I can find out."

"Okay."

He walked around the bed and set her phone next to her, then sat down. "Don't tell anyone about this."

This time she frowned. "Why not?"

"Because I can take care of it."

More like, he didn't believe her, and he knew everyone else wouldn't believe her either.

BOLT DIDN'T WAVE in greeting at Charlotte when he walked into the station. Why should he? It's not as if she cared about him anyway. Thinking him pathetic and not worthy of the badge. Not liking his girlfriend—because that's what they were, weren't they? She was having his baby. She was living with him.

Yes, his girlfriend.

His girlfriend who had a choice to make.

What the hell did that mean?

Why did he sense Cherry knew what it meant? Because if she didn't, why hadn't she woken him up the minute she received it? Why wait until the morning to tell him? Well, he should be grateful she even told him. He couldn't be mad about that.

Hell, he didn't even want to be mad she held it back from him. But the thought someone had been outside, watching her, watching the house, scared the shit out of him. The person was so close yet kept their distance. Why?

Why didn't she have faith in him that he could handle it?

He knew he had hurt her when he told her to keep it to herself, but he had said it to protect her. Everyone already doubted her. This would only add to the doubt.

He paused right outside Logan's office.

Last time he went off on his own looking for evidence, looking for the one thing to break a hole in Aubrey's case, he got shot. He proved to everyone how much he couldn't work as a team. Though his mind told him to keep this to himself, his gut screamed he should trust Logan.

He knocked on the doorframe.

"Can I have a word?"

Logan ushered him in, waving at the seat in front of his desk. "I'm glad you stopped by. I wanted to apologize. I never want you to think I don't have your back. I do. Cherry means a lot to you, and I understand. If you believe in her, then so do I."

A weight lifted off his shoulders hearing that. If Logan was one thing in this world, he was an honest man. He didn't say things he didn't mean.

"I'm glad you said that. Because Cherry got two text messages last night and one doesn't sound...good."

Logan leaned forward, resting his elbows on the desk while clasping his hands in the air. "What did they say?"

"Well, the first one said, 'I see you.' Someone was out there, in the woods. She didn't wake me up."

Logan nodded but didn't respond. Bolt was grateful. Nothing he said would've soothed his nerves about that.

"The second one said, 'You have a choice to make.'"

Logan's brows dipped low. "What choice? What does that mean?"

"She doesn't know. She has no idea what this person is talking about. They didn't send anything else."

"What's the number? We'll trace it."

Bolt shook his head. "Unknown. We got nothing."

"Could it be Dean? Making a choice about coming back home?" Logan sounded hopeful, like it'd be something simple as that.

Bolt knew better.

"Could be. Highly doubt it."

Logan slumped back into his chair, sighing. "The whole thing is odd. This person keeps to the background for two months, watching her, giving her the creeps. Now, all of sudden, they're reaching out. Sending a cryptic message."

"I don't know what to say." Bolt tensed. "To be honest, I didn't even want to tell you."

"I'm glad you did."

"Could you keep it between us for now?"

Logan didn't look happy about that.

"You might not be saying it and just thinking it, but everyone else will say it out loud. They'll say she knows what it means. They'll say she's hiding something and lying. I'm this close" –Bolt held his thumb and pointer finger close together— "to losing my shit on all of them."

"I hear what you're saying Bolt, but we work better as a team. We always have."

"Sorry to say it, but this team is falling apart. I don't feel a part of it anymore."

"Bolt..."

It was the truth. He felt so disconnected from everyone, he was damn close to turning in his badge, convincing Cherry to leave, and make a new home far, far away from everyone.

For the first time, that sounded like the most solid plan.

He stood up and unclipped his gun from its holster.

Logan tensed. "What are you doing?"

"What I should've done months ago."

A KNOCK SOUNDED on the bathroom door, making Pepper jump.

"Be right out."

Seth was never good at giving her space, knowing the moment she said it she didn't want it. He opened the door.

There was no hiding the evidence now. Not that she had intended to do so.

"Shit. What happened?" Seth grabbed her hand, holding it gently, as he stared at the Band-Aid that looked like it needed to be changed already. The blood was seeping through.

"I cut myself."

He eyed her critically. "I can see that. How did it happen?" He tore the Band-Aid off, wincing. "Shit, Pepper, it looks like it needs stitches."

It looked deep. The edges were about a quarter inch apart and the blood hadn't stopped flowing, despite her holding toilet paper to it for a good long while. She grabbed more, pressing it to her hand since he had taken the Band-Aid off.

"It's fine. It'll die down."

"How did you cut yourself?"

No use hiding it.

She picked up the towel from the toilet seat and grabbed the kitchen knife hiding below it, setting it on the counter next to them.

"I did it on purpose."

Seth's eyes rounded in shock. "Why in the hell would you do something so stupid?"

She set the wad of toilet paper down and pulled up her sleeve, showing the cut on her upper left arm. Then she pulled up her pant leg, showing the cut on her right ankle. One was also on her left thigh, a tiny one on her stomach, and an awkward cut on her back. That one had been hard to reach.

Seth shook his head, tears welling in his eyes. He grabbed the wad of toilet paper, pressing it hard to her hand.

"Why?" he whispered. "Why would you do this to yourself?"

Seeing the pain he was in, the tears on the edge of escape, she felt her own build. "I won't let her get away with it again. I won't let her pretend to be me."

Her gaze sought the mirror; his eyes followed her. She

traced the outline of her cheek. "I even thought about cutting here."

"Don't. Don't you dare do it. No more cuts. I would never fall for that again. I know you." He turned her around, cupping her cheek. "I know you, Pepper. She would never fool me again."

A weak smile appeared. "Now it'll be even easier for you."

"Come on." Seth pulled her out of the bathroom and toward the front door.

"Where are we going?"

"That cut on your hand is deep. I'm telling you, you need stitches." He paused by the door, caressing her cheek slowly as if envisioning a cut there as well. "I don't want you to have any scars from this. A reminder of your sister hurting you like this."

"I did this. Not her."

"Only because you fear her. That's her fault."

Seth placed her hand over the toilet paper and pressed hard. "Hold that. Hard."

He grabbed the keys, waited for her to exit, then set the alarm and locked the door.

She knew it had been a dumb thing to do, but at the time, when the knife was slicing her skin, it had felt like the right thing to do. Her sister couldn't hurt her anymore. Not if she didn't allow it. These wounds would heal and disappear. She didn't make them that deep. Well, she failed on her hand. The rest were superficial. They'd disappear and her sister would never be able to hurt her again. Hurt the ones she loved again. Because she knew how much it gutted them that they had fallen for her act. Now, she couldn't repeat the same thing over. She hadn't allowed it.

Seth pulled into an empty spot in front of the doctor's office.

Before he could exit, she stopped him.

"I'm sorry. I know you don't understand, but it's something I had to do."

He reached across the console and cupped her neck, kissing her. "No, I get it. I do. I just don't like seeing you like this. In pain."

"It doesn't hurt."

He cocked a brow in disbelief.

She chuckled, even though it wasn't funny. She couldn't help it. "Okay, it hurts. But it's a bit of pain that will go away. I feel better already. I feel more confident in the situation. I have the upper hand this time. Not her. So that's why it doesn't hurt."

"No more, okay?"

She nodded, then kissed him. "No more."

He opened the door to the clinic, and Pepper winced when Kat rushed around the counter.

"What happened to your hand?" Kat lifted the wad of toilet paper and grimaced. "That's deep."

"It's a long story." Pepper didn't want to defend herself again.

"Well, I have time while I stitch you up." Kat did not look happy at the prospect.

"Maybe I'll tell you after you're done." Pepper wasn't sure it was wise to tell Kat she had done this herself.

"Not a chance."

No one argued with Kat.

18

"PUT YOUR GUN BACK. NOW, BOLT."

Bolt didn't reach for the weapon he had laid on Logan's desk. He grabbed his badge next.

"Stop it, Bolt!" Logan shoved out of his chair. "You're not quitting. I won't have it."

"You have no say." Bolt laid his badge next to his weapon. "I quit."

He turned around, startled to see Charlotte standing in the doorway with her arms crossed.

"You want to leave, you'll have to get through me first."

He wouldn't knock her over, and Charlotte knew that. Why was she pretending like she cared whether he stayed or not?

Logan rounded his desk, nodding in approval at Charlotte. "You're not quitting. We can talk about this."

"About what? The fact none of you have faith in Cherry. That none of you even believe she's pregnant. Like you need to see the damn stick she peed on or something. I don't need that kind of proof. The fact she's been throwing up her guts all night and this morning is proof enough for me. Hell, her simply telling me she was pregnant was enough for me to believe her."

"We're not trying to make her the bad person." Charlotte said it quietly, as if she wasn't sure she should even speak.

"You haven't liked her from the beginning. You turned your distrust and put it into Deke. He's normally a level-headed guy. Makes decisions himself. You're doing exactly what you set out to do, Charlotte. What you always do."

She took a few steps inside the office, holding up a hand for Logan to let her go first. "I'm sorry I doubted you about Aubrey. I don't know how many times I can say I'm sorry. My distrust of her has nothing to do with you. Lillian—"

"She's never met her! She's not the villain here. She's scared and afraid and just wants whoever is messing with her to stop."

Charlotte swallowed. "What if you're wrong, Bolt?"

"I might've gotten shot in those woods, but I wasn't wrong to go out there. Wayne was out there. I was right to go look."

For the first time, those words really penetrated his senses. He hadn't been wrong. He'd been ambushed. He'd been surprised and paid the price for it, but he hadn't been wrong.

"I wasn't wrong about Lillian trying to pretend to be Pepper. I was the only one who noticed the difference. The only one! So don't ask me if I'm wrong. What if you're wrong, Charlotte? Did you ever think about that? Or is it always all about how wrong stupid old Bolt is?"

"I don't think you're stupid."

"You also don't have faith in me. If you did, you'd trust I know what I'm doing. You'd trust that Cherry is good because I said she is."

"And I do trust you," Logan said as he shoved his gun and badge into his stomach.

Bolt was forced to grab them when Logan let go.

A throat cleared behind Charlotte, prompting them all to look in that direction. Danny stood there with a crooked grin.

"What am I missing here? Looks intense."

"Bolt's trying to quit." Charlotte threw her hand in his direction for Danny to take a look.

Like, look at the idiot.

Whatever. He didn't need this bullshit.

Danny frowned. "Why?"

No way. He wasn't going through it all again. "Because I can."

Then he turned around and laid his gun and badge back on the desk.

He met Logan's gaze. "Try and stop me again. See how I react."

Logan chose not to say a word. He brushed past him, glared at Charlotte, who looked actually stricken with guilt for the first time. Danny stood in his way.

"Let me by, Danny."

"I will. For now. But you're family, Bolt. I can see you're hurting right now and want your space. I can understand that. But it won't keep me away." Danny leaned closer. "It won't keep any of us away."

Again, whatever. They could talk his ear off, but he was done listening to them. He was going home to get Cherry and they were ditching this town for good.

OKAY, maybe Bolt was right and she needed to see the doctor sooner. Her stomach hurt so badly from all the puking going on. Even her throat burned from everything coming up the wrong way.

She washed her face, brushed her teeth, using as little of the toothpaste as she could. Even the slight minty favor played havoc on her senses. She could feel the bile wanting to make another appearance. Damn it, she'd been sitting by the toilet for the entire time Bolt had been gone.

Water sounded nice, but she was afraid to drink any. Even that didn't want to stay down. But if she didn't keep her fluids up, she'd get dehydrated. Even she knew that.

She poured herself a glass of water, sipping it slowly.

A knock on the kitchen door had her jumping and her grip on the glass loosening, but thankfully not enough where it fell out of her hand. No need to let whoever it was know they'd frightened her.

Her heart pounded as she turned around toward the door. She screamed at the man standing on the other side with a cocky grin on his face. He had a heavy beard and a black knit hat that had her insides twisting with unease. A ski mask? Though that was silly. If it was, he'd have it pulled down over his face, and it wasn't covering his face. It didn't feel cold enough outside to be wearing a hat.

Why was she worrying about the dumb hat? How did he get past the cameras without the alarm sounding? She glanced at her phone sitting on the counter.

"Tsk, tsk, Cherry. It's too late for that. Open the door, darling. Would ya? I don't feel like breaking the glass," he goaded, tapping on the door again.

She wished the door didn't have a glass panel so she wouldn't be able to see him. The dead look in his eyes said if she even touched that door, he'd hurt her.

"Come on. Let us in. We only want to chat."

We? She didn't see anyone else. Stepping closer would give her a better angle, but she didn't want to get too close to the door.

She jumped, the glass slipping from her fingers this time when Pepper stepped into the frame.

No!

What was going on?

Pepper laughed, her eyes sparkling like the devil was playing a merry tune.

Oh, God.

Not Pepper.

Lillian.

"Gosh, it's my sister." Lillian slapped the guy's shoulder. "Would you look at that? That's my sister. Well, half-sister, but hey, a sister is a sister, am I right?"

Lillian's fingers tapped on the windowpane. "Open the door, sister. I want a hug."

No way in hell.

"You should go. Bolt's on his way."

Oh, she hoped so. Or she was so screwed.

Another maniacal laugh echoed through the door. "No, he's not, silly. Your phone didn't ping, did it?" She tsked like the guy had, shaking her head with laughter. "We disabled the cameras. No one's coming because no one knows we're here. You can't keep me out. No one can. Hell, they can't even keep me in!"

She jumped with joy, giggling like the crazy woman she was.

"Now let us in. We have much to talk about."

"No. I won't. I have nothing to say to you."

"Oh, dear." Lillian looked at the guy with a mock frown. "I guess we're going to have to do this the hard way."

The guy threw her a wicked grin before shoving his hand through the window, shattering it.

Cherry didn't need any more warning than that. She took off for the front door and threw it open, running out of the house without any shoes. She didn't even have on decent clothes. A tiny tank top she'd slept in and the only pair of PJ shorts she brought with her. Her ass cheeks spilled out, and she wore them for Bolt knowing how much he liked seeing them on her. Not because they kept her warm or anything.

The brisk air brushed across her skin as she raced down the driveway, the pebbles jabbing the soles of her feet. It hurt to run but she had no choice but to run for her life.

The sound of footsteps behind her had her picking up the pace.

She couldn't stay on the gravel driveway. It hurt too much. Switching directions, she raced into the woods, slapping branches away from her face as she ran. Twigs and leaves crunched beneath and still caused her pain, but not as badly as the gravel had. If she stayed straight ahead, she'd hit the main road. Someone had to be driving. She'd flag them down and jump in, getting away from the evil sister who wanted to kill her as much as Pepper.

The crunching sounds behind her said he was still in hot pursuit. She didn't turn to look. It wouldn't help to look, and it would ruin her focus. *One foot in front of the other. Keep going. Pick up the pace.*

Those things screamed in her head as she ran.

The road appeared in the distance. Safety was only fifty feet away or so. She'd make it. And luck was on her side. Bolt's truck was coming this way.

Why was he coming home so soon?

It didn't matter.

He sensed something was wrong and he came to her rescue. She knew he would.

She pushed herself harder. He was about to pass her and turn into the driveway before she would reach the road. That wouldn't help her. Maybe he had the windows open. Probably not, but it couldn't hurt to scream for help.

"Bo—oomph!"

She went down hard. The man shoved her into the ground, clamping a hand over her mouth. No matter how much she wiggled, it didn't move him. He was like a mountain sitting on her back, his knee digging in.

"Tsk, tsk, Cherry. That was very naughty. I wasn't in the mood to run. You're going to pay for that later."

She screamed through his hand, though the sound didn't carry. Bolt wouldn't hear that.

"Enough of this."

Pain exploded in her head, then nothing but blackness.

SHIT. He was running late. Danny had called him fifteen minutes ago, saying he was heading to the station, and Deke had said he'd be out the door in two. What a lie.

He'd been scrolling through his phone, looking at the reports the Florida field office had sent over of all the information on Lillian's escape. Not much to be had. The guard had let her out of her cell at one in the morning during his rounds and let her out the back door. Or what they called the service entrance for deliveries. Nobody had noticed either were gone for thirty minutes, when the alarms were finally sounded. That had given them plenty of time to get far enough away from any roadblocks.

Lillian could be anywhere right about now. On her way

here. On her way out of the country. Though Deke doubted she'd run. She would want to finish what she started. Lillian wasn't a woman who walked away from a challenge. They'd won, and she despised that.

He poured out his coffee into the sink, then set the mug down, sighing. Time to go. No more wasting time. He'd like to say he was taking a second—third—okay, like fiftieth look at the case, but in reality, he didn't want to go in. He didn't want to keep seeing the pain and anger on Bolt's face.

Bolt might not be able to see the dangers Cherry posed, but they could. Maybe she wasn't hatching a plan with Lillian. Maybe she was in town doing exactly as she said.

But maybe Charlotte was right and they couldn't trust her yet.

When it came down to it, he'd support Charlotte any day of the week before he'd support a woman he'd met a little over a month ago. Bolt had to understand that.

Problem was, he couldn't see that. Deke felt bad for hurting his friend. He was tired of seeing the pain in his eyes. He'd cool it for today. If Bolt wanted to believe in Cherry, then fine. He'd give him that. For the day, anyway. But he'd stop at nothing to keep his friends safe. If that meant showing Bolt the truth of who Cherry really was, then so be it. He'd be the bad guy.

He'd just use the bathroom and then leave. A few more minutes wouldn't hurt. He was already late.

***

A LOW MOAN echoed in the cold room. Cherry raised a hand to her forehead, wincing at the pain when she swiped at the cut. Her fingers were coated in blood when she pulled them away. Her head throbbed. She was bleeding, and as she looked around at the dirty, dark, cold room she was in, she knew she was in more trouble than a simple headache and a small cut.

He'd knocked her out with his fist. If her memory served correctly, she had noticed rings on his fingers when he tapped on the door. Obviously, one of his rings had cut her when he punched her.

She'd come to in the trunk of the car wherever they had been taking her. They hadn't driven far from Bolt's. At least, it didn't feel far when she woke up jostling to and fro in the trunk, stopping a few minutes later. Of course, she feigned she was out, hiding the cringe she felt when he pulled her out of the trunk and threw her over his shoulder. He could've been gentler with her. She was pregnant!

Oh, no. Her baby.

Her hand dove to her belly, though she didn't feel any different. She felt nauseous, but that could be from the morning sickness or the knock to her head.

She'd have to pray everything was okay with the little one inside her belly. She'd die if anything happened to their baby. Bolt would take it just as hard if they lost it.

There was a small window on the far side of the room, light peeking through. It gave enough for her to see the room, but not enough to keep the heebie-jeebies from entering her system. The room creeped her out. She sat on a small, dirty cot that smelled like it had been pulled from the garbage. Even thinking about what she might be sitting on made her want to throw up. Besides the cot, nothing else was in the room.

What did it mean?

Did they plan to keep her here for a while? They took anything out of the equation for her to escape. The cot did her no good to get out of here.

Though it gave her some comfort, despite the lumps she felt under her butt, it grossed her out.

Crawling on her hands and knees, she got off the cot, cringing when the cold concrete hit her palms. She'd freeze to death if they didn't give her a blanket. Her clothes didn't cover much of her at all.

She crawled until she hit the wall, slumping against it. Her arms wrapped around her knees, trying to keep the heat in, failing miserably. She couldn't control the shivers that wracked her body.

The doorknob twisted and the door slammed against the wall. It frightened her, but she managed to contain the terror by not jumping or reacting. That's what they wanted her to do.

"Oh, look at you." Lillian frowned, though every inch of the expression wasn't real. "You poor thing. I did ask nicely for you to open the door. It didn't have to come to this."

"What do you want from me?"

Cherry hated how weak she sounded. How scared each word echoed out of her mouth. She needed to stop letting them think she couldn't handle this. She put a hand on the wall and pushed herself up. It hurt like hell, her feet boiling with pain as she put pressure on them. That's what she got for running for her life with no shoes on.

"You won't get away with this."

"Oh, you're so cute. This little delusional world you live in. Isn't she cute?" Lillian asked the guy standing next to her, laughing. "Of course I'm going to get away with this. I might make a mistake once, but I don't do it twice. I'm no dummy. You were so close to freedom. Bolt was right there." Another chortle split her lips. "I almost laughed, but I didn't want to give myself away. He might've heard me. It's too bad I couldn't stick around to see his panic at you gone."

"I don't understand why you're doing this."

"Because I can." The smile she threw Cherry's way made the goose bumps lying in wait on her arm stand on end.

This woman was the devil incarnate. Cherry feared she was right. She would get away with this. Bolt had no idea where she was.

But she knew he'd never stop until he found her. She had to hold on to that hope. Hopefully, she wasn't dead when he did.

"So you kidnapped me because you can? That's it. You're going to hurt Pepper because you can? That's insane."

Lillian shrugged. "She means nothing to me. The world will be a better place when she's gone. She's pathetic. A loser. Nobody likes her. She knows it. If anything, I'm doing her a favor."

"And me? Why me? You don't even know me."

"I know." Lillian nodded, pursing her lips as if perplexed by that. She slapped the guy on the shoulder. "I had this one follow you around. His reports to me made me laugh. How scared you'd be. How you'd look around and not see him. I didn't tell him to torture you like that, but I did get a kick out of it."

So this had been the unknown entity lurking, creeping in the shadows. Well, at least, now she knew. Lillian had been behind it all along.

"I wanted him to tell me all about you. The things you did. The people close to you. I was surprised to learn you knew about Pepper. Then you had to go and ruin everything and come here. I'm the better sister. You should've come to me!"

Just showed how little Lillian knew her, understood her.

"How did you find out about me? I stumbled upon you two."

"Oh, I always knew about you. People think I don't pay attention. That I'm a dumb blonde or something." Lillian twirled her finger around a strand of hair, with a cheesy smile on her face. "I can be when I want to be. My father wasn't good at keeping secrets. Pepper was so absorbed in herself to notice anything. I never cared about you. I don't care about you. Seeing as you've taken Pepper's side, fallen into bed with the deputy, you made your choice whose side you're on. It isn't mine. That's too bad."

Was that what the text meant?

You have a choice to make.

That implied she could still make it. Was Lillian giving her the option to change her mind? To jump on her bandwagon instead of Pepper's?

Because no matter what these two did to her, she never would. She'd never betray Pepper like that.

"You're wrong. I picked the better sister," Cherry said with complete confidence. "I don't regret that."

"Yes, well, yay you." Lillian mimicked like she was waving pompoms in the air. "I'm going to give you a choice. Maybe you won't regret that either. I guess we'll find out."

Here it was. The moment of truth.

Lillian stared at her, the wicked smirk growing until Cherry couldn't stand to look at her any longer. Her gaze tore to the floor.

"I'll give you an hour to make your choice."

Her head shot up.

"But you didn't tell me what it is."

"Oh, silly, me." Lillian laughed like it was the funniest thing in the world. "You can either save your precious baby that's barely a pea inside you. Or you can save Bolt. But only one will survive today. The other will die."

Cherry rushed forward, then stopped before Lillian was

within arm's reach. She'd be dumb to try and attack her. She wouldn't win a fight when it would be two against one.

"Why? Why would you do that? Why would you make me choose something like that? I've never done anything to you. I don't even know you!"

"That's very true. But Bolt knows me. He helped hurt and kill the man I loved. I can't let that slide. But since you are my sister—well, half, that still counts for something—and you fell in love with him, I thought I'd offer an olive branch. So you can see I can be nice too. I'm not killing the baby *and* him. I'm letting you keep one. Seems fair."

"I'll never forgive you for this. Take your olive branch and shove it up your ass," Cherry seethed.

"So you want me to take the baby and him? Is that what you're saying?"

God, no. She didn't want to lose either of them.

"No. No, please, no."

"It's pathetic to beg. Don't beg, Cherry. I was almost starting to like you there for a brief moment. I'll stick to my word. You can make a choice. I'm nothing but true to my word."

The guy turned around first, and Lillian followed.

"Wait! Please don't do this. Where are you going?"

"Oh, you don't think I'm just out to get you, do you? Oh, no. I have to kill Pepper. Bitch deserves to die. I have to kill Deke. So many people to take care of today. I'm not wasting any time this time around. They all die today. I'll be back when I'm finished. I'd say you have about an hour or so. Maybe less. Choose wisely."

Then the door slammed shut, leaving her alone in the cold, dirty room once again.

Banging echoed around the room, drowning out her cries as she pounded on the door.

No one answered. No one would. Not for an hour.

How could she make such a decision? If she chose for the baby to die, didn't that mean she'd die too? How else would she kill the baby if not by hurting her?

Tears streamed down her face as she slid her back against the door until her butt hit the floor.

She had no way to escape. Nothing to do but ponder her dilemma.

Her baby, or Bolt?

19

———

BOLT PULLED INTO THE DRIVEWAY, then slammed on the brakes. The front door was wide open. He glanced at his phone, hitting the screen to light it up. No alerts showed. Not even him pulling into the driveway, which meant the camera system wasn't working.

Shit!

He darted out of the truck, running into the house screaming Cherry's name.

"Cherry!"

He ran from room to room.

"Cherry!"

He halted when he came across the broken window in the kitchen, the glass littering the floor.

"No, no, no. Shit!" He slammed a fist into the wall, wincing from the immediate pain.

Damn it. That had been a bad idea. His hand throbbed, but it didn't matter. Nothing did but finding Cherry.

He walked back outside, looking around the yard. Nothing looked out of place.

"Cherry!" he shouted, cupping his hands around his mouth.

Nothing answered back but the wind lashing at his face.

Maybe she ran and hid somewhere. He rushed to the backyard to his shed, though it was locked from the outside. She wouldn't be in there. He walked around the yard, looking for signs of anything. Heaven help him, even blood. Thankfully, he didn't see any of that. That had to be a good sign. She was alive. They took her alive.

He stalked back to his truck, on the verge of screaming at nothing.

Now what did he do?

Go back to the station and grovel for forgiveness. Beg his friends for help.

Help finding a woman they didn't trust.

"Shit!"

He slammed his hand on the hood.

So much for his plans of getting out of town.

His heart raced as he climbed back into the truck and grabbed his phone. The pressure from squeezing it hurt, especially after slamming his fist into the wall, but he didn't stop. He deserved the pain. Leaving her alone had been the worst decision he could've ever made. Why had he done that? Those texts should've been clue enough someone was out there. Waiting for their moment to attack. They barely waited. He hadn't been gone more than an hour.

She was gone.

"Get it together, Bolt. You got this. You're not an idiot. You can find her."

His pep talk did nothing to soothe the ache crushing his chest. But it gave him the courage to call the one person he had to believe would care.

"Hey, Bolt." Pepper sounded agitated.

Did someone already tell her that he quit? That he walked away from everyone? Of course, if they had, why would she care either? She had seemed off last night, as if she had doubted Cherry as well.

"Bolt? Are you there?"

"Yeah, I'm here." He swallowed, then blinked a few times. *Get it out!* "Cherry's gone."

"What? What do you mean gone? She wouldn't leave. Not now."

"No, I don't mean that kind of gone. Someone took her. My front door was wide open when I got home. The camera system is down. The back door window is broken. She's not in the house."

"Oh, my Go—" Pepper's voice broke, then she inhaled and blew out a breath. "I'll be right there."

"No, I'll meet you at the station. There's nothing to do here. I looked everywhere. I didn't find anything. There's no point in looking for evidence. We know who did this. Lillian. Now we just have to find her."

"Okay, I'm almost done at the clinic. I'll meet you at the station."

"Why are you at the clinic?"

Pepper sighed. "It's a long story. We'll find her, Bolt. We will."

They'd better. Or he didn't know how he'd live without her.

OKAY, now he was being ridiculous. He had to leave. Danny would rip him a new one if he didn't get there soon. Danny had already given him an earful for laying it so heavy on Bolt.

He wasn't trying to be a dick about it. So sue him for caring about his friends. Making sure they didn't do something to get themselves killed. They'd all been in a tight spot this past year, and he was sick of it. No more. He wasn't losing another friend. Not that he'd known Derek as well as Logan and everyone else had, but he felt his loss as hard as everyone because *they* had known him. They had cared about him.

His phone rang, indicating Danny was tired of waiting for him.

"I know, I know. I'm late."

"Dude, what are you doing?"

Go with the truth, or lie? Danny would detect a lie in a heartbeat.

"I'm sorry I don't see things how Bolt does. I hate making him mad, but I also can't keep it to myself. I was delaying my departure, okay."

A heavy sigh echoed in his ear. "You won't have to worry about that this morning. Bolt quit. Turned in his gun and badge."

Deke paused with the key still in the doorknob just waiting for him to twist it to lock. "What do you mean? Why would he do that?"

"I guess he's sick of everyone being on the other side. He has a point. We half opened our arms to Cherry, and the first sign of something bad, we jump ship. We point the finger at her. I'd tell us to go to hell too if I was him."

This was his fault.

For getting on Bolt's case too hard. He shouldn't have been so intense about it.

He needed to apologize. He still had reservations about Cherry, but he could keep them inside, keep them to himself, at least when Bolt was around. Bolt couldn't leave.

He was a damn good deputy, and the county needed him. Their group, their tight-knit family, needed him.

"I'll go talk to him."

Deke finished locking the door, the keys dangling in his hand as he jaunted to his car.

"No, I'd give him space right now. He looked pissed when he left. Get in here so we can figure out how to find Lillian before she does anything crazy."

"Yeah, okay. I'll be right there."

He had one hand holding the phone while the other slipped the car key into the lock. The ominous click that didn't sound right registered immediately.

"Shit!"

The phone dropped from his hand as he dove for cover when the car exploded.

PEPPER STOPPED NEXT to Seth at the terror on Danny's face, the door still half open to the station.

A loud boom echoed in the distance, shaking the ground some.

"Deke! Deke!" Danny hollered into his phone.

Charlotte raced around the counter, grabbing at Danny. "What was that? What happened? Please tell me that boom doesn't have anything to do with Deke. Danny!"

Pepper stood frozen, watching the chaos unfold in front of her. She had thought getting the call from Bolt was a lot to handle. Whatever was happening here just made it all worse.

All because of her psycho twin. She knew Lillian was behind all of this.

"Danny!"

Charlotte shook Danny by the shirt, yet he wasn't hearing her. He kept staring at his phone.

"Seth, do something," Pepper whispered because she had no energy. She didn't know what to do. All of this was her fault. She brought this terror to this small town. To these wonderful people.

"Hey, Charlotte, back off." Seth grabbed her from behind, but she shook him off.

"Don't touch me!" Charlotte pointed a finger at Danny. "Make him talk."

Logan joined the fray. "What's going on?"

Danny rubbed his chest. "I was just talking to Deke. I was talking to him." He nodded, as if reassuring himself that's what he was doing.

"Okay. And?" Logan prodded.

Danny finally looked away from his phone to Logan. "Didn't you hear the boom? The ground shake. That was the bomb's shockwaves."

"What bomb?" Logan whispered. "I didn't feel or hear it."

Odd. They had all felt it, though Logan had been in his office, not near the front door she still held half open. She stepped inside, not wanting to appear like she was preparing to run when that was all she wanted to do. The door shut quietly behind her.

"The bomb that..." Danny's lips twisted in pain. "That...I was just talking to him. He got away. I was just talking to him."

"No, no." Charlotte backed away, bumping the counter. "No, he's fine. He knows better than to die on me."

This couldn't be happening.

Pepper couldn't believe this was happening.

First Cherry. Now Deke.

She'd be next.

Her sister wouldn't leave without killing her too.

"He killed Brett."

All eyes turned to Pepper still standing by the door. But at least she was inside the building, not half out of it.

"Deke hurt Brett and he died from his injuries. She wouldn't let something like that slide."

Choked sobs tore from Charlotte's throat. Pepper winced at the sound but didn't cower. She couldn't. Not when all of this was her fault. Maybe she shouldn't have voiced it, but it was the truth.

They needed to hear the rest of it.

"Bolt called me a few minutes ago. He should be here soon. Cherry's been taken. The house was broken into. Lillian has her. She's probably dead too. And I'm next."

"Hell, no!" Seth hollered, taking two steps before the doors behind Pepper imploded.

Gunshots rang out.

Everyone dove for cover. Pepper managed to get behind a chair meant for visitors. Logan and Danny had no choice but to rush to the hallway. Seth and Charlotte were closest to the counter, diving behind that.

Pepper didn't go anywhere without her weapon, pulling her gun out from the ankle holster she wore. She knew Danny and Logan were armed. The sound of a shotgun being cocked told her Charlotte had a weapon near her where she sat. Unless she handed it to Seth, he was the only one not armed. Not able to help them fight the onslaught of bullets raining down on them.

CHERRY SCREAMED and scuttled away from the door when she heard the lock disengage. The door swung open.

Evan walked in.

"Are you okay?" He rushed to her side.

She shied away from him, but if he was here to hurt her, there wasn't much she could do to fight him off. Her energy was slowly depleting.

"I'm not with them. I'm not here to hurt you." He raised his hands in surrender, backing away, but still crouching near her.

"Then how'd you know...how'd you know I was here?"

"I was running late to opening the garage this morning. This building is on my dad's property. I saw a car turn down the road that they shouldn't be on. What can I say? My dad has been into some really shady, bad shit, and I wasn't going to let it happen again. I followed them. I saw Pepper with this guy, then he pulled you out of the trunk. I waited until they left to come inside."

Her head shook as if she were spinning and couldn't stop. "That wasn't Pepper."

"Lillian." Evan cursed underneath his breath. "Should've known."

He stood up and held out his hand. "Come on. We should get out of here before they return. Unless you like being in this cold-ass room?"

No, she didn't like being locked in here. Evan, while Bolt didn't trust him, was the lesser of two evils right now.

She took a hold of his hand and let him pull her up. Her legs were so wobbly, he had to help her out of the small cabin. There was no furniture anywhere, as if it had been abandoned a long time.

"It's a bit of a walk. I parked my truck where they wouldn't see it. I couldn't exactly pull right up."

She bit her lip, not daring to look at her feet. If she did, she'd cave, dropping into a ball of terror on the floor. The pain was starting to get to her. She hadn't looked in the room, but it felt like a few pebbles were embedded in the soles of her feet.

"I can carry you," Evan offered, glancing at her bare feet.

"No, I'll walk."

She had her limits. While she was grateful for his help, she refused to look like a coward, some damsel in distress.

A loud boom shook the earth, startling her into Evan's arms.

"Shit. What was that?" He wrapped an arm around her shoulder. "Come on. Let's go faster. Shit's going down and I don't want to be stuck here."

They traipsed through the woods as fast as she could, the whole time she ignored the fire breathing through her feet and up her legs. She cried with relief when she saw his truck. He helped boost her into the seat and then raced around the front, hopping into it like someone lit a fuse under his ass.

"I'll take you to the sheriff."

She nodded. Going back to Bolt's would be silly. He might not be there, and it would only waste time.

Evan peeled out of his hiding spot, crushing tiny trees and bushes, scratching the sides of his truck from the large branches that hit it as he drove. His tires squealed when he hit the pavement.

She threw a hand out when they got closer to Main Street. "Stop!"

He slammed on the brakes.

"Do you hear that?"

He rolled down both windows, making it much easier to hear the gunfire erupting.

"Holy shit, it sounds like a damn war zone," Evan muttered. He ran his hands through his hair and then hit the steering wheel hard. "We can't drive into that."

Bolt could be there. He could get hurt.

Which meant Lillian lied to her. She didn't let her make a choice like she said she would.

She whipped open her door, grimacing as her feet hit the pavement.

"What are you doing?" Evan jumped out of the truck, meeting her in front of it.

"What does it look like I'm doing? Bolt's in town. He needs me."

"You're insane. He's a deputy with a gun. He knows what he's doing. You barely have any clothes on. You can't walk into a gunfight."

Her eyes trailed down her minuscule outfit. He was right, but it didn't sway her mind. What did her outfit make a difference anyway? She'd fight naked if she had to. Protecting Bolt was all that mattered.

"Thank you for rescuing me. I'm sure I'd be dead if it wasn't for you. I appreciate it. I'm sorry you made mistakes and they won't forgive you for it. You seem like a decent guy."

Then she started walking toward town.

"Wait!" Evan rushed to her side, falling in step with her. "Bolt will kill me—if he's not already dead—if I don't stay with you. Not much of a rescue if you walk right back into danger without help."

She smiled but didn't respond.

He was wrong in one aspect.

Bolt wasn't dead. He could handle this. He told her all the time, and she believed him.

20

BOLT SAT CROUCHED behind his truck, trying to peek around the corner to get a good look at the men firing into the sheriff's station. He'd made it onto Main Street at the same time the SUV swerved in front of the sheriff's building and three men hopped out, firing without hesitating.

He braked hard, angling his truck in the road as well. If they made a run for it, they'd be blocked by his truck. It didn't mean they couldn't put the SUV in reverse and escape the opposite way.

What the hell was going on?

First Cherry, and now this.

And he was useless. He couldn't even help his friends trapped inside the building. He'd handed in his gun and badge. Unlike Pepper, who liked to wear an ankle holster, he didn't. The weight on his leg bothered him. Made him feel off-kilter, so he never wore one.

His truck was empty of weapons as well.

If they noticed him sitting in the middle of the street and started raining bullets down on him, he'd be a sitting duck.

Not his brightest decision, quitting today. But how in the hell was he supposed to know all hell would break loose?

"Bolt. Psst."

He glanced to his right, his eyes bulging at the sight. Mrs. Dunburry had the shop door open, crouching low with a shotgun in her hand.

"I don't see a gun on you. Do you need this?"

Yes, he did. Right now, he was not going to be embarrassed that she was helping him out.

He nodded, smiling.

She shoved it hard, and the sound of it scrapping against the concrete made him wince. No way any of the men would've heard that, not with the way they hadn't let up on firing. But it didn't mean he liked the sound permeating the air.

"Oh, can't forget this." She waved a box of ammunition with a giddy smile like this was something that happened in their small town all the time.

The box slid the same path.

"Thank you," he mouthed, not wanting to risk talking loud.

He checked the weapon, groaning that she had shuffled a loaded gun—with the safety off—in his direction. He also wanted to know why she even had the shotgun in her store when he didn't recall her having a permit for it, but now wasn't the time to worry about it. It had come in handy.

He shoved his hands at her, shooing her back into the store. She was bound to catch a bullet sticking out like she was.

Walking low with the shotgun in his right hand and the box of ammunition in his left, he headed for the front of his truck, peering around the corner. Now only two men were firing, hiding behind the SUV, occasionally popping up and firing into the building. One guy was down in the street, not moving.

Good for them. They were returning fire and managed to hit one. Two more to go.

He could see the two remaining, but he didn't have a good shot from this angle. He wouldn't have a good one from the back side of the truck either.

There wasn't a break in the attached buildings until two more stores down. He could jaunt that way, cut through the alley, run down the opposite way, and come up behind them where another alley lay directly where he needed to be.

It was the perfect way to finally ambush them for once. But damn it, he only had a 12-gauge shotgun, which was generally used for hunting around here. It held three bullets max. It didn't give him ample time to take two people down. His shots had to be precise. One shot for each. Because as soon as he fired, they'd turn and fire at him.

It didn't matter. He had no other choice here. His friends needed him.

He ran low but fast down the street, staying in the middle with his truck for cover. As soon as the alley appeared, he darted to the left without looking at the men. His breaths were even and steady, thanks to the running he enjoyed doing on his days off. He made it to the other alley right behind the men in no time. This was where it got tricky.

They hadn't heard him, so he kept going until he was safely behind the large garbage bin that needed to be picked up. The stench was enough to make him want to hurl. A quick glance said he needed to be closer if he wanted his aim to be decent. There wasn't much for him to take cover to get that close.

Again, it didn't matter. His friends' lives were on the line.

These guys were prepared with an insane amount of ammunition. They barely stopped shooting to give anyone a break.

He eyed the small, short round garbage can sitting close to the edge of the alley. It wouldn't be much cover, but it'd have to suffice. He'd rush up to it, fire off his three shots, duck down and reload, hoping he'd be able to do that in record time—if he didn't knock both of them down right away.

The bullets scattered to the ground when he dumped the box upside down. He pocketed as many as he could, shoving three for easy access in his shirt pocket. One deep breath released, and then he was running like a bat out of hell to the front of the alley.

They didn't hear him approach. He raised the shotgun, aimed, and fired all three shots in quick succession, hitting the first one in the back and the second one in the stomach when he turned at the sound of the first shot.

They both went down like flies on a flyswatter.

Wow. That went easier than he expected.

Not the loser like they thought. Not the idiot who couldn't get things done.

His heart pounded as he stepped out into the open, the alley walls no longer a safety net. He glanced in both directions, not seeing any other signs of people with weapons. The streets were empty except for him.

It was over.

Maybe. He couldn't take the chance. He pumped the weapon, releasing the last cartridge, and dug into his shirt pocket to reload.

"Uh-uh, I wouldn't do that if I were you."

Chills ran down his spine at the voice.

Bolt looked up to see Lillian in front of him, a gun

pointed at his chest. She had materialized out of thin air. He hadn't even heard her footsteps.

"Nice shots. I'm impressed. Though you killed my friends and that pisses me off."

The vicious smile on her face said he'd regret what he had done.

If he died today, at least he died protecting his friends. He couldn't find fault in that. Though thoughts of Cherry made his gut clench. She was alone somewhere. Scared, possibly hurt. If she managed to survive this, she'd be alone raising their baby. Agony punched him in the gut as the thought rolled through.

"Where's Cherry?"

"Now why would I tell you that? You murdered my friends."

This woman was delusional. Why she hadn't been locked in a psych ward was a mystery to him.

"I defended my friends. I defended this town. Please, tell me she's alive."

"Oh, she is. I wouldn't kill my sister."

Bolt's brows puckered into confusion. "Really, because you tried killing Pepper. What do you call that?"

"Well, she's a bitch and deserves to die. It's a totally different story."

"Let Cherry go. I don't care if you kill me. Just let her go."

"Oh, you're so sweet. She's so lucky to have found you." Lillian wiped an imaginary tear from her eye. "That's how I felt about Brett." Her smile vanished in the blink of an eye. "And now he's gone. That makes me very unhappy. I'm lost without him. I was lucky to have found him. Now what do I do? Now who do I get in trouble with? It's not as fun without him."

She waved the gun at him. "You were there. You hurt him."

Not exactly true. Deke had shot him and shoved a chest down the stairs that knocked him so hard he went into a coma. She was so far gone in her grief, it wouldn't matter what he said.

"The question is, what do I do? Do I kill you here and now? Do I wait? I never go back on my word. Not with family. Not with my sister. I have a feeling she's gonna be one to really grapple with the choice she has to make. It's only sisterly of me to help her out. I don't want her to struggle like that."

Goose bumps flushed his skin as her smile grew into the evilest smirk he'd seen yet.

"Bye, bye, Bolty."

"No!"

He turned at the sound of Cherry's voice.

The gun went off.

Cherry pushed him out of the way, crying out in pain and falling hard to the sidewalk.

"Cherry? No, no, why would you do that!"

Bolt rolled her over, grimacing at the blood soaking her shirt. "No!" He shoved his hands hard down over the wound, the blood seeping through his fingers like a raging river not deterred by rocks in its way.

She groaned, raising her hand, but it fell before it could lift even an inch off the ground.

"Wow. Not the decision I expected. But good for her."

Bolt shot his gaze at Lillian who had lowered the weapon.

"A deal's a deal. It's your lucky day." Then she winked and turned around.

"Bolt..." Cherry whispered.

"I'm here. I'm here. You shouldn't have done that."

A wisp of a smile touched her lips. "I chose you."

What the hell did that mean?

Then her eyes closed.

"Cherry, stay with me. Stay with me!" Bolt looked up, wondering where everyone was. Why weren't they out here yet? "Help! I need help!"

The SUV blocked the station's door, but he heard it whoosh open and feet pound on the pavement a few seconds later. Pepper rounded the vehicle first.

"Bolt, what happened? Oh, Cherry. No." Pepper dropped to her side, swiping a hand across Cherry's cheek, but her eyes were still closed.

She needed to open her eyes. Say something. Anything. Even that she hated him for leaving her alone and letting her get taken.

She'd be fine. He only had to pray she'd be fine.

"Lillian did it. She shot her. She went that way," Bolt said, tossing his head in the direction she had walked off. "Go get her, Pepper. Don't let her get away. I got this."

"I know you do. Thank you. Don't let her die."

Not if he could help it.

He saw Seth rush off with Pepper, while Danny and Logan crouched near him. He didn't ask where Charlotte was.

"How'd she get here?" Danny asked, pulling off his suit jacket. He pushed Bolt's hand aside. They pressed the jacket over the wound, which was high enough above her stomach that he had high hopes the baby was okay. But it was also too close to her heart that it might not even matter. He could lose them both. It couldn't happen.

Not to Cherry. Not the sweetest, brightest, happiest woman in the world. The woman who walked into a room with one smile and everyone would return the smile because that's what she did. She brought the happiness out of others. She brought the light back into his world when it had been dark for so long.

"She just appeared behind me. She shoved me out of the way. She took this bullet for me." Bolt's voice broke, he pressed his lips together to keep it all inside. Keep all the anger and fear that wanted to break free. He couldn't break down now. Not in front of everyone.

Logan's hand clutched his shoulder. "Charlotte ran to get Dr. Matthews. She'll be in good hands."

He nodded, noticing for the first time Deke wasn't around. God, did he get hit inside the building?

"Where's Deke?"

Agony brushed across Danny's face. "He might be... a bomb went off when I was talking to him. I should go check on him. He might need medical attention too."

Danny stood up and Logan joined him. "You can't go alone, Danny."

Before he could hear them arguing, the sound of footsteps pounding on the pavement echoed behind him.

Dr. Matthews and Kat were ready to tackle Cherry, and he felt helpless as they pushed him out of the way. He had to do something. Anything.

Charlotte stood quietly to the side, watching everything but not seeing it. The paleness in her face said she was barely hanging on by a thread.

"I'll go with you, Danny."

Danny shot a surprised look at him. "You should stay with Cherry."

"I can't see her like that. I can't do anything for her. It won't help me. We should know if Deke's okay."

Now he understood why his brother never visited him in the hospital when he'd been shot. It was hard to see the one you loved hurt, in pain, dying. At least, he'd like to think that's how his brother felt. That he loved him, even if he had a hard time expressing it.

"Charlotte, you stay with Cherry. Call in reinforcements. Just in case more people come. And we need help cleaning up. Keep your gun by your side." Logan looked broken as he stared at the mess everywhere.

"Bolt, go with Danny and check on Deke. I'll catch up with Pepper and Seth. We need to find Lillian. Everyone, stay on their guard and ready for anything."

Logan waited for someone to argue. No one did. Not even Charlotte who Bolt could see was on the verge of losing it. He understood her pain well. He wanted to lose it right along with her. She was smart not to insist going with Danny. If Deke was dead—and with a bomb as the culprit, it didn't sound promising—she shouldn't see him like that.

He walked away without looking back once at Cherry. He couldn't. He'd fall apart seeing her die like that. Only good memories were all he wanted to see. If he lost her, he'd make sure he'd forget all the memories. Because living without her would be too painful otherwise.

"I'M SORRY ABOUT CHERRY."

Pepper froze, slapping Seth in the chest. "Don't say that. She's going to make it."

Seth nodded with a short smile, but she knew he didn't believe her. Hell, the words sounded forced. But she had to think positive. Losing her sister now after she had started feeling like she had a sister for the first time would be devastating.

And she had to apologize to Cherry for not having more faith in her. For not sticking by her side as firmly as Bolt had.

They kept jogging down the street, keeping an eye for any sign that Lillian was around.

"She went that way and turned right!" Mrs. Dunburry shouted, pointing her finger in the direction where the park lay.

"Thank you. Go back inside until we know for sure it's safe." Pepper ushered her back in with her hands and picked up the pace.

Seth didn't lose a beat running with her.

Lillian probably stashed a car this way. A quick getaway on the off-chance things didn't go as planned. They hadn't. Lillian was losing again. If Pepper didn't stop her now, it would never end. She'd live with one eye over her shoulder her entire life, and she couldn't live that way.

Her weapon was gripped tightly in her hand. Seth had a gun of his own, which made her feel better. Two against one. Not that he was as good of a shot as her. They'd been to the range together many times in the past few months. He liked to go with her. It had turned into a challenge of sorts. Who could hit the bullseye the most? She always won.

The park came into view. The playground equipment was empty, strollers abandoned. Good. Everyone was smart enough to run for cover, not sure what was going on.

Lillian thought this kind of coordinated attack would make them falter. She'd been wrong.

At the end of the park on the opposite side, she saw a black, nondescript car sitting. That had to be it.

"Go that way." Pepper gestured to the right, then she tossed her head to the left. "I'll go this way. I don't see her, but that has to be her car."

They separated, and she felt the disconnection immediately. Knowing he wasn't by her side made her heart beat faster, her insides quiver with trepidation. If she lost Seth…

She had to remain positive. About everything. They'd come out on top. She had to believe it.

Pepper spotted movement the closer she got to the car. Some of the playground equipment must've skewed her view of Lillian running for her escape. Now she had eyes on her.

"Stop, Lillian!"

Her sister froze, then twirled around with a vicious smile on her face.

"Oh, look, the worst half right in front of my eyes. Long time, no see, sis. You look terrible."

Pepper wouldn't disagree, but she also wouldn't tell Lillian how much she was right. She hadn't slept well last night, the fear causing havoc in her mind. To the point she cut herself everywhere as if that would solve part of her problem. Well, it did. It made her feel more secure in the knowledge that, even if Lillian got away, she could never pretend to be Pepper again. No one would ever fall for her shenanigans again.

"You're going back to prison."

Lillian's lips turned down in a mock frown. "Are you sure that's wise? You know I'll get out again. I'll do this again. I won't stop until you're dead. I got Deke. Check." She giggled. "Bolt gets to live because, well, Cherry made her choice. She picked him over the baby. Shocker. Isn't that surprising?"

Was that what the cryptic text had meant? For Cherry to choose who lived, Bolt or her baby? How much more diabolical could her sister get? That was a disgusting thing to do to someone.

"Now, all I have to do is kill you. I said I would, and I never go back on my word."

Pepper's hand was steady as she held the gun straight in Lillian's face. "I'm not like you. I don't kill people. I don't like to shoot my weapon."

"Then you're going to wonder and worry and go insane thinking of when I'll strike next." Lillian shrugged, laughing. "I'm okay with that." She thrust her hands out. "Lock me up, sis. Take me in."

She would, but she didn't have any handcuffs on her. It hadn't been her day to work. They'd only been in town to see the doctor. She never went anywhere without her gun, something that would never change. Not after all of this.

"Turn around and put your hands on the hood of the car," Seth's voice boomed more strength than she felt she had.

She wasn't alone in this. They could bring Lillian back together, handcuffs or not.

Lillian rolled her eyes. "Oh, look, the knight in shining armor is here. Sound the trumpets."

"Now," Seth demanded.

His hand looked as steady as hers as he held the gun toward Lillian.

Another eye roll, but Lillian obeyed. She propped her hands to the hood, wiggling her ass.

"Search me, handsome. But don't cop a feel. I don't think Pepper would like that."

She shared a look with Seth. He grinned, even though nothing was funny. It helped calm some of the anxiety coursing through her system. Because he wasn't grinning at

Lillian's ridiculous words. He was smiling to let her know she had this. They won. Lillian lost.

Pepper shoved her weapon back into her ankle holster, then patted Lillian down, removing the gun behind her back. No other weapons were found. She checked the clip, then tossed Lillian's weapon behind her back.

Pepper grabbed Lillian by the shirt and turned her around. "Let's go. You're under arrest."

"Oooo, so testy. Not surprising. You always were a bitch."

"Walk."

Pepper didn't want to hear her say anything. Because no matter how much she tried to pretend Lillian's words didn't hurt, they did. They gutted her each time. She knew she shouldn't take Lillian's words to heart, but it was hard. So damn hard.

Seth walked next to her with Lillian leading the way. Pepper made sure to keep the distance between them short. Lillian could make a run for it. It would be dumb as there were two of them and only one of her. But in case she thought it'd work, Pepper wanted her close.

"You know, I changed my mind."

"Stop talking." Pepper shoved Lillian in her back.

Lillian bent forward, then out of nowhere she swiped out a leg, bringing Seth down with one swipe, his gun flying out of his hand. With another swift move, she punched Pepper in the face, dropping her to the ground. Her face throbbed and for a moment, her eyes blurred. Then Lillian was on top of her.

"I'm not going to prison, and I'm killing you now."

Not without a fight.

Pepper fought back, swinging her fists at Lillian. They rolled around the ground, both trying to get the upper hand. Then Seth was there, trying to grab Lillian off her. He managed to throw her aside, grabbing Pepper's hand and pulling her to her feet.

Lillian pushed herself off the ground and stood as well.

Pepper felt the gun still tucked behind her back, bringing her hand around to grab it when Lillian's hand raised with the gun she'd picked up from the ground. The gun she'd kicked out of Seth's hand.

How had this turned so quickly against them?

Pretty simple. She underestimated her sister. Like always.

"Game over, Pepper. I'm going to kill your boyfriend too for the hell of it."

A gunshot rang through the air. Pepper flinched yet felt no pain. She gripped Seth's shoulder, yet he stared at her in wonderment because he wasn't hit either.

Lillian's mouth opened, yet no sound came out. Absolute shock coated her face. Then she crumbled to the ground, the gun slipping from her grasp.

Logan stood behind her, lowering his weapon.

"Are you two okay?" Logan asked, walking closer to Lillian, kicking the gun away.

Though it wasn't necessary. Pepper could see the light gone out of her eyes. Her sister was dead. It was officially over. The sense of relief that hit her was overwhelming. She had thought it'd be better if Lillian ended her days rotting in prison, paying for her crimes the correct way. But Lillian had been right. Pepper would've been looking over her shoulder her entire life, and now she didn't have to.

Seth's arm, trembling yet solid, wound around her shoulder. "We're fine. We're okay."

Logan stared at Lillian, then met her gaze. "I'm sorry, Pepper."

"Don't be. She was dead to me a long time ago. You saved

our lives, and you shouldn't be sorry about that. How's Cherry?"

A wince crossed his face. "Dr. Matthews and Kat are taking care of her. Bolt and Danny went to check on Deke."

Hopefully, Deke made it out alive. A bomb... Well, she'd keep her positive attitude intact because it helped in this moment. It could help him as well.

21

BOLT DROVE them to Deke's house. Danny was barely hanging on by a thread with the thought his best friend was dead. Bolt wasn't hanging on any better, but doing the simple task, keeping his eyes on the road, steering the wheel to move forward, helped him focus on something other than Cherry. He needed that.

When they pulled into the driveway, he could feel the heat of the fire burning the car, even with the windows closed. Not a piece of it was untouched. It had been a massive bomb.

They exited the truck, leaving their doors wide open. Almost trance-like, they circled the car, looking at the destruction, keeping their distance from the intense heat. Roiling with anger and fury, laughing in a way at them. "See the mayhem I caused," it taunted.

"He must be in the car. There's no body on the ground," Danny said with no inflection in his tone. "The flames are too wild to get closer. He's gone. Deke's gone."

Bolt put a hand on Danny's shoulder but remained

silent. What did you say to someone in a moment like this? No words would make any of it better.

"How do I tell Charlotte?"

She already knew. Danny wouldn't have to say anything. She knew Deke was gone.

"How do I tell his family?"

That one would be harder.

"You don't have to. I can. Logan can. Someone else can do it."

Danny tossed his head back and forth. "No, I'd never pass it on to someone else. This is my responsibility."

"Come on. We should call the fire department."

Not that it mattered, other than to douse the flames so they could retrieve Deke's body. Danny hung his head, walking back toward the truck. Bolt stood for a moment longer, staring into the flames.

At least his death had been painless and immediate.

Bolt turned to leave, stopping when a sound echoed from the trees a short distance away. He took a few steps, taking his time. Then rushed forward when he heard the low groan.

Just on the outskirts of the tree line, Deke lay on his side, moaning.

"Danny!"

Bolt rushed to his side. "Deke, can you hear me?"

Parts of Deke's face were red as if the flames had given him an intense sunburn. His clothes were singed in places, but nothing too terrible that said he had horrible burns. His hand clutched his right leg, which looked bent in a bad way.

"Holy shit! Deke!" Danny dropped to his side. "Deke?"

It took a while before Deke finally opened his eyes. "Danny?" he croaked, blinking rapidly before his eyes hit him. "Bolt."

"We're here. You're alive. Shit, man, you're alive." Danny laughed, halfheartedly mingled with a sob. "Only you would survive a damn car bomb."

Deke grinned. "I live for suspense, man." He groaned. "Or not. My leg is on fire."

They both looked at it, but no flames were visible. Obviously, the pain was immense.

"It looks broken," Bolt said. "You don't look like you have many burns."

"It sure in the hell feels like it's on fire," Deke whispered. "The flames felt like they engulfed me. I heard the click of the bomb go off and I tried to run. I didn't get far before the blast threw me through the air."

"You got far enough away to survive. That's all that matters," Danny reassured him.

"So if you're here, it means you didn't quit, right, Bolt?"

Now wasn't the time to get into that. He had no idea where he wanted to go from here. So much had happened in so little time, he'd yet to process any of it.

Danny clapped him on the shoulder. "Hell, no, he didn't quit. We all wouldn't be here if it weren't for him."

Maybe not true. They'd had protection in the station. The gunfight would've lasted longer if he hadn't taken down the two men. If he had waited, Cherry wouldn't be fighting for her life right now.

"Let's get you to the hospital." Bolt stood up and pulled his phone out, calling for an ambulance.

The rest of the day went by in a blur. Deke went into surgery to have his leg reset, the bones broken in too many places. Most of his burns were superficial, though some on his back were pretty bad. Everyone was relieved he had survived.

Everyone was grateful the nightmare was over. Lillian was gone and couldn't enact revenge ever again.

Charlotte, Danny, and Kat were with Deke while he stayed planted in a chair in the waiting room, hoping for good news about Cherry. Pepper, Seth, Logan, and Aubrey sat with him, though they must've sensed he didn't want any of them to talk to him. He couldn't. The tears would come if one word tried to get out.

She'd lost a lot of blood before getting to the hospital. Of course, Kat and Dr. Matthews had done everything they could to help her. The amount of time she'd been in surgery, Bolt feared it hadn't been enough.

Bolt looked over at the doors when they swung open. He stiffened in his seat when the last person he expected to see walked in.

Carson.

Not even his parents were here. Though not for the lack of trying. They had wanted to come, and he told them not to. That it wouldn't help for everyone to be waiting on pins and needles for the news.

The bad news he knew was coming.

Carson sat down in the seat next to him.

Bolt relaxed some, but still felt the tension in his body. It floated between them like an invisible barrier.

The others were on the other side of the room; even they didn't say anything.

A few minutes went by in silence.

Bolt couldn't take it any longer.

"Why are you here? You didn't even show up when I got shot."

Carson didn't look at him. "Because I didn't want to see my brother like that. If you died, I wanted to let out my rage alone, not in front of people. But you made it, and I didn't have to do anything stupid."

So he had been right. His brother did care—in his own way.

"Why are you here now? You won't go in rage over Cherry?"

Carson glanced at him out of the corner of his eye. "I'm here for you. So if you want to go into a rage, I got your back."

"She's pregnant, you know."

"Mom and Dad told me."

Carson didn't say congrats, and Bolt didn't mind. There might not be any congrats to offer anymore.

"I love her. I've never loved a woman like her before."

Silence filled the space again. Yeah, it was an awkward conversation for them. They didn't have these kinds of chats.

"I was shot once."

Bolt jerked. "When? Does Mom and Dad know this?"

"No. I never told them. Anyone. It was overseas. It hurt." Carson shrugged. "You know. You've been there."

Bolt sighed. "A lot must've happened over there. It changed you."

"Death and destruction does that to a person." Carson looked him directly in the eyes. "I might not be the old Carson you seemed to like, but I'm still your brother. I still love you. I'm sorry I can be an ass."

"Thanks for being here. It means a lot."

Carson nodded and went back to staring at anything other than the people in the room, including him.

A few painful hours later, the doctor finally entered.

The news was good. Cherry made it through surgery.

His brother left right after.

His departure didn't hurt as much as it would've in the

past. Bolt understood him more now. He cared, but in his own way.

Cherry might be the same. She might never love him, not knowing how to love, but he knew she cared about him. She took a bullet for him.

He planned to show her for the rest of his life how much he loved her—if she'd still have him.

IT HURT TO MOVE. She felt like she'd been hit by a truck, even though it'd been a tiny little bullet. Despite the pain echoing all over, she pretended like it didn't hurt. She held in the squeaks of agony every time she shifted. She held in the winces that wanted to touch her lips.

Pepper was no dummy. She knew she hurt.

"I knew you'd be okay. Chapmans are strong."

Cherry squeezed her hand, then let it go. "How are you?"

"Stop," Pepper said, waving her hand in the air. "You are not worrying about me."

Well, she couldn't help it. She saw the bandage on Pepper's hand. Had asked about it, and Pepper gave a short response that she simply cut herself. No more explanation than that. How? Had Lillian done it? While she knew she shouldn't be agonizing over these little things she couldn't help it.

Pepper had been the first person she laid eyes on when she woke up. She'd given her a brief rundown of everything that happened. Lillian was dead. Deke was okay, albeit with a broken leg. Bolt was waiting to see her.

Then why wasn't he in here yet? She'd been awake for a while now and still no sign of him. The only person to visit her had been Pepper. She'd yet to leave her room. She didn't take it personally that not even Seth stepped in. Or Logan or any of the others. So much had happened, she knew the cleanup would be horrendous. They had more important things to do than check on her. A nobody.

"You can go, you know. You don't have to stay with me all day."

She'd rolled out of surgery late last night and didn't wake up until this morning. The drugs had knocked her out, plus the loss of blood. She could go for more drugs, something, anything to erase the pain weighing her down.

"I know. Deal with it. We're sisters. This is what sisters do. They hover when you're sick." Well, Cherry wasn't exactly sick, but she understood what Pepper was saying.

Her eyes drifted closed after she couldn't take it any longer. Her eyes felt heavy like the rest of her body. The nurse popped in, giving her more pain medication. She could've cried with relief.

The door swung open an hour later. Bolt walked in with his hands filled with bags galore. She couldn't keep the smile off her face.

Pepper stood up. "Now I'll go. I'll stop by later."

Bolt dumped the bags on the empty chair, then stopped next to her bed. The indecision on his face had her insides melting to a puddle of goo. This man. One moment so strong and in her face. Other moments, shy and afraid to act. Such an interesting contrast, and she loved everything about him.

Wow.

Yes, she loved him.

At least, what felt like love.

His smiles brightened her day, making her want to smile. The way he took care of her filled her heart with joy. The way he believed in her when no one else did. If that's what love felt like, then she wanted to grab it with both hands and never let go.

She patted the bed. "Sit. Please."

He listened, threading his fingers with hers. "You scared me. Don't do that again. Don't ever step in front of a bullet again. Okay?"

She was never very good at following directions. So many teachers had told her so. Maybe because her mother never instilled the good sense into her.

"I'd do it again in a heartbeat."

Bolt's free hand touched her belly. "Even if it risked our baby?"

She placed her hand over his. "Don't think it was an easy decision. Honestly, in that moment, when she had the gun pointed at you, I wasn't thinking about anything other than I didn't want to lose you. So yes, I'd do it again."

By some miracle, her choice hadn't ended like Lillian wanted it to. Her baby survived. She survived. Bolt survived. They could still be a happy family. If he still wanted her in his life.

The fact it took so long for him to show up had her very nervous she was going to lose him, despite everything she'd done.

"Well, I'm going to need you to promise not to do it again. I can't go through what I did. Sitting in that waiting room, wondering and worrying I lost you. I can't do it. So promise me?"

"Only if you promise never to get hurt or shot again. I might not have been here when it happened, but the thought of it happening again scares me. You think I like watching you go into work every day, that gun strapped to your hip. Well, I don't. I hate it."

"I quit yesterday."

Pepper hadn't told her that.

"Why?"

He smiled. "Because I chose you."

Her eyes watered as his words flowed through her. She'd said the same thing to him right before she passed out. To hear those words said back to her was more than she could've ever hoped for.

She closed her eyes, willing the tears to remain at bay. Crying was the last thing she wanted to do, especially in front of Bolt. Then she opened them, directing her attention to all the bags he'd brought into the room. A distraction. Just what she needed.

"What is all of that?"

Bolt's grin widened even more, letting go of her, and reached over for a bag. He pulled out a yellow onesie that said, "Nothing but a ray of sunshine."

"Some are baby clothes. Baby toys. I know it was silly to buy the baby stuff, but I couldn't help myself. A few books, in case you're here longer than we'd like. I know how you like a good romance to cheer you up. Some snacks." He chuckled, wincing. "The hospital food is not the greatest. Basically, anything and everything you need until I can take you home."

Concern flitted across his face. "You do want to come home with me, right?"

She clutched the baby onesie to her chest, then grabbed the front of his shirt, pulling him closer, ignoring the pain that stretched across her body.

Then her lips met his and the pain didn't feel so bad. Not when his touch soothed her with one simple caress.

"I would rather be with you than anywhere else in the world. I'm not sure what love is supposed to feel like, but if it's this intense emotion that makes me go crazy thinking I'll never see you again, then it has to be love. I love you, Bolt."

"I love you."

His lips dipped in again. Sweet, slow, and tender.

"Now let's talk about your job."

He frowned.

"You can't quit."

Laughter touched his eyes and lips. "I already did."

"Well, unquit. Because it's something you love to do. It's something you were born to do. They need you. I need you too, but it's a part of you, and I would never want to take that away from you."

"Logan asked me to take my gun and badge back. I told him I couldn't. Not yet."

"Well, I'm telling you to do it. If it's what you want."

"Would you be happier in another town? A bigger town?"

Her hand found his once again, sliding her fingers until they were clamped together. "Small-town life has grown on me. I'm happy here with you."

"Okay." Then he brushed her cheek and leaned in for one more kiss.

What did that mean? That he'd ask for his job back? Or he'd find something new to do.

22

BOLT PULLED open the door before anyone could knock. The curtain in the living room was wide open. Cherry liked the sunlight shining through during the day, and it made it easy to see all the vehicles pull into the driveway.

It looked like everyone had shown up.

Logan and Aubrey reached him first, Aubrey pulling him into a hug. "I brought some pot roast. I felt weird coming empty-handed."

"Thanks. That's nice of you. Cherry needs all she can eat. I feel like she's lost too much weight."

She'd spent five days in the hospital, nibbling on her food, even the snacks he had brought. This was her first day home, and obviously, everyone couldn't hold back any longer. They'd all visited her in the hospital but hadn't stayed long. Pepper had, but no one else had.

Even Deke had wheeled into the room to say hi and check on her. His leg was stuck in a cast and would be for a few months, but that was better than losing his life.

Logan watched Aubrey walk in, touching his shoulder. "I want to talk later." Then he followed her inside.

Danny and Kat stopped and grabbed a hug. Then Seth and Pepper. Charlotte and Deke came last. Deke took his time, hopping on one foot with the help of his crutches. He looked awkward and uncomfortable, but overall, very good for someone who had survived a blast from a bomb.

"Need help up the stairs?" Bolt asked, figuring Deke wouldn't, but he wouldn't be the jerk who didn't offer help.

Deke nodded, smiling in appreciation. He tried to hide his wince as he hobbled up the two steps with help from Bolt but didn't let a sound of pain out. Bolt knew it hurt.

"You didn't have to come. You just got out yourself."

"I made a lot of mistakes in the past few weeks, and I'm not doing that anymore. I'm sorry I hurt you. I'm sorry I didn't have faith in you, even if I had my doubts. It's unforgivable." Deke sounded contrite.

Bolt didn't think the wince touching his lips had to do with the pain in his leg. He meant every word.

"No, it is forgivable. I appreciate you coming. Friends still?" Bolt held out his hand, knowing it would be an awkward handshake. But Deke wouldn't want him to treat him like he couldn't handle something simple like that.

Deke shocked him by dropping a crutch and leaning in for a hug. They clapped each other on the back, the hug strong and a little longer than he'd hugged anyone else.

"I'm glad you're still here," Bolt whispered.

"You and me both, man."

Charlotte held out the crutch to Deke when he leaned away, looking the most apprehensive out of everyone. Deke nodded at her and walked inside the house.

"You don't have to say anything, Charlotte."

"Because you won't believe a word I say anyway?"

That garnered a chuckle out of him. "It would be ironic if I did. But no. Because you are who you are. You've always been that way. Strong in your convictions and never backing down. I understand why you felt the way you did, but it doesn't mean I liked it. Cherry will always come first for me. Always."

Charlotte smiled. "And she should. If you love her that much, she should. These past few days have opened my eyes. I thought it was bad when Deke got shot months ago. The pain and the terror...the thought of losing him. This was a thousand times worse. I think part of me died in that moment I thought he was gone. Nothing I can say will make it better between us. I know that. Making your favorite cupcakes again won't help either. I know that. But I'll do everything I can to bridge the gap between us. It might seem like I don't have faith in you, but I always have. But, yeah, maybe that faith cracked a little here and there. For that, I'm sorry. I'm really glad that Cherry is okay."

Bolt was grateful they all were okay. It could've ended so much worse. One of them could've been void from the world altogether because of one deranged woman.

"Come on, let's go inside."

The room was lively, filled with chatter and laughter. Cherry looked happy and content relaxing on the couch. Deke sat next to her with his leg propped with a pillow on the coffee table. Bolt wished he had a better way to make him feel comfortable, but that would have to do for now.

The day moved along at a fast pace, the daylight turning into evening. Aubrey's pot roast smelled divine, and based on all the eager looks on everyone's faces, they were ready to eat. Instead of eating in the dining room, they ate scattered around the living room. It would be hard for Deke to sit at the table, so not to exclude him, they ate near him instead.

Bolt helped clean up, getting shooed out of the kitchen

by Kat and Aubrey who insisted they'd do the dishes. He wouldn't complain.

Logan and Danny stopped him in the hallway as he tried to make his way back to the living room.

"So it's time for that chat, uh?"

Danny leaned against the wall on one shoulder, his arms crossed with a shit-eating grin on his face. "I'm only here to step in if need be. Carry on."

Logan chuckled, shaking his head. "I want you to come back, Bolt. I'm hoping you do."

His conversation with Cherry about it swirled through his brain. She was right. He loved being a deputy. When he graduated high school, he thought he would've hightailed it out of town so fast to get away from it all. The looks, the laughs, the teasing he could never escape. Instead, he'd found himself stuck in a place he hated, then morphing into a position he'd never imagined he'd be in. There, he found his place in life. Yeah, he might not always make the best decisions when it came to his job, but he loved it. He loved being a deputy. Despite its annoying intricacies sometimes, he loved this small town.

"In the moment, quitting was the right thing to do. Emotions were high and I was pissed. Cherry will always come first for me."

Danny tensed as if waiting for the bad news. Logan didn't look happy either, prepared to argue with him.

"I'd like to come back. It's where I want to be."

Logan swiped his hand behind his back and pulled out his gun and badge he'd been hiding there the whole time.

"Glad to have you back."

Then Logan pulled him into a hug after Bolt took his things, clutching them like the lifeline they were.

Danny blew out a breath, grinning. "So glad that went the way I wanted it to. Let's have a beer to celebrate."

They had one more beer before everyone decided to call it a night. He carried Cherry to the bedroom when it looked like she was ready to fall asleep. It'd been a busy, chaotic day. Fun and entertaining, but probably too much after just getting out of the hospital.

He put his hand on her hip like he usually did right before she fell asleep. He loved watching her eyes close and the sleep take over. Sometimes, he imagined it could happen as easily for him. One of these days, it might.

"How's Evan?"

Bolt frowned, surprised by the question. "I have no idea. I haven't spoken to him."

"I forgot to tell you. I never told you how I escaped."

He had never asked. The last few days, not much talk had occurred about Lillian. What was there to say? She brought death and mayhem to their small town. Everyone, even the townspeople, wanted to forget it.

"Evan had something to do with it?"

She nodded. "He saw their car go on his dad's property and he followed it. I would've been stuck in that room if it weren't for him." Her hand touched his chest, right over his heart. "He followed me into town. You didn't see him that day?"

He saw nothing but her bloody body on the pavement. The death surrounding him. The chaos one woman created.

"I didn't."

"I'd like to visit him tomorrow. Tell him thank you."

For once, Bolt didn't disagree. He owed Evan a ton of thanks. Instead of losing her to a bullet, he could've lost her in a completely different way. No one, not even Lillian, survived that day. If Cherry had still been locked up, they would've never known where to find her.

"Of course. We'll do it together."

Then his lips were on hers, his hand smoothing a path up and down her body. He knew nothing more could occur, not yet. But it wouldn't hurt to show her a bit of love before she closed her eyes.

***

CHERRY'S FINGERS brushed Bolt's cheek like they were a tip of a flower petal. Soft and slow, not wanting to wake him.

He felt the movement anyway.

His eyes drifted open, a smile gracing his relaxed face.

"Morning," she said before kissing him.

"Good morning."

"Did you know you slept in today?"

A deep chuckle floated around her. "Highly doubtful."

Her brow cocked as she gestured toward the clock on his nightstand. He twisted, swearing, then laughing.

"It can't be nine o'clock. I haven't slept that late in...I don't remember."

She brushed his cheek again. "I know. You slept great all night. It was so nice to see."

He frowned. "What are you talking about?"

"I'm not a dumb blonde, even if I can play the part sometimes. I know you have trouble sleeping. I never wanted to bother you about it. I sensed it was a sensitive subject."

"I've tried everything. Nothing seemed to work. I even thought sleeping next to you might help, and sadly, it didn't." His hand wove down her side and planted in its customary spot on her hip. "If you noticed me sleeping last night, it must mean you didn't sleep well."

"It could've been better. Why do you think you slept so well last night?"

His shoulder lifted in a careless gesture. "I have no idea. Maybe I just feel content for the first time in a very long time. Nothing was weighing on my mind."

So her talk about Evan hadn't stressed him out. She'd worried about bringing it up, but Evan deserved the recognition after helping her. Her situation would've been much more dire without him.

"I have the week off. I told Logan I didn't need that much time, but he insisted. What do you want to do all week?"

"Whatever you want to do."

She didn't have a care in the world anymore. She had a man who loved her, who would do anything for her, a baby on the way, a sister by her side. What more could she want?

"I'll make you breakfast in bed, and then we can go see Evan."

"I love the sound of that plan. As long as it's not bacon."

He grinned before kissing her, then rolled out of bed. He made her a bagel with a side bowl of Cheerios and a large glass of water. She'd had a lot of toast and bread in the hospital. It was the one thing that seemed to stay down without a problem. She'd also munched on a lot of Cheerios. Not the honey nut kind, but the plain kind with very little flavor. She couldn't even add sugar without feeling nauseous. Dr. Matthews had also prescribed her nausea medicine to help her keep food down.

They stopped in town to grab some cookies, then pulled into Evan's garage. He strolled out to meet them, wiping his hands on a rag.

"Here. I brought you cookies. I didn't make them." She winced. "Trust me, they wouldn't be good. But it's the thought that counts, right?"

She held out the container of chocolate chip cookies with the brightest smile she could manage. Evan hesitated before taking it from her.

"Thanks. You didn't have to, but thanks."

"Well, you didn't have to help me either, but you did. I know it's not close to being the same thing, but you know what I mean. Thank you."

She forced the tears she could feel building in her eyes to stay at bay. Breaking into a blubbering mess was the last thing she wanted. She wasn't sure if it was because of all the intense emotions they'd been through lately or pregnancy hormones. She hoped it wasn't pregnancy hormones because then it meant she was in for some very long, trying months ahead.

"Cherry didn't tell me until last night how you helped her. If I had known, I would've been by sooner." Bolt held out his hand. "Nothing I say will be able to express my gratitude. Thank you."

Evan eyed his hand suspiciously, as if Bolt had intentions to shake his hand then slam him to the ground or something. Cherry waited with bated breath until he finally shoved his hand into Bolt's and gave him a tight shake, then let go right away. Her breath released, the tension flowing out of her like the light breeze blowing around them.

"I did what anyone else would've. No big deal. Glad you're okay. Even without shoes, you run fast." Evan smiled, remembering how when she'd seen Lillian with a gun on Bolt, she'd darted down the street like she'd suddenly sprouted wings.

He would've never been able to stop her if he had tried. Nothing would've stopped her from protecting Bolt.

"So, we'd like it if you came over sometime for dinner or

something." The offer came out stilted, but she was proud of Bolt for doing it instead of letting her.

He'd insisted it should be him, and she didn't argue. She knew the animosity between him and Evan. Between Evan and everyone in town. It had been something Bolt felt compelled to do and who was she to stand in the way of that?

"You don't mean that. What would Seth and everyone else think?"

Bolt popped a shoulder up and then down. "I don't care what everyone else thinks anymore. I'm going with my gut from now on, and my gut says we'd like to have you over for dinner sometime."

Evan stared at him, darted a look at her, then back to Bolt. He remained silent, the confusion littering his face.

"We all make mistakes, Evan. Some more terrible than others. I'd like to think we should all get a second chance. When I found Cherry was missing, I would've done anything to get her back. I didn't understand your reason before, but I do now. Maybe I'd feel differently if my friends hadn't made it out alive, but it all turned out okay. They're okay. And..." Bolt sighed. "I'm sick of it all. I want to move on. I want a second chance at things as much as you." Bolt slid his hand into Cherry's. "I have one with her. Come over. Don't. It's up to you. Just know the invite is there."

Evan nodded, his lips pressed together as if holding his emotions back. Maybe tears like she still wanted to release. He offered a half-hearted smile and lifted the cookies. "Thanks for this."

"You're welcome. Also, I'm looking for a car. Do you have any cheap ones I could buy?"

Evan's smile brightened into a real one as he tossed his

head to the right. Cherry's old yellow car sat looking sad and lonely.

"I have a car that just got a new engine. Doesn't run like brand new, but it works."

Cherry's eyes pinned to her baby. The car that got her out of hell in Florida and to a new beginning in Minnesota.

"You fixed it? I thought it had too much wrong with it."

Evan laughed. "It did. I had an old engine lying around. I tinkered around with it and got it working again. I have lots of parts just hanging around here. I have lots of time on my hands. I like working on cars. It's yours if you want it. Five hundred."

"That's too cheap. Now you're just being overly nice."

"No, I'm being a friend."

Cherry jumped up and down giggling and smiling, then moaned, regretting it when the pain in her chest where she'd been shot pulsated with agony.

She bent over, holding her hand to her chest.

"Cherry." Bolt's hand smoothed down her back, his whispered plea of only her name said everything he wanted to say. Are you okay? What can I do? How badly does it hurt?

She stood up, pasting on a smile. "I have to remember not to get so excited like that yet. I'll take it. I've missed her."

Evan looked stricken, then his features smoothed out and he forced out a grin. "Okay. Good. I'll get the paperwork ready. You can have a cookie too."

"They are for you. We'll be back with the money. Thank you so much, Evan."

Then she rushed forward, crushing him into a big hug. He stiffened as if not used to people showing him affection anymore. Well, she'd change that. It would be her new mission—and Bolt's. Because they were in this together.

She kissed his cheek for added measure. He blushed, averting his eyes, especially from Bolt's view as if he'd be mad. How silly.

They said good-bye and left, going home to grab the money and come back for her car.

"Did you have to kiss him on the cheek?"

Her hand slid into his as he drove home.

"You know it meant nothing. He's so lonely. I feel bad for him." She pulled his hand to her lips, kissing it. "And I'll kiss you everywhere you want when we get home."

Bolt's lips curled into a delicious grin. "Not until you feel better. I'll do the kissing for right now."

When they got home, he showed her exactly what he meant, the car forgotten for a brief moment in time.

Cherry had found a home for the first time. She'd make sure to cherish every single memory.

EPILOGUE

2 years later

THE DOOR OPENED, and a brisk, cool draft brushed across his skin, making him shiver. He was not going to see this as a bad premonition, just because it was Friday the thirteenth.

"Get in here. It's colder than I thought," Bolt said, ushering his hand in, shutting the door quickly.

Evan chuckled, wiping his boots before slipping them off. "They say there's snow in the forecast next week."

"Bite your tongue, man. I don't want snow that fast. Cherry's already purchased three Halloween costumes for Ashton, unsure of which one to use. I don't want to go trick-or-treating with him if there's snow on the ground. He just started walking. He suddenly hates to be carried all the time because he likes walking on his own. So independent already."

"Where is that rascal?" Evan asked, peering around the corner into the living room, which was empty.

"Cherry's giving him a bath. I told her it's silly because he'll need one tonight after the party."

Silence coated the air for a moment. Though Bolt and Cherry had accepted Evan back into their lives without an issue, nobody else in their group had. Despite their vocal protests, they had even named Evan Ashton's godfather when he was baptized last summer. Cherry had insisted. Bolt couldn't disagree. If not for Evan saving Cherry's life, Ashton would've never been born. Cherry herself would've died in that cold, empty room with no one having any clue where to find her. Bolt owed Evan a lot.

In the past two years, Evan had done everything he could to make amends with his old friends—with the town. No one but Bolt and Cherry had given in. For the most part, as far as Bolt knew, Evan had accepted it. It didn't mean moments like this weren't a bit awkward.

Later in the afternoon, Bolt, Cherry, and Ashton planned to attend Rosalind's birthday party. Kat and Danny's little girl was turning two. On Friday the thirteenth of all days. In the month of October. It didn't get creepier than that. At least in Bolt's eyes, not that he'd ever say anything to anyone. Well, he would with Cherry; she'd understand. She'd get him.

She *did* get him. Every small, tiny broken piece inside of him.

"Well, I can't stay long. Devon is opening up the garage, but I told him I'd be there later. I wanted to stop and give this to you."

Evan held out a white plastic bag. Despite the townsfolk not opening their arms wide open and letting him back in, his garage was doing great. People still needed their vehicles fixed, and he was one of the best mechanics in the business. It was hard to ignore that. Devon, a recent college dropout who moved into the area a year ago, started working with Evan soon after he arrived. He was as good with machines as Evan was. Though there were a few years between them, they'd become best of friends. Bolt was glad Evan had someone other than just him and Cherry to rely on.

Bolt took the bag, opened it up, and chuckled. "Another Halloween costume?"

Evan grinned, shrugging. "I saw it and thought of Ashton. I had no idea Cherry's been buying up all the stores, but it doesn't surprise me."

Bolt pulled out the one-piece costume and shook his head, laughing some more. It was fuzzy and brown and the hood with the adorable ears meant if it was cold out, Ashton would be warm. As his room was animal themed, like a zoo, this was a perfect outfit for him—a big teddy bear.

"She's going to love it. The other costumes aren't an animal."

"Well, even if he doesn't wear it on Halloween, it'll keep him warm on other days. Keep it regardless."

"Thanks, man." Bolt handed him the costume and tossed his head toward the bathroom. "Why don't you go show Cherry? I'll put on another pot of coffee. You can take one with you."

Evan nodded in appreciation and headed down the hallway.

Bolt started the simple task of brewing another pot, taking two phone calls while doing so. One from Kat to remind him the party started at two o'clock. He knew it, though didn't say so in an irritating way. Kat was Kat. The bossy-loving woman who had to have everything perfect. At least since Rosalind had been born. She doted on her daughter like a mother should—sometimes maybe too much, but he'd never be the one to say it. He couldn't talk. He doted on Ashton just as much.

When the time had come to learn what they were

having, he almost wanted it to be a surprise, but Cherry insisted. The moment he had learned they were having a boy, he'd been elated. Then terrified he wouldn't know how to raise a boy. Each new day, he learned something new. Sometimes about himself. Sometimes about life. Sometimes about how precious each moment truly was. Though they hadn't talked about it, he was itching to have another. This time a girl. A spitting image of her mother, one he knew would bring as much light to the world as Cherry did.

He was pouring coffee into a to-go mug when his phone rang again. Seeing the sheriff's number was always a fifty-fifty kind of thing, especially on his days off. Either Logan wanted to shoot the breeze, or he needed to go into work.

"Hey, what's up?"

"Neptune needs us. You remember Officer Anders and the dead body you helped with last week. Well, his girl-friend is missing. They need all hands on deck. Looks like it's that Clarence fellow who took her. He's already killed a few people."

Bolt's stomach dropped.

He'd been following the cases, considering Neptune was only a town away. Three women murdered—brutally murdered. Every time he thought about them, his mind ventured to Cherry and what he'd do if he ever lost her, especially in such a vicious way. He knew how Jake felt. That feeling of hopelessness, knowing the woman you loved was gone, missing.

He'd do anything he could to help Jake out. To take that horrid feeling away.

"I'll be right there. Where are we headed?"

"I'll text you the address to Clarence's house. That's where the chief of police is setting up base."

Bolt disconnected, rushing to his room to change. When he popped his head into the bathroom, he couldn't help the smile that brushed across his face at Cherry laughing at Ashton splashing and Evan grinning at the spectacle.

Her laughter died when she saw he was dressed in his uniform. She stood up, frowning. "What happened?"

"Missing woman. Fellow officer's girlfriend from Neptune. I have to help."

Cherry placed her hand over his heart. "Of course you do. We'll be here when you get back." Then she kissed him on the lips, sealing the words as if written in stone.

Bolt looked over her shoulder when she leaned in for a hug, making eye contact with Evan. "Coffee's on the kitchen counter."

But he knew Evan saw the worry, the fear, even though he knew he shouldn't be frightened leaving her alone. Some things were harder to get over than others. His worry about Cherry would never cease to exist.

"Thanks. Maybe I'll stay a bit longer if that's okay."

"Yep."

That's exactly what Bolt had wanted. He wouldn't stress as much if Cherry wasn't alone.

Then she kissed him again, saying without words what she wanted to say.

I'm okay. You're okay. We're all okay. Bad memories are best forgotten. It was something she said every so often, just to remind him the past was in the past and that's where it needed to stay.

"I love you," Bolt whispered against her lips.

"You can show me how much tonight." Then she sealed those words with a kiss as well.

Is reading this book the first one in the series for you? No worries! They can all be read as a standalone. Start the first book today with <u>ESCAPING MEMORIES</u> and find out how Logan and Aubrey met!

For Logan & Aubrey's story
Escaping Memories
A Lucky Town Novel, #1

Her past is a deadly puzzle she must solve...before it's too late.

Stumbling into a stranger's isolated cabin, she's terrified—her memories a dangerous blank slate. The only thing her instincts scream is to trust the ruggedly handsome Sheriff Logan Caldwell who found her. With his protective nature and gentle touch, he also makes her feel safer than she has in...well, as long as she can remember.

As shadows of her forgotten past close in, Logan becomes her only ally against an unknown enemy. Every recovered memory brings more fear than answers. As passion ignites between them, one thing becomes clear: if her enemy finds her, she'll meet a fate worse than death.

*With nail-biting suspense and smoldering romance, plunge into the danger and desire with the first book in the **Lucky Town series** today!*

FOR DANNY & KAT'S STORY
DANGEROUS MEMORIES
A LUCKY TOWN NOVEL, #2

Has the nightmare returned or is this a darker threat?

Agent Danny O'Rourke's greatest wish is for his sister, Aubrey, kidnapped months ago, to finally come home. Though he couldn't save her then, he'll do whatever it takes now to help her heal and bring her back into his life. Except one thing is standing in his way—the Caldwell family.

When a new case links to the Caldwells, he's determined to find answers, even if it means facing off with the alluring Kat Caldwell. Though he tries to hate her, Danny can't deny the intense attraction burning between them.

As the body count rises, Danny has the chilling realization that Kat is the target of this twisted predator's obsession. Haunted by the failures of his past, he'll risk it all to protect her. But one question remains: is the danger they're facing now linked to Aubrey's disappearance...or is an even more sinister force at play?

As Danny follows the clues down a rabbit hole of lies and depravity, there's only one thing he knows for certain: losing Kat is not an option. As their passion flares white-hot, the killer's trails turns deadly cold, and Danny must confront his greatest demon to rescue the woman he loves...before she's taken from him forever.

For Seth & Pepper's story
Stolen Memories
A Lucky Town Novel, #3

Some secrets are worth killing for...

Seth Caldwell has always been the family troublemaker, but he's ready for a change—starting with his best friend Evan. But before he can talk to him, Evan goes missing and his boss turns up dead. Despite the lies between them and Evan being the prime suspect, Seth knows he's no killer. Now, in order to find him, Seth is forced to turn to feisty new deputy Pepper Wilson for help.

With her razor-sharp instincts and ability to unnerve him like no other, Pepper quickly becomes a temptation he can't resist. But Seth senses she's hiding her own secrets behind that alluring smile. As the danger grows closer and they spiral deeper into a twisted web of deception, one truth becomes clear—some will go to brutal lengths to exact revenge.

Grab this enthralling thrill ride that will leave you gasping for more today!

FOR DEKE & CHARLOTTE'S STORY
DEADLY MEMORIES
A LUCKY TOWN NOVEL, #4

Love is scary...death is terrifying.

Deke Sumnter only has casual sex. Anything beyond that, he's not interested. Until Charlotte. She's smart, sexy, and something he's always craved. But one time was all he could give her. He should've known it wouldn't be enough. Now, she won't even talk to him. He'd take just being friends over the silent treatment.

When trouble starts brewing again in their small town, this time targeting the woman he swears he doesn't love, he won't let anything stop him from protecting her, even if everything inside of him says he needs to stay as far away from her as possible.

Captivating suspense and electric romance unite in this emotional thriller that will leave you breathless. One-click now to start reading today!

ABOUT THE AUTHOR

I'm a *USA Today* Bestselling Author that loves to write contemporary romance and romantic suspense novels, although I am partial to romantic suspense. I even dabble in paranormal. Honestly, I love anything that has to do with romance. As long as there's a happy ending, I'm a happy camper. And insta-love...yes, please! I love baseball (Go Twins!) and creating awesome crafts. I graduated with a Bachelor's Degree in Criminal Justice, working in that field for several years before I became a stay-at-home mom. I have a few more amazing stories in the works. If you would like to learn more about me and my books, head to my website by scanning the QR code. Thanks for reading!

Scan me